Baker's Dozen

A Lexi Fagan Mystery

Autumn Doerr

This book is the product of Autumn Doerr's imagination. It is a work of fiction. The characters in this book, with the exception of Stella Brooks, are made up. Though Stella Brooks was an actual person, she did not say any of the things within these pages because it's made up. Any other resemblance to actual persons, living or dead, actual events and locations is purely coincidental.

Kindle ISBN 978-0-9861209-0-9
WGA Registration 1451600

ISBN: 098612091X
ISBN 13: 9780986120916
Library of Congress Control Number: 2017911080
Autumn Doerr, Pasadena, CA

Book design by Barbara Lebow
Author photograph by Josh Fogel

For Ruth Shein and Robin Hall, both gone, but not forgotten.

TABLE OF CONTENTS

1

LATE DECEMBER, 1983 – JERRY STEVENS

Lexi sat at the kitchen table she had rescued from an alley near her apartment on Russian Hill. Saxman Bite, the 15-year-old black-and-tan cat she had brought with her from Alaska to San Francisco two years earlier, sat licking herself, legs splayed unladylike across the floor, her head buried in her belly. Lexi was 19 and could hardly remember a time without Saxman in her life.

Lexi had awakened just before her alarm was set to go off. It was another day that reminded her of what she'd lost—memories only sleep could erase. She showered, then dressed in slacks and a blouse before wrapping her uniform, a glorified apron, around her like a lab coat.

She waited impatiently for the sound of the newspaper thud against the front door of the building.

After draining the lukewarm tea at the bottom of her mug, she turned off the transistor radio that sat near the window. It was too early for Metro Dave to give the first traffic report of the morning, not that she cared since she bussed or walked to the bakery. She just liked his voice. Her pony-tailed hair was still wet, forming a large curl dampening her uniform at the neck and making her shiver. Instead of messing with the heater in the hall, she put on her coat and looked at her watch.

"The paper has to be here by now, Sax."

She walked into the hall and glanced at a mirror next to the front door. Her intelligent and unblinking eyes looked back at her. She tucked away the unruly tendrils forming around her head despite the ponytail.

As expected, three papers were tossed over the steps and so close to the door that they slid across the marble as she pushed the door open. She grabbed one and hurried back inside. Hers was apartment number one, the first door on the left as you entered the building.

With only 10 minutes before it was time to leave for the bakery, Lexi returned to the kitchen table with the paper. She first shook, then smoothed out the front page. Scanning the headlines, she stopped to read every word of the article she had been waiting for: "Murder Investigation Opens in Cathedral Hill Fire."

She pulled the coat around her like a blanket and continued to read what looked like a follow-up story:

> The December 19th Cathedral Hill fire claimed three lives. It was believed that each of the victims died of smoke and fire-related injuries, but new evidence suggests that one of the victims died under suspicious circumstances. According to Detective Robert Reiger, the first African-American detective in the SFPD Homicide Department, firefighter Jerry Stevens's death is under investigation after forensic evidence collected at the scene indicated injuries unrelated to the fire. "We are investigating Jerry Stevens's death based on evidence collected at the scene which is inconsistent with fire-related injuries," Det. Reiger told reporters at a news conference Tuesday afternoon at the police headquarters on Bryant Street. Mr. Stevens's body was discovered near the first-floor Mezzanine where the fire is suspected to have originated. Det. Reiger cited the ongoing investigation when declining to answer further questions.

Lexi crumpled the paper as if to obliterate the news. She had moved to San Francisco to escape her past, but death had followed her here. Saxman looked up, her gold eyes watching Lexi as she slumped in her chair and thought back to the day of the fire, to a time before she had discovered things about her friends, and about herself, things that would change everything. Was it really only a few days ago? So much had happened in such a short time. She forced her mind to go further back to the days she and Jerry had spent together, when they had fallen hard for each other.

Jerry's face broke into a wide smile as he handed Lexi a motorcycle helmet. It was cool, only in the mid-50s. She saw he was only wearing a gray T-shirt under his leather jacket. His jeans were well worn and faded, as were his boots. His face was smooth shaven, his dark blue eyes looked almost black. He had a full mouth and a dimple on his chin. She took the helmet and lowered her head, stuffing her curls inside before fitting it over her head and settling behind him on the bike. Her jeans were tight from eating too many donuts at work so, to sit more comfortably, she pulled the legs of her jeans toward her knees and away from her crotch. She justified to herself that no one would resist eating donuts hot from the oven; besides, she walked to work most days, and it was a hilly commute. The snugness of her jeans, however, signaled that her donut-to-walking ratio was way off.

"Should I bother asking where we're going?" she yelled into his ear as he pulled away from the curb onto Larkin Street. He shook his head, pulling her hands tighter around his waist as the bike gained speed.

They rode the Suzuki in silence, the bike making its way to Lombard and toward the Golden Gate Bridge. It was a beautiful day. The sun was high. Clouds puffed their way across the azure sky above the bridge's towering steeples. They rode past signs for Sausalito, Marin City and Mount Tamalpais before reaching a hilly two-lane road that seemed to go on for miles.

They leaned together as one body into curves, sat up for straightaways and slowed for traffic, Jerry's driving steady as the woods sped by. Light and shadows alternated through the trees, coming and going like waves on a shore. Lexi had never been on a motorcycle before and took note of Jerry's watchful caution. She wondered what it would be like without a helmet, the cold wind on her head and face, turning her hair into a tangled mess.

"How ya doing?" Jerry yelled over his shoulder.

She gave him an affirmative squeeze. His hand drifted from the handlebar to her hand and weaved in between her gloved fingers. Her cheek flushed and her heart pounded. While they had been on only one other official date in the short time they'd known each other, Lexi had been attracted to Jerry from the first time they'd met. She was giddy with anticipation.

A sign for Muir Beach appeared on their way down a steep hill. Jerry pulled the bike into a parking lot, a rocky beach stretching before them with the sea beyond. He turned off the bike and Lexi reluctantly took her hands from his waist. Though she wore Frye boots, and a leather jacket over her sweater, Lexi was shivering. Jerry took off his helmet, his short military-style cut undisturbed.

"Let me help you," he said, reaching for her helmet. She lowered her head and shook the helmet off into his hands. Her hair tumbled out and over her shoulders. She pulled strands out of her face before getting off the bike, her eyes meeting his. She remembered the first time she'd looked into those eyes at the bakery, and how they had reminded her of the deep blue of blueberries she had picked as a child.

He set the helmet on the seat and stepped forward. He was so close she could feel his warm breath. It smelled like coffee. He took her chin and raised it, leaning in for a kiss. The cold she had felt in her bones only moments earlier dissipated.

Lexi hadn't paid attention to the saddlebags hanging over the back wheels of the bike until Jerry pulled out a heavy plaid blanket and a paper bag. He walked toward the ocean. Lexi followed, her legs wobbly from the ride and from having a proper kiss, the kind of kiss that emitted a glow she could feel throughout her whole body. As she caught up to Jerry, she realized that she was starving and hoped there was food in the bag.

They sat on the blanket Jerry had spread on the ground and shared a lunch of fresh turkey sandwiches on Dutch crunch rolls, along with cucumber and tomato salad he had packed in bowls covered in Saran wrap. Lexi knew the food hadn't come from a deli, so it must have been made at his apartment, or perhaps the firehouse where they'd had their first date. As they had done at their firehouse dinner, they washed down their food with bottles of ice-cold Coke.

They were mostly silent as they ate, enjoying the water rushing towards the shore before retreating out to sea again. At that moment, there was no world for Lexi beyond the beach; the two of them sitting on a blanket dusted with sand with their lunch and the ocean for company. Lexi felt at home in this raw beauty and was comfortable with Jerry. When their eyes occasionally met, they smiled at one another until one of them would laugh at their obvious and giddy infatuation. They ate and smiled and laughed until the sun was well over the water.

After they finished eating, Jerry packed away the salad bowls and utensils and tossed the empty sandwich wrappers and bottles in the trash. He then returned to the blanket, extending a hand to help Lexi up. Picking up the blanket, he shook the sand away and wrapped it around Lexi's shoulders before encircling her in his arms.

"That was the best lunch I've had since moving here," she confessed.

"How about dessert?" he asked, searching her face. His eyes moved to her mouth, then to the halo of hair flying in the wind and finally back to her eyes.

This time Lexi took Jerry's chin and lowered his mouth to hers as she leaned in for a kiss. He pressed his hands into her back. Lexi was on the tip of her toes, her hands caressing his face as he lifted her into his arms.

The sound of children laughing suddenly flooded the air. Jerry set Lexi down gently as they looked around and saw a family walking along the water. Two young girls were calling, "Emma! Come Emma!" as a chocolate-colored Labrador bounded out of the water. He shook sand and seawater all over the girls who screamed with delight.

The beach that had been deserted during lunch was now full of life. Lexi took Jerry's hand as they walked to the parking lot. Back on the motorcycle, Jerry headed north, winding along the two-lane highway that hugged the coast. The seemingly endless road took them inland where oak trees and bishop pines replaced the shrubs and grasses of the sandy earth closer to the ocean. As they drove, the afternoon sunlight gave way to the gloaming of early evening. Lexi clutched the blanket tightly to her.

Jerry slowed onto Sir Francis Drake Boulevard. Lexi saw a sign for Tomales Bay. They stopped outside a small inn with a painted sign that read "Manka's Inverness Lodge." She peeled herself away from Jerry and the bike, stretched and shook the tension from her arms and legs before taking off her helmet. Jerry was unpacking another saddlebag.

"I hope your cat's going to be okay without you tonight?" he said with a sheepish grin. The plan had been for a day at the beach, but Lexi had felt the thrill of adventure as daylight turned to dusk and they had continued north, away from the city.

"Why, Mr. Stevens, are you kidnapping me?" Excited and nervous, Lexi let him take her hand as they walked up the stairs. "But I don't have any clothes." He looked back at her to check if she was teasing. She caught up to him and hugged him close, squeezing his hand before letting go and taking the steps two at a time, beating him to the landing.

Lamps giving off a dim light hung from the rafters of the porch. She could barely make out a large hole cut into the porch to accommodate an enormous crooked pine tree reaching for the sky.

It wasn't any brighter inside. There were dark wood-planked walls, a stone floor and no furniture except a rustic wooden bench along one wall and a desk at the far side, next to stairs leading to the second floor. No one was at the desk.

"We're expected." Jerry put his bag on the bench before reaching behind the desk for a key. "It's dinner service in the restaurant and it's only Milan and Manka running the place." He picked up the bag and moved to the stairs. "Let's clean up before dinner."

"Sure. It won't be the first time I've brushed my teeth with my finger. Or I could use your toothbrush," she teased as she followed Jerry upstairs. She took off her glove and put her finger through the belt loop of his jeans.

On the second floor, the smell of wood fires burning in the damp air grew stronger. There were only four rooms off a narrow hallway. Jerry opened the door to number 3 and moved aside for Lexi to enter first.

The room was small but comfortable. There was a fire in the fireplace. Lexi took in the low beams of whole tree trunks overhead and the blocky wooden chairs and table. The bed sat high against a wall facing French doors leading to what Lexi presumed to be a deck. It was now pitch black out, with the only light in the room coming from the fire.

Jerry set the bag on a chair and turned to Lexi. "If any of this makes you uncomfortable, I'll get my own room. I mean it. Whatever you want."

Lexi put her hand on his shoulder and pulled him to the bed. "What part of this amazing day makes you think I'm uncomfortable?" She rummaged in her coat pocket, pulling out a crushed white bag and handed it to Jerry. "If we get hungry, I brought cookies." She opened the bag, and they looked inside. "I mean crumbs," she laughed.

"And as far as my cat goes, Saxman can take care of herself for one night. She's a scrappy little thing."

Lexi gave him a long, deep kiss as they disappeared under the covers, any thoughts of dinner forgotten.

In the morning, Lexi woke, only partly covered by the thick comforter. She moved her cold body toward Jerry, who was radiating heat. He stirred, and they made love again. This time, Lexi felt more alive than ever. Jerry touched, licked and kissed every part of her body. They lingered and teased, embracing and caressing each other to the point of agony, followed by release, both eventually dozing in a tangle of bedding and limbs.

When Lexi woke the second time, she sat up and stretched. The sun was shining through the windows of the French doors, and just beyond the silver-grey deck of weathered redwood she recognized Tamales Bay. She watched as the blue water ran slowly between the banks of the surrounding yellow hills. There were patches of purple and sand-colored grasses and a few ducks looking like decoys in the water.

"God, I'm hungry," Jerry said as he jumped out of bed and, in a few steps, threw open the doors. Cold air rushed in as Lexi pulled the comforter closer. She smiled as she watched Jerry on the deck underneath the outdoor shower. He turned on a spigot. Water poured from the largest showerhead she'd ever seen.

"Come on. It's heating up." Steam rose from his lean body as the water rained down. Squealing in anticipation of the cold, Lexi threw off the blanket and ran outside to join him under the water.

"You said it was warm!" They hugged close as they heated up well before the water.

Lexi and Jerry were the last guests to arrive for breakfast. Like the rest of the inn, the dining room was paneled in dark wood, and light poured in from the many windows. Jerry leaned close to Lexi and whispered, "It's a good thing we skipped dinner. It's never good. I love the Prokupeks, but their food is usually heavy and tasteless."

She looked at the couple clearing tables. "That's too bad; they seem so nice." Jerry pointed to the man. "That's Milan." Milan wore riding boots and a white blousy shirt, something Lexi imagined a Cossack would have worn. Next, Jerry pointed toward the woman. "Manka." Her thick arms swept across a table as she was clearing away condiments and dishes.

Jerry smiled fondly as he watched the couple move around the room before returning his gaze to Lexi. "They are nice. I've known them since I was a kid, but have you ever eaten oxtail soup and stuffed cabbage?"

"It sounds awful." Lexi giggled. "At least this looks good. It's an unusual breakfast, but I bet it's delicious."

On the table were honey and jam, a plate with brown bread, sliced salami, hard cheese, whole hard-boiled eggs and some white paste that looked like a mayonnaise of some sort. After taking a bite, Lexi realized the white paste was homemade cottage cheese.

She spread it on the warm, heavy brown bread. The breakfast was not the best she'd ever eaten, but it was satisfying.

After they'd finished eating and pushed away their plates, Milan gave Lexi a quizzical smile, his thumb pointed up before catching Jerry's critical eye. Milan then grimaced and hesitantly turned his thumb down.

Jerry said, "Okay, you old goat, I know. We would have missed breakfast if Manka hadn't taken pity on us. It was not bad." Milan's wide smile looked as though he had been given a four-star review.

Jerry then stood while Lexi grabbed her coat. "Don't give us the bum's rush. We're leaving." Jerry walked over to Milan and kissed him on each cheek.

"She is lovely girl, Jerry." Turning to Lexi, Milan said, "What are you doing with this guy? He's rotten boy. Steals bread from kitchen and gets mud on Manka's floors."

Manka laughed as she joined them. Jerry gave Manka a squeeze and she pinched his cheek before hugging Lexi so hard she couldn't breathe. "This beauty too good for you."

"Tell me about it. I'll tell my folks you send your love. Thanks for everything."

"Není za ." Milan gripped Jerry's hand, his watery eyes winking with affection at the young couple. Jerry beamed back at Milan.

"Let's take a walk before heading back." Jerry traipsed down the stairs, opened the saddlebag and threw in the overnight bag. Lexi followed him to the motorcycle. He turned and hugged her. "How about the pier?"

"Lovely."

Lexi wanted to stay as long as possible. They had been lucky to have the same weekend off. Her bakery job almost always included weekends, and Jerry was usually on call if he wasn't already scheduled on a Saturday or Sunday. She thought of how to describe him to her friend from the bakery, Beverly. *Jerry is easy to be around. He's confident and what's the word? Mature.* He was also great in bed, but she would keep that to herself. Beverly would be relieved that Lexi had a boyfriend since, despite Lexi's protests to the contrary, Beverly suspected her lover, their boss Victor, had a thing for Lexi.

As they walked together toward the pier, Lexi's hand was entwined with Jerry's, both inside his flannel-lined jacket pocket. She gazed toward the end of the pier and could see something out there, though she wasn't sure what it was.

As they got closer, she recognized that there were rocks in some kind of pattern. As they reached the end of the pier, she could better make them out: A heart made of large white stones. Inside it were smaller black stones that formed the letters "JS + LF."

"When did you do this? Did you get up in the middle of the night?"

"Someone else got up. I trained with a guy from the Point Reyes Fire station. Luckily, he's a romantic sap like me."

Lexi was overwhelmed. "I don't know what to say."

"Then don't say anything." They leaned into each other and kissed until they nearly fell over, catching their footing and each other at the same time.

2

DECEMBER 19, 1983 – THE FIRE

McCracken's was an old-school bakery with a warehouse in the back, separated from the bakery itself by a swinging door. The warehouse was where the sugar donuts, custard éclairs, the breads, the jelly thumb-print cookies, pastries, and cakes, including a heavy German Chocolate cake, were made and distributed to the two other stores in the city. The windows along the side of the bakery faced Chester Alley. At the front was a large picture window that faced Van Ness Boulevard, the main artery that cut across San Francisco from the Mission District to the Marina on your way to the Golden Gate Bridge.

This time of year, McCracken's had a few Christmas decorations that had seen better days taped to the walls. A wreath hung above the table where steaming pots of coffee and hot water for tea sat on burners. Customers helped themselves to plastic cup holders with paper inserts. The pale pink walls had no picture, and the only display was the faded Styrofoam wedding cake case near the door.

The room had tables and chairs for customers as well as fixed stools and a low counter in front of the windows. On a normal day, customers would sit and watch traffic as they ate donuts and pastries and tried not to spill coffee as the paper cups turned soggy.

By 8:00 on this cold Monday morning, McCracken's Bakery had been open for an hour. Lexi was behind the counter, giving change to a customer when she heard a crash outside and looked up. Smoke was coming from a window on the first floor of the Cathedral Hill Hotel across the street. Dense black clouds poured from the south wing of the hotel. A window exploded, shooting glass onto the pavement. Lexi ran to the bakery's office, located in the warehouse just behind the bakery. She looked for the phone under a stack of papers to call 911, but before locating it she heard sirens screaming up Van Ness Boulevard. She ran back to the front of the store.

A few tables near the front window of the bakery faced the hotel. Lexi knew the people sitting there watching the fire were probably tourists, but they were definitely not guests at the hotel. The Cathedral Hill Hotel was known for its excellent continental breakfast, and no hotel guest would bother crossing the six-lane road to pay for donuts.

Smoke poured from the windows. The blare of sirens grew more insistent as fire trucks and an ambulance raced up the street toward the hotel. Lexi hoped that no one was hurt, but things were looking bad. Everyone inside the bakery was quiet. The flames were now visible through the gaping windows, spreading quickly across the first floor and lapping at the floor above.

When the fire trucks stopped, the sirens went dead, but the lights continued rotating in eerie silent circles. The sound of more breaking glass, the smell of the roaring fire and what Lexi thought might be screaming entered the once peaceful bakery through the crack in the front door. She flinched and quickly moved back behind the counter to help a customer, who kept looking over her shoulder at the horrific scene across the street. From where she stood, Lexi couldn't see anyone coming from the hotel.

"What could have started it?" asked a woman with a thick accent, standing near the bakery's front window. It was not a question that could be answered. Lexi came around the counter to where the woman stood and they both stared across the street. The stench of smoke and burning debris wafted in as a customer opened the door. The smoke mixed unpleasantly with the scent of fried oil and sugar inside and Lexi nearly gagged. She also felt the familiar and uncomfortable strain of her uniform ties against her belly. The sourdough bread and glazed donuts hot out of the oven were taking a toll. She loosened the ties and said helplessly to no one in particular, "I don't know; I'm seeing what you're seeing."

The few customers in the bakery continued to stare at the burning hotel. Lexi turned and asked the woman who had spoken, "Where are you staying?"

"Next door," she said with relief, pointing to the International Hotel to their right. That makes sense, Lexi thought, no breakfast.

McCracken's Bakery was at the edge of several neighborhoods. The run-down Tenderloin district almost touched the nice apartments and churches of Cathedral Hill. Respectable car dealerships and hotels were a block from the seedy end of Polk Street. It made for a diverse mix of customers and was one of many reasons Lexi enjoyed working at the bakery.

It was supposed to have been Lexi's day off, but she was filling in for another employee. It was easy to pick up extra shifts around the holidays; besides, she wasn't sure she'd have anyone to spend Christmas with.

Lexi's grandparents, who had raised her, lived in the tiny coastal town of Ketchikan in the panhandle of Alaska where it runs along the Canadian border, and the cost of a ferry ticket to Seattle plus an airline ticket were beyond her meager budget. Jerry was a very new romance and, while Lexi was hoping they'd spend some time together, she didn't want to presume he'd invite her to a family get-together. They hadn't seen each other since their day at the beach and the night at Manka's. It had only been a week and they had made plans to get together on Wednesday the 21st. Still, she was hoping he'd call her before then. Since his work was firefighting, she was sure he must be across the street.

By now, the half-dozen customers inside the bakery had been joined by about a dozen more people milling around on the street in front.

Just then, the power cut out.

Lexi pondered the situation. Should she close? She didn't need power to operate the cash register because it was from the turn of the century, with large round push buttons. Most mornings when they were busy, the cash drawer was left open because the buttons were a hassle and often stuck and jammed. The cash drawer was open now. The bakery was as out-of-date as the register and didn't even take credit cards.

But she also had to consider the baked goods. Each glass case was still nearly full; cookies on the right, donuts in front for customers to see as they approached the counter, puff pastries in the corner next to the register in a refrigerated case. A lot of cakes were already out. The baking racks that held silver trays of Danish pastries used to restock the counters were still half full. She couldn't close with so much bakery sitting unsold.

No. Staying busy was a way to put Jerry and his safety out of her mind.

Without taking her eyes from the fire, Lexi moved the last tray of pastries into one of the glass cases.

Doing something familiar calmed her and the smell of almonds from the bear claws helped clear her mind. Though it was a cold day, beads of sweat formed along her forehead, matting her bangs.

Two bakers, who were nearing the end of their shift, swung through the warehouse door and came into the bakery. Ben, the older of the two, was first; his eyes were sharp, sweeping the room as if in search of prey. He pushed Lexi out of the way, knocking her into the register. Dean followed and gave Lexi a sympathetic look as he trailed behind Ben, who stopped near the front door, watching the fire. Dean kept his distance from Ben who, with narrowed eyes, scanned the destruction across the street.

According to bakery gossip, when Ben had come back from Nam, he was a changed man. The employees kept their distance, all except for the owner, Victor McCracken, who went out of his way to protect Ben. No one knew the real story behind Ben's volatile temper or his relationship with Victor; there was only whispered speculation.

More sirens blared up Van Ness. The lights from two more fire trucks, a second ambulance and three police cars blinked as each vehicle screeched to a halt.

Lexi recognized Dean's weary look; his eyes were on Ben. Ben slammed through the front door and was now standing on the street outside. Dean turned toward Lexi and lifted his shoulders to his ears in an impish shrug. Dean's smooth brown skin and high cheekbones were the opposite of Ben's sallow, pockmarked face. Physically, they were opposites as well. Ben was tall and bulky with muscles like a body builder, whereas Dean looked more like Bruce Lee—small and wiry. Lexi had thought Dean was a teenager when she met him on his first day of work around the time that she had started and Dean had thought the same thing about Lexi.

Lexi saw Ben look up and down the street before taking off running. Dean and Lexi watched as he disappeared toward Geary Boulevard.

"Looks like Ben's gone rogue." Dean said wearily.

"Nothing new there." Lexi stared across the street at the fire. She was having a hard time focusing.

"Let's just hope he keeps it together until Victor gets here." Dean turned to Lexi. "Did he hurt you when he knocked you into the counter?"

"No." Lexi said rubbing her arm. "I just hope everyone's okay over there."

"What are we going to do?" asked Dean.

"I don't know *what* to do."

"I know," Dean said. "I feel like an ass just standing here."

Lexi looked at the cakes in the cold counter. "The freezer's out. Should we move these cakes to the walk-in? It might keep things colder for longer."

Dean opened the door and slid a cake topped with strawberries onto the counter. "At least the whipped-cream ones." It seemed futile to worry about cakes at a time like this, but Lexi wanted to do something.

Ben ran back into the bakery, nearly knocking over the wedding cake display next to the door. The cloudy plastic case rocked and a Styrofoam rose fell to the dusty bottom.

"The power is out for the entire block," he said, panting.

"We're staying open until I can reach Victor." Lexi surprised herself with a decision she wasn't conscious of making. Victor was often late and sometimes didn't show up for work at all, but she had never dealt with anything this dramatic before. She was sure Victor must have heard something about the hotel fire on the radio and would be rushing to the bakery at any moment.

Besides, she was reluctant to leave. Lexi thought there would never be a more exciting day to be at McCracken's than today when the Cathedral Hill Hotel was going up in flames. The firefighters were on the scene and she assumed the guests were being evacuated, though she hadn't seen anyone come out. Standing in the middle of the bakery, Lexi looked out of the large picture windows at a perfect view of the fire.

Her immediate problem was Ben. She needed to calm him. Even on a good day, Ben could be emotionally unstable. Lexi needed to keep him busy so he wouldn't focus on the chaos across the street or fret about the people who began to fill up the bakery to get a front row seat as the fire grew worse. It might not be the best idea to leave Ben with customers, she thought, but this was an emergency.

"Ben, watch the front while I call Victor. Dean, come with me." Lexi pushed through the swinging door to the warehouse with Dean at her heels singing, "It's raining men, Hallelujah! It's raining firemen!"

Once in the office, Lexi and Dean scanned the flour-dusted interior to figure out how to contact Victor.

"Where's Victor's number?"

The office was a tiny room built into a corner of the cavernous warehouse. The desk was overflowing with paperwork and was now even more disheveled from Lexi's first attempt to call her boss. Some of the drawers stood half open with files spilling out. Every shelf was stacked with invoices, order slips and pieces of paper with notes scribbled across them. The wedding cake toppers were haphazardly piled on the filing cabinets.

Dean lifted a stack of receipts that buried the telephone. A slow puff of dust and flour rose around them. A clipboard with sheets of orders was halfway off the desk. Under the clipboard was a ripped, coffee-stained piece of paper taped to the desk.

"Here it is, conveniently under"—Dean laughed—"stuff."

Victor's name and number were faded but readable. Lexi dialed the number. No answer. After what seemed like 50 rings, the machine picked up. She left a message and dialed two more times without registering the futility of trying to reach someone who was obviously not home. Dean's finger cut the line on the cradle.

"Honey, you left a mad man in charge of the asylum."

"Shit!" Lexi slammed the phone down, just missing Dean's finger, and they ran to the front. Ben stood behind the register. His large hands were pressed to his sides. Customers crowded the counter in front of him, talking at once. Business had really picked up; clearly, the fire was making everyone ravenous.

"There's a donut left right there," said a customer, pointing meekly.

"That's a fancy buttermilk cruller, you idiot," Ben said before addressing Lexi. "You'd better get things squared away." He turned and walked into the warehouse.

"Sorry about him." Lexi handed the cruller to the bewildered customer. "No charge."

Across the street, the growing fire had now engulfed the first floor along one whole side of the hotel. A wall of flames shot out in angry bursts and was moving toward the next tower. The firefighters broke several windows to the right of where the flames were headed to keep the glass from exploding. But that action sent a shower of shattered glass onto the emergency crews below. Another ambulance barreled up Van Ness, made a U-turn at Post Street and stopped in front of the hotel's garage.

The crowd in the bakery continued to stare out the windows, all except Ben, who straightened cookies and muttered about how sloppy they looked. He seemed to want to help, but didn't know what to do. Lexi needed to get him back to where he felt safe in the warehouse with cake tins and frosting.

"I'll take over now, Ben," Lexi said in as soothing a manner as she could manage. As if released from a strong magnet, Ben turned and, in two long strides, disappeared. Lexi watched as the swinging door banged back and forth in his wake. Dean began moving cakes to the walk-in fridge and Lexi could barely keep up with the flow of customers, emergency workers and reporters. The bakery was getting cleaned out quickly.

Lexi had an idea. "Dean, let's start cutting those cakes and bring me more paper plates and plastic forks, please." She figured she could sell the cakes by the slice.

When the line of customers temporarily thinned, Lexi noticed the sky was smudged with smoke. She watched as firefighters in full gear—helmets, yellow fire jackets and thick black boots—scrambled around the trucks. She was sure Jerry was over there, but she couldn't make out individuals under the protective uniforms. A ladder from the biggest fire truck extended toward a window. Two firefighters ran to the hydrant on the sidewalk. Manipulating huge pliers, they uncapped the hydrant at two ends and attached the hoses. After the hydrant was turned on, it took two firemen on each hose to control the gushing water. A smaller hose attached to one of the trucks was hauled up the ladder. The fire was so intense they couldn't get near the hotel so, instead, the ladder was suspended in the air with a fireman near its top. She hoped Jerry wasn't that guy.

Despite the commotion across the street and the power outage on the block, the bakery regulars started to squeeze their way in between the gaping tourists, the car salesmen and office workers from the neighborhood.

Lexi couldn't believe that less than two hours had passed since she opened the bakery. Stella Brooks, one of the bakery's most faithful customers, barely gave the fire a glance and went straight for the coffee table near the front door. Waving at Lexi, she pointed to the cups. Dark sunglasses covered her eyes, but Lexi guessed the question.

"It's probably lukewarm," Lexi said.

Stella had been coming into the bakery long before Lexi had worked here. She had been a jazz singer for most of her career, but a lifetime of singing in smoky clubs had caught up with her. When she spoke, her words rasped out in painful barks. Since it was hard for her to talk, she shrugged at Lexi and poured a tepid cup of coffee. Then she pushed her way through the crowd by the window and sat down at the far end of the counter.

Stella's weak voice and tiny frame added to the impression that she was fragile, until she let go with a string of profanities. Lexi guessed she was in her 80s. She wore jeans and a turtleneck every day of the year no matter the weather. When she wasn't covering her eyes with sunglasses that engulfed her small face, Stella wore thick black-rimmed glasses that magnified her eyes to comic proportions. Her hair was cut in a severe pageboy, a few dark streaks breaking the silver sheen.

"Hair that stands up to any weather San Francisco can throw at it," Stella had mused at one of her daily visits. Today she shook out *The Chronicle* she'd plucked from the top of a garbage can, which was her habit—"The news is always so bad, I hate to pay for it," she'd once told Lexi—and began to read. She acted unperturbed even as firefighters shouted orders and dragged hoses across the driveway just a hundred feet from where she was sitting. Lexi noticed that, unlike the scene across the street, the paper's headline for December 19, 1983, was uneventful.

To Lexi's surprise, another regular, Tiny Timm, appeared at the counter. A lifetime of using crutches had pushed his shoulders close to his ears and hunched his small frame. Since his legs were immobile, he walked by swinging his legs forward while balancing on his crutches. His face was creased after years of pain, but his eyes were soft and gentle. Despite his withered legs and deformed body, or because of it, Timm went out of his way to dress well. He wore dark tailored suits with button-down shirts in shades of pink and purple.

When Lexi had met Timm during her first week at the bakery, he had thrust his hand up and said, "Tiny Timm with two m's, short for Timmothy, with the same double m's. My parents had a sense of humor, and so do I. I came up with the 'Tiny"—very Dickensian, don't you think?"

Timm looked at the crowd in the dark bakery. "What happened, *ma cherie*?"

"I don't know how the fire started. I heard a crash and thought it was a car accident. The power is out, as you can see."

"It looks serious. That's some firestorm."

"I know one of the firefighters. Remember the guy who helped me with my epic nosebleed? I think that's his company." She tried but failed to sound matter-of-fact.

Timm pretended to be struck by the news. "Ah, your new boyfriend. Then you're not coming with me to ze Kasbah?" Timm clutched at this heart.

"Not today." Lexi didn't know why she'd even mentioned Jerry. She wasn't doing a good job of putting him out of her mind.

"What can I get you? How about anything but your regular Russian tea cookie? There's not much else left, but the cookies aren't fresh today anyway. How about a cream puff?" She wanted to push the cream pastries before they went bad.

"No. No. No." Timm took out his wallet from his pocket, took out two dollars and stretched his arm to the counter. "Your best Russian tea cookies and coffee, too, please."

Lexi took change from the open register and handed it to Timm. He pocketed it and moved the crutches under his arms, maneuvering his way to his spot at the counter in front of the windows facing Chester Alley. He looked over his shoulder at Lexi and said, "Is there any hot coffee?" She pointed to the darkened overhead lights and said, "The power..."

"Cold coffee goes best with tea cookies. Just like in mother Russia."

Lexi put two cookies on a paper plate, poured Timm's coffee and set them in front of him.

"*Ma Cherie,*" he said as a thank you. The place was filling with people again, so she couldn't visit with her regulars, but that was a relief. The only way she could keep it together was to be busy. The more she tried not to think about Jerry fighting the fire the more he came into her mind.

Lexi's watch read 9:20 a.m. Every table was filled with customers and every seat at the counter near the window was taken. There was only a cup or two of coffee she had saved in a thermos in the warehouse after the power went out and a few Old Fashioneds left in the donut case. Even the cakes Dean had cut into slices that she had sold for donut prices, were almost gone. The cookies were disappearing, too.

"I guess you know what donuts people really like when supplies dry up," she said to Dean as she surveyed the almost-empty glass cases. "Plain cake was the last to go."

"In a disaster, "said Dean, "what are you going to go for? Frosting? Hell yeah. Forget plain, go for the sprinkles."

Lexi, feeling the heat from where her thick hair gathered into her ponytail, just wanted to take her hair down and shake it loose. Her matted bangs had given up, forming a frizzy crown along her hairline. She loosened the ties of her wrap-around apron even further and took a deep breath.

Across the street, rivers of water from the fire hoses disappeared into the gaping windows of the hotel before gushing back out, down the driveway and onto Van Ness Boulevard. The fire was under control now. Firemen started coming into the bakery. The first guy fumbled around to pay, but Lexi waved him off. She was happy to give them whatever was left. Though she couldn't help but feel a pang that it wasn't Jerry.

She didn't recognize anyone from the night she'd had dinner at the firehouse, and she was too embarrassed to ask about him now, with the building across the street being destroyed. People were probably hurt, or worse. Maybe she was wrong and Jerry's crew hadn't been called, but it seemed impossible that he wouldn't be at a fire of this size in this area of town.

"You're going to be let go for giving those firefighters free donuts." Henry's voice came from his usual table in the middle of the bakery.

"Henry, I'm sorry. I didn't see you. Give me a sec." She ran to grab the last of the coffee from the thermos in the warehouse that she'd been saving for him in case he made it in. He was one of her favorite customers.

When Henry entered a room, people noticed. His elegant hat and gray suit fitted his slim frame. He wasn't tall, but seemed so. The first time they met, Henry handed Lexi three dollars for an éclair. That's when she saw the frayed edges of his shirt cuff under his coat sleeve. She took the money and made a point not to look at his cuffs anymore. After that first day, she never charged him more than a dollar for his regular order.

"The coffee's pretty cold," she apologized.

"I've been through worse, my dear." He put his cool dry hands over hers as she set the cup on the table. His eyes were soft and cloudy, rimmed white from cataracts. Though his eyesight was not good, his mind was sharp.

He reached into his pocket for his wallet, but she demurred. "I can't accept anything for this dreck." She didn't want to embarrass him but wasn't about to take his money on this dreadful day.

Lexi had always felt a twinge of guilt about undercharging her favorite customers, until she noticed Victor leaving one night with a bag full of donuts and loaves of bread that had been left over that day. She'd followed him as he dropped the food off at the homeless shelter around the corner. After that, Lexi's philosophy was that charity begins at work.

Lexi noticed several customers at the counter looking around helplessly.

"Gotta get back to work." Lexi squeezed Henry's hand and jogged around the tables, picking up empty cup holders and throwing the coffee-stained inserts away. She'd forgotten a towel, so she brushed crumbs onto the floor with her free hand.

An hour later, the paramedics and firemen had cleared out and were back across the street. In the crush of men, Lexi saw a yellow arm making semi-circles in the air, waving toward the bakery. Jerry? Unsure and feeling a bit silly, she ran outside and waved back, but the person who had waved a moment before had melted back into the sea of uniforms. Her heart was beating fast. Where was Jerry? Was he safe? The fire had started several hours ago.

She walked back inside the bakery. The clock on the wall was stuck at 8:12; that's when the power had cut out. According to her watch, it was now 10:02.

The power was still out; the donuts were long gone, and she even sold most of the cut-up cake slices. Lexi thought she might have to close. Where was Victor?

"I'm afraid we're out of almost everything." Lexi said to a new group of people who came in.

Paula, who owned "Paula's Keys" just up the street from the bakery, squeezed in past some German tourists. "I just came to see how you're doing. I can't make keys without power, so I had to close up shop. Anything left for the locals?" Paula asked, gliding to the counter.

"I might have a crumb for you." Lexi reached into the refrigerated counter for a slice of pineapple upside down cake. The temperature was only a few degrees cooler than the room.

"I hope it's still good," Lexi warned her.

"Oh, I like living dangerously," said Paula, picking up the plate. Lexi could see the deep callus worn onto Paula's index finger from polishing keys with a whirling bundle of wires.

"I'll just watch the show from here," Paula squeezed in next to a couple of Japanese tourists and gulped down her cake.

Lexi guessed that Paula was in her late 20s. They were about the same height but that's where the similarities ended. Paula had a boy's body. No hips, flat stomach, no chest to speak of. Lexi mused that Paula's hair, which changed color frequently, looked like the pineapple upside down cake she was now eating, bright yellow ends with brownish roots.

Lexi helped the German tourists, but with little to sell and the bakery at a slower pace than normal since there was still no power, Lexi pulled the cash drawer from the open register and walked back into the warehouse. It had turned into a big moneymaking day, and she didn't want to be robbed on top of everything else.

Before disappearing into the back, she called over her shoulder to Paula, "Can you watch the front for me?"

"Sure thing, toots!"

The back door of the warehouse was open. She could see Ben and Dean sitting on metal folding chairs, smoking. They looked like a couple of teenagers with their floppy hair and tight jeans. She dropped the cash drawer in the office safe and walked outside. By scissoring her fingers she motioned to Dean that she wanted a drag of his cigarette.

"I didn't know you smoked." He seemed surprised.

She shook her head, took a drag and said, "I don't." She took his pack and shook out a cigarette for later.

Leaning against the wall, Lexi announced to them, "Even though Victor is MIA, I think you two should go home."

"Who died and left you queen?" snapped Ben. Lexi inwardly shuddered at the idea that this guy used to carry an automatic weapon. He seemed to snap at the slightest provocation.

"Here we go." Dean sighed. "Don't mess with Lexi." He ducked away from Ben as if expecting to be whacked.

Surprising them both, Ben responded in a much softer tone. "Victor's not home. His poker night ran long."

"Why didn't you tell me that before?"

"You didn't ask." Ben crushed his cigarette butt under his foot even though there was a canister for ashes and butts right next to him. He walked toward his motorcycle that was parked in the alley behind the warehouse.

"I'm telling you," Dean looked disgusted. "That guy is like Rambo in *First Blood.* He's going to pull a gun on us some day."

"He is scary." Lexi sat down heavily, jarring her tailbone on the cold metal chair. "I have to get back up front but…" She paused.

Dean waited for her to continue. They watched the Triumph pull away.

"It's Jerry. The guy I've been dating—" Lexi trailed off, not wanting to say more.

"Oh, yeah, the handsome fireman. You lucky dog. I don't think he's your type. Except I don't know what your type is. Tall, dark, short, sweet? As long as he's handsome, honey."

Lexi couldn't help a brief smile. "Dean, he's got to be over there."

"Jerry's fine. He knows what he's doing. The guy you should worry about is Mr. Rambo. He was late this morning. Of all mornings."

"No way. Rambo would never be late. He's down to the military minute. Victor, yes, but not our Ben." Lexi took another drag of Dean's cigarette before handing it back.

"Wait, do you think he plays poker with Victor?" Lexi asked, though she couldn't fathom it.

"I'm imagining it's not so much poker as 'Deer Hunter' and Ben's Christopher Walken with a gun at his head, and people betting if he's going to blow his brains out."

Lexi shook her head. "Go home. I've got to get back in. There'll be a riot soon. We're down to cake slivers and crumbs."

"You're a clever girl. You'll figure something out." Dean took a long drag and stubbed out his cigarette butt in the sand on top of the canister that propped open the door.

It was 10:35 a.m. and still no word from Victor. Lexi pushed an empty baker's rack toward the swinging door leading to the back when she felt someone behind her. She turned and was face-to-face with Trevor Hayes.

"You scared me," she said, looking into Trevor's steady eyes. He was the fireman who had cooked dinner at the fire station for her and the crew on her first date with Jerry.

Trevor was standing close to her. She stepped back.

"I'm afraid there's nothing left to eat or drink." She couldn't figure out why he was behind the counter. "Do you need to use the phone?"

"No, lass," Trevor said. His Scottish accent seemed more pronounced than she remembered. He continued, "It's a madhouse over there, but it seems that all the guests made it out safely."

"That's great," she gushed with relief. "Is Jerry with you? How is he?"

"He's fine."

Trevor walked back around to the customer side of the counter. Lexi felt herself unclench. It had been the longest morning of her life. Now that she knew Jerry was fine, she could finally relax.

"Jerry's on the 'A' team on the front lines." Trevor laughed. "They keep me and the rest of the cooks on easy duty. They don't want to take a chance they might not get their next meal."

"I can understand that," Lexi said. "Your dinner was delicious, like something you might expect at a four-star restaurant."

"Five stars, lass," Trevor winked, and then reached across the counter. Her hands disappeared beneath his dirty gloves. He squeezed firmly, looked into her eyes, and said with a cool smile, "I came in to thank you from all of the guys."

She blushed. "No problem. Donuts and lukewarm coffee were the least I could do."

Then he dropped her hands, turned and was gone, but her hands still smarted from where he had nearly crushed them in his vice-like grip. It was strange behavior, but this was an unusual day, and she remembered thinking that he was an intense guy when she had first met him. Lexi hadn't been able to tell if he was trying to impress her, or if he was just pushy. She had wanted to make a good impression at dinner and took her cues from Jerry who didn't seem to take Trevor seriously.

Realizing she was famished, Lexi grabbed a few small thumbprint cookies. She sat down for the first time since she had left home that morning and quickly ate them.

3

DECEMBER 19, 1983 – VICTOR MCCRACKEN

Victor finally lumbered into the bakery at 11:30 that morning as if nothing had happened. His face reminded Lexi of a photo she had seen in a magazine of the Kennedy's. A family photo at their compound in Maine showed open faces with warm, easy smiles. Only Victor's Irish was more of the "black" variety—blue eyes and dark hair with competing cowlicks.

"Didn't you get my messages?" Lexi asked in an exasperated tone.

"I knew you could handle it. Besides, Ben would have called if there was anything to be really concerned about." He gave Lexi a sheepish grin, the crevices next to his mouth deepening into parentheses.

"Ben!" Lexi's face reddened. "I left *you* messages. We don't have power. We don't have donuts. You weren't concerned about that? And how about the fire? People could have been killed." There was rising panic in Lexi's voice as she spoke. She knew she was talking about Jerry. Now that she was no longer in charge, her emotions didn't need to be put into a box until later. It was later.

"You worry too much," Victor replied and then promptly disappeared into the back before Lexi could say anything else.

Lexi was too tired to argue. The truth was that there wasn't much Victor could have done; he couldn't magically make donuts without electricity. She had done a good job. The tourists and the regulars had been taken care of. The only regular who hadn't made it in was Howard, her most challenging customer. She figured that the chaos on the street had kept him away. It would be hard to maneuver a wheelchair while the sidewalks and bakery were so crowded.

Beverly, a co-worker and friend and one of Victor's two girlfriends (though no one was supposed to know that), arrived just after Victor. The freckles on her brown skin were hidden by a deep flush. Lexi and Beverly both had freckles. It was one of the things they shared, and it had bonded them as friends. Lexi assumed that Beverly and Victor had arrived together but, thinking that they were being discreet, had walked in separately. So much for poker night. Victor had a full schedule that often didn't include work.

The gold bracelets Beverly wore every day jangled as she and Lexi got down to bakery business. The few remaining cakes in the counter were room temperature and needed to be tossed out, along with the two that, even though they had reached their sell-by dates, Lexi hadn't yet had time to throw away.

Lexi saw a gurney being wheeled out of the hotel and into a waiting ambulance. She watched as it sped away with sirens blaring.

"Have there been many injuries?" asked Beverly.

"That's the first one I've seen." Lexi was sorry that Trevor had been wrong. She and Beverly stared across the street at the hotel's gaping hole. The guts of the rooms were exposed like a honeycomb with charred edges.

Beverly's smooth skin crinkled into a frown. Lexi noticed a faint red circle on Beverly's forehead between her brows. She thought it was the remnant of a bindi. Beverly had told her that young girls from the town her parents had come from in India wore them like a beauty mark was worn in the West. A red smudge on Beverly's hands confirmed she had tried to rub henna off in a rush to get to work. Maybe she had been to a wedding. Lexi had only recently learned about bindis and henna tattoos when Beverly had explained the custom.

She turned to Lexi and said, "It's not too busy so I'll check on Victor." Beverly's black braid bounced on her back as she pushed through the door to the warehouse, her slender dancer's limbs disappearing into the back.

"I'll bet you will," Lexi muttered to herself.

She was bone tired. Walking to Henry's table, Lexi took off her apron and wrapped it into a ball before sitting down.

"It used to be the old Jack Tar Hotel back in the 1960s when it was built." Henry motioned to the hotel. "Those boxy sections look old now, but were very modern at the time. I remember there was a sign on the roof that had three sides. It rotated very slowly and said 'Jack,' 'Tar' and 'Hotel' on each of its sides."

One of the other regulars interrupted, "My Frankie, he designed that sign. The letters were called Franklin Gothic." Her voice broke off. Lexi thought of the group of women who came in nearly every day as "the widows." They dressed in drab housedresses that buttoned up the front, their knee-highs sagging below the hem. Henry said many of them lived in his building in the Tenderloin, and that once a month when their social security checks arrived they put on fresh dresses and splurged at the corner grocery store. Between checks, they spent their afternoons drinking weak coffee and watching traffic outside the bakery while complaining about the weather.

Lexi leaned closer to Henry and whispered, "Her 'Frankie' has been gone for who knows how long, but she talks about him like he were still alive."

"I think she just misses him." Henry's cloudy eyes met hers.

Lexi felt ashamed. She had spent her childhood living with older people, her grandparents, and knew they sometimes lived in the past. Looking at Henry dressed in his once-fine clothes she couldn't blame him or the widows for wanting to dwell on better times.

Lexi changed the subject. "Why did they change the name of the hotel?"

"I don't know. One day it was the Jack Tar and the next it was the Cathedral Hill Hotel. Maybe because it's across the street from all those churches."

"What churches?" asked Lexi.

Henry laughed.

"On Franklin. There's a big Unitarian Church right on Franklin, and down the street there's Saint Mary's Cathedral on Geary. That's why it's called Cathedral Hill. Lexi, how long have you lived here?"

"Two years," she said sheepishly. "There are so many places in San Francisco that I'd love to explore, but I guess since I never have customers from over there, I never paid much attention to that area."

"The front of the hotel is actually on the other side, on Franklin Street. You should walk over there. It's a busy street, like this one, but there are nice buildings and the churches are worth a look. Van Ness is the back entrance to the hotel, where people collect their cars."

"That's a relief. No wonder I haven't seen guests leaving the hotel." Her body relaxed a little until she remembered the gurney.

Stella croaked, "You know what Jack Tar means?"

"I thought it was someone's name, like the owner of the Hilton Hotels," Timm said from his side of the room. Henry, Stella and Timm were talking to each other but looking at Lexi.

"No. Jack Tar isn't a name," said Henry. "Jack Tar is what they called sailors because their coats were covered in tar to repel the water. I imagine they smelled to high heaven!"

Stella added, "I remember during the war, if you were in North Beach you couldn't spit without hitting a sailor." Her voice trailed off to a whisper.

"You would know, my dear," said Henry. "Did you sing in the clubs then?"

"Mind your own business, old man," Stella snapped, though with a smile. They were looking at each other now.

The lights flickered on. Lexi walked to the coffee table and started a fresh pot.

"How about a donut?" Stella asked.

"Today you want a donut. There's barely a cookie left."

Lexi was always trying to tempt Stella to eat, but most of the time she had only coffee. Like most of the bakery's customers who weren't tourists, Stella lived on a fixed income in a studio apartment in the Tenderloin

District. It could have been a lack of money that kept her from eating, but, unlike the other customers with limited funds, Stella didn't splurge on the 15th of the month when her social security check arrived.

As far as Lexi could tell, Stella was stoned every day, but unlike every stoner Lexi had known, pot didn't give Stella an appetite. Her habit was to sit at a table by the front window out of earshot of the widows, nursing coffee and reading *The Chronicle* that Lexi brought to work every morning.

By 3:30 p.m., the fire was completely out. Damp smoke hung in the air like the smell of wet cigarettes. Fire hoses were collapsed and stacked, ladders retracted, equipment stowed and reporters and their news vans long gone. The entire first floor of the hotel's left wing was a gaping, wet, black hole. Lexi watched as several of the fire trucks pulled away.

Lexi should have been off work at three, but she was so wound up and had hoped Jerry would come over once the fire was under control, that she'd stuck around long after her shift had ended. Victor sat in the office. Lexi listened as he cancelling the day's cake orders. He barely fit in the old banker's chair. His big hand swallowed the phone at his ear.

"I'm sorry, Mrs. Greely," he said in his soothing deep voice, "but the fire has destroyed your chances of happiness. Your precious son's birthday cake will not be ready at four."

He gets away with murder, thought Lexi. And it sure pays to be Victor's friend, if your name is Ben. Victor hung up the phone. Lexi said, "I'm going to head out soon, okay?"

Victor looked at her and said, "Sure. You did good today." Lexi smiled and stood up tall, acknowledging her first compliment in two years. Victor started to straighten papers on the desk, but only seemed to make things messier. He asked, "Didn't you have a date with a fireman recently?"

"Who told—" Lexi paused. "Oh, Beverly. Does everybody need to know my business?" Victor put his hands behind his head. Lexi gave in. "If you must know, I have been seeing a certain fire fighter."

"So, how old is he? How long has he been with the SFFD?"

"What difference does that make?" Lexi said. She playfully pushed his chair with her foot. It didn't budge.

"Did you see him today during the action across the street?" Victor asked, ignoring her response.

"No, but they were pretty busy over there fighting a fire." She was irritated more at Jerry than at Victor. He might not be used to having a girlfriend to check in with but that didn't excuse Jerry from making a call. She felt bone tired. The adrenaline had left her body, and she was shaky and needed to eat real food. She stuffed her sticky balled-up uniform into her purse. "I gotta go. I'm sure there's a bus somewhere I'm missing."

She swung her purse over her shoulder and marched out of the office and through the swinging door into the front.

Beverly was restacking cup holders at the coffee table. She looked at Lexi. "Would you help me with this before you go? It's like a bomb went off in here."

As tired as she was, Lexi wasn't ready to give up the idea that Jerry might show up. She glanced across the street. It was still all aftermath and not much action. She grabbed a stack of paper cones and started stuffing them into cup holders.

"So, I guess you told Victor about Jerry."

"Not the intimate stuff."

"Well, that's something to be grateful for at least." Lexi continued, "You know, Victor is amazing. He was just on the phone cancelling orders. He insults people and makes fun of them, and they love him. He's kind of a genius that way."

"I know," Beverly said. "It's sexy."

"Ewe," Lexi gave Beverly a gentle bump on the hip as she finished one stack of cups and began working on another.

"Speaking of sexy, where's your fireman?"

"Victor asked me the same thing." Lexi made big eyes at Beverly. "He never came in. This place was crawling with firemen, but not him. I think he waved at me, though."

"Waved at you? From where?"

"From across the street."

"From across the street?" Beverly was indignant. "I thought this place was crawling with firemen?"

"If Trevor was right and Jerry was on the front lines of the fire, I'm just selfish for being upset that he didn't come over here." Lexi looked down. "Or maybe he doesn't feel the same way about me?" Lexi tried not to cry. Beverly put her arm around Lexi's shoulder.

"Oh, honey," Beverly hugged her. "You're exhausted. Of course he fell for you."

Lexi looked up and saw the last of the fire trucks disappear down Van Ness as her bus drove by. Giving Beverly a weak smile, she said, "Thanks for the pep talk" and ran out of the bakery after it.

It was cold in Lexi's apartment on Larkin Street. She turned on the wall heater in the hall and sat at the kitchen table. In the cupboards were a few dishes, and she had a couple of dull silver forks and knives that she had picked up at a flea market stuffed into a drawer that stuck every time she tried to pull it open. Next to the table above the sink was a big window that never fully closed. After a previous tenant had moved out, the building manager painted a fresh coat of white latex over the old coat, making it impossible to close the window completely. Lexi could feel the cold air seep in through the opening at the top of the window.

She lit a cigarette that she had bummed off Dean and took a deep drag. She always told herself she wasn't a real smoker since she rarely bought a pack, and there were plenty of people to borrow from. They didn't seem to mind that she never returned the favor. Lexi watched as the smoke slowly curled toward the crack at the top of the window that beckoned the smoke outside.

She put her head down, yanked the rubber band from her ponytail, and let her hair spill over her head. It smelled of sweat, sugar and a damp, burned chemical residue. Saxman rubbed against her leg.

"Oh, Saxman Bight," she said, lifting her hair off the table with her forearm.

After smoking half the cigarette, she stamped it out and gave Saxman a distracted rub as she watched the sun disappear and the kitchen go dark.

Eventually, she got up and prepared dinner. Pouring the boiling water and spaghetti noodles into a colander, Lexi watched the steam rise above the sink and fog the window.

She wrote "Jerry" in the steam with her finger and thought about the day they'd met.

"Hello, Susan." Timm had used his crutches to pogo stick his way to the counter.

"Now, don't you start teasing me. I don't even know who Susan Hayward is, and I don't want to be compared to some old actress." Lexi gave a fake frown.

"Susan Hayward was a great beauty," Stella croaked.

"That's what I mean," Lexi said. "Don't talk about me in front of my back like that."

The day Lexi had met Jerry, it was getting late in her shift, and she didn't feel well, so she popped a few garlic pills for her headache. One of the other bakery clerks, Claudia, had told her garlic was an old Russian remedy for whatever ailed you.

The only thing left to put out were the cookies that were replenished once a week. Lexi pushed the older chocolate chip, oatmeal and sugar cookies to the back of the tray to be sold first and started filling in the fresh cookies nearest the glass. At the end of the month, when the widows' money was running low, they bought one or two cookies for 10 cents instead of donuts, so there were more cookies to replace than usual this week.

She put the fresh-baked goods into place. The widows were on their second cups of coffee and finishing off their cookies. Henry's éclair was half eaten, and Lexi was checking the date written under the doilies of the cakes when a drop of blood landed on the counter top. She put her hand to her nose.

"Beverly, I have a nosebleed." Lexi ran to the back and grabbed a handful of butcher-block paper towels. She wanted to protect her uniform, so she quickly stuffed toilet paper up her nostrils. It was soaked with blood before she even took her hand away.

Lexi went to the bathroom and put her head back to try and stop the bleeding. Salty warm blood dripped down her throat. She felt as if she were drowning and wondered if drowning people could taste the water. This was bad. Grabbing a handful of toilet paper, she backed out of the bathroom and tilted her head down just enough to see the floor under her feet. She leaned against a wall and put her head back. Blood dripped down her throat. After what felt like an hour, Lexi walked back out front as she continued to nurse her nose.

Out front, Dean was standing at the register punching buttons.

"Where's Beverly?" Lexi asked.

Without blinking an eye at the state of Lexi's face, Dean said, "She's even a bigger mess than you are." He pointed to the swinging door. "She's back there somewhere, probably in a fetal position crying over guess who?"

"Victor?" Lexi felt light-headed. Dean looked relieved to see her. He pulled a small garbage can from under the register and handed it to Lexi for her to discard the soiled paper towels in her hand.

She stared into the muck of wet coffee grounds and cigarette butts. Even with a nose full of blood, she could smell the stench of rotting food and old tobacco. She felt as if she was going to throw up. Her head started to pound.

"I hate blood." Dean practically ran out of the room. She called after him, "Dean! I could use some help here." But he was long gone.

"Okay, I'll take over. Got it," she announced sarcastically to no one in particular.

The customers were staring at her. Blood stained her hands and a wad of soaked toilet paper covered her nose and mouth. A young man in a Members Only jacket and jeans stood up from where he was sitting near the front of the store and walked to the counter.

"I notice you're having a little problem."

"It might only be a little problem if I could get it to stop."

"I can tell you how to stop a nose bleed if you'll let me. Leaning back is the wrong way to go."

Lexi nodded weakly. The young man came behind the counter and led Lexi to the back, eventually stopping at Victor's office. He was a good three inches taller than Lexi.

"Sit in the chair." Lexi did as she was told.

"Pinch your nose at the bridge right here." He put his index finger and thumb on the bridge of her nose near her eyes and pressed hard.

"Now keep pressing that spot, and put your head between your knees."

Lexi placed her fingers where his had been and pushed as hard as she could.

She looked at him suspiciously. "It works, I promise. I'm a fireman, and we're trained to handle every kind of emergency. Even nosebleeds."

Lexi swung her head between her knees. She hadn't recognized him, but he didn't look like he'd come from the methadone clinic or like he'd been hustling on Polk Street. Maybe he really was a fireman.

She was afraid to remove the toilet paper from under her nose to see if the bleeding had stopped, so she left it dangling.

"I'm Jerry, by the way."

"Lexi," she said. Her voice was hoarse from the blood that had run down her throat. "I sound upside down." *I must be losing a lot of blood,* she thought. *That doesn't even make sense. You can't sound upside-down.*

Jerry chuckled and gently placed his hand on her shoulder.

It felt like a long time, but must have been only a few minutes before Lexi sat up, releasing her fingers from her nose. Slowly she removed the blood-soaked paper and waited nervously. She looked at Jerry and noticed for the first time how handsome he was. He was slim. His jeans were tight, and he wore cowboy boots. He smiled.

"You're all right," he said reassuringly. "My donut awaits."

"Thanks. I've got to get cleaned up and back out there. People get angry when they see pastries they can't get to. There could be a riot."

She returned to the bathroom and threw the bloody wad of paper towels into the trash. Lexi then stared at herself in the mirror. She looked as if someone had punched her in the face; her nose was crusted with dried blood, and her cheeks and chin were spattered with red dots. Thankfully, her uniform hadn't been too bloodied, but her hair had escaped from its ponytail and was sticking up awkwardly. She washed her hands, wiped her nose and face, and patted her hair as flat as she could. She rushed back to the front where customers were waiting at the counter. Jerry was gone.

After the crowd had cleared, Timm grabbed his crutches and made his way to the counter.

"What happened to you? You look like you've been in a fight, *ma cherie*."

"I had the mother of all nosebleeds, and I didn't even take aspirin. I had garlic pills."

"Garlic pills!" shouted Timm. "They thin your blood as much as aspirin. Probably more. You're like a walking open wound."

"Oh," Lexi said weakly. "I was trying for a natural remedy. I thought only aspirin thinned blood."

"Nose bleeds are natural, and see where that gotcha?"

Beverly came from the back, wiping her eyes and, not noticing Lexi's condition, said, "Why don't you take a break, Lex? I'll take over."

Timm and Lexi looked at each other and smiled.

Saxman meowed for her dinner, snapping Lexi out of her reverie and into the present. Standing at the kitchen sink, Lexi smiled at the memory as she watched the letters spelling "Jerry" fade from the window as the steam from the water cleared.

"Ok, Saxman. I'm hungry, too."

4

DECEMBER 20, 1983 – AFTERMATH

The day after the fire, Lexi took the daily deposit to the bank. Lexi hadn't heard from Jerry, and, though disappointed, she had talked herself into not being surprised. It had been the biggest fire in San Francisco in many years. There were people crawling over the scene, and the blackened beams where rooms had once been were still wet.

Lexi walked from the bakery down Van Ness. McCracken's was six blocks from the city center of San Francisco: The gold-domed City Hall, the block-long federal building, the library, the Opera House and the new Symphony Hall. But over the years, the city's power brokers had shifted their offices to the Financial District down Market Street toward the Ferry Building. Lexi walked past corner liquor stores, pawnshops and dirty store fronts before the Tenderloin District gave way to luxury cars on display behind large picture windows, print shops and apartment buildings as she neared City Hall.

The bank was just past City Hall on Market Street near the "Civic Center," ironically named since it had a large courtyard near the BART and metro stations where the homeless, drug addicts and the disaffected gathered daily in full view of city government. Since moving from her small town of Ketchikan, Alaska, to San Francisco, there was nothing about the city Lexi had seen that she didn't love; even the gritty Tenderloin and homeless encampments, though not her favorite areas, were part of her adopted city. She spent a lot of time at the main library on her days off and admired City Hall across the mall. San Francisco's library was like the Library of Alexandria in ancient Egypt to Lexi. It was the center of all knowledge compared with the tiny library in Ketchikan.

After making the bank deposit, she walked back toward the bakery on the hotel side of the street to get a closer look at the damage. There were six lanes of traffic on Van Ness, split by a wide median with scrawny shrubs and a few anemic trees separating McCracken's from the hotel. This close, the hotel looked so altered that it was like a different building entirely.

The left tower's second-floor rooms were destroyed while the hotel's right side was completely undamaged. From a birds-eye view, the hotel was shaped like an "H" and took up half the block.

The cleanup crew that she had seen earlier was now gone. Glass had been cleared away. The pavement was a pool of gleaming wet blacktop, and a trickle of water ran down the driveway and into the gutter. She noticed a large garbage container bursting at the seams and spilling over with burned wood, black waterlogged mattresses, broken chairs and gnarled metal bed frames.

Lexi had read in the paper before work that the hotel had 400 rooms that ran the block from Van Ness to Franklin. At least the fire had started during the day while, Lexi assumed, most of the guests were out and about. She thought of Jerry and hoped he'd come in to the bakery after his shift today. She didn't want to go back to work yet and decided to visit Paula's Keys further up the street from the bakery

Though the newspaper was delivered to her apartment each day, Lexi liked to keep it and cut out articles to send to her grandparents in Alaska. So, every morning, she also took *The Chronicle* from outside Paula's store for the bakery. The stack of papers had been delivered twined together. Lexi shook the top paper back and forth to loosen it from the ties.

Today she would pay Paula for a week's worth of papers. This was mostly a gift for her customers, Stella and Henry, who each read the paper cover to cover, Henry first, then Stella. They each would fold it neatly into sections and stack it on top of the garbage can near the front door when they had finished. When it was slow, Tiny Timm read Herb Caen's gossip column to Lexi. Timm was a big fan and would finish reading it with, "And that's the news from the Sugar Cane!"

As she approached the key store, Lexi saw Paula through the window. She was sitting at the engraving machine. Above the door was a sign with a caricature of Paula's face with her signature frameless, star-shaped, pink-tinted glasses with "Paula's Keys" painted underneath. The bell rang as Lexi opened the door.

"Hi, Paula."

Paula didn't look up. Instead, she continued to concentrate on engraving a gold metal plaque secured in the machine's vise. Her glasses were halfway down her nose. Her bangs looked like she had cut them herself, their choppy ends clinging to her hairline for dear life. Paula's baby-doll T-shirt exposed her pronounced collarbone and ribcage. A faded decal of "K-C and the Sunshine Band" stretched across her tiny chest. Lexi noticed a purple bruise on Paula's right forearm just below the sleeve. It wasn't the first time Lexi had seen bruises on Paula's arms in shades of deep purples, or hints of yellow as they healed.

The first time Lexi had ever gone to Paula's Keys was when she needed an extra key for her apartment. That day, Paula had had a black eye. Trying not to seem too nosy, Lexi ignored it. Sometime later, Paula told Lexi that was why she had wanted to get to know this "cool redhead from Alaska"; because Lexi hadn't even raised an eyebrow at Paula's black eye. Paula was close in age to Lexi, who didn't have many friends her own age. While she loved her customers at the bakery, they were mostly her grandparents' age. It was Lexi's familiarity with older people that made her ignore Paula's black eye. Not only had she been raised by her grandparents, she had also worked in an old-folks home during high school. The residents often fell down and bruised easily. You didn't want to overreact or make a fuss. It made the people she had grown to like feel out of control and embarrassed them. As long as there was no question of abuse, you let it go. The result was a habit of underreacting to things that would alarm others.

There was another reason Lexi took things in stride. Lexi's mother and father had died in a seaplane accident when she was a baby, that was the reason her mother's parents had raised her. For most of her life, Lexi had felt she was more of a caretaker of her grandparents than a child, and she had had little time for friendships. Even when she began school, her free time was often taken up with making sure her grandparents were well cared for, that they took their daily medications and got to their doctors' appointments. Each year there seemed to be more pills and more appointments.

Paula wanted to be friends with Lexi, and that was a good enough reason to become friends.

Her co-worker at the bakery, Beverly, was a few years older than Lexi, but since Beverly was dating Victor and studying pre-med at San Francisco State, she had little time for Lexi. Like most of her San Francisco friends, it was a work-place friendship.

It wasn't long after they'd met at the key store that Paula invited Lexi for drinks to what Paula called a "fern bar" on Polk Street. The bar was actually named after a tree, not a fern: The Royal Oak.

"It's like a fern jungle in there." Paula had explained. "They are spider plants everywhere. Who knows why this silly trend started, but they have a good happy hour, so I put up with excessive greenery in my face."

They had sat at the bar at The Royal Oak and ordered drinks. Paula's attention-grabbing glasses always did the trick. People noticed her. Her hair was punk-black at the time and looked butch next to Lexi's hair with its long curls tied back with a blue ribbon.

As Paula had warned, bushy fern fronds poured from pots near Lexi's head, threatening to entangle themselves in her hair, which got tangled enough without help from outside tendrils. The bartender took their order, eyeing them with interest. There were a few people perched on Victorian couches, sitting in circles of patchy light under Tiffany lamps. Smoke clouded the room and made everything look out of focus. Several customers stared at them. The bartender set two Brandy Alexanders on the bar in front of them and started wiping the counter with a clean towel.

The alcohol burned in Lexi's throat. Paula looked around the room.

"They think I'm your girlfriend."

Lexi choked on her drink. "My what?" She caught the bartender's eye. He gave her a sly grin.

"So, what's your story?" Paula leaned away from Lexi, taking in her second-hand-store men's jacket, ripped jeans and ankle boots.

"I don't have much of a story, really. I grew up in Alaska with my—" Lexi started to say before Paula interrupted.

"Two more of these!" Paula yelled, making a circle with her arm in the universal symbol for another round.

"Alaska," Paula leaned closer to Lexi, her breath boozy. "This is going to be fun. She nodded toward the bartender, who was trying to hide his interest in Paula and Lexi. "He also thinks we're lovers."

"Why?" Lexi felt the dull veil of alcohol after draining her glass.

Paula put her arm around Lexi and winked at the bartender, who nodded approvingly while grabbing bottles from the speed bar without once taking his eyes off the seemingly happy couple.

"Don't worry, sweetie," Paula said, keeping her arm on Lexi's shoulders. "You're not my type. I like a man in uniform."

Paula let go and leaned back, giving Lexi the once-over before she asked, "Where do you live, anyway?" Paula's mischievous we-are-a-couple prank seemed to have played out.

"Larkin and Union."

"Russian Hill." Paula said as a customer at the other end of the bar caught her attention. "Fancy. You come from money?"

"Oh, no!" Lexi said. "I'm from a one-horse town. My parents were teachers."

"Are they retired?" asked Paula.

"They died." Lexi laughed. "I can't believe I just laughed. My parents are dead! I'm tipsy."

"You were drunk after your first sip, Alaska."

A few drinks later, they exited the Royal Oak—much to the disappointment of the bartender, who had seemed overly interested in them—and then hopped into a cab, which sped down Polk Street before abruptly stopping at the curb in front of a building South of Market. Paula had told the driver to take them to the "Cool Whipped Club."

"You're going to be blown away!" Paula, a bit tipsy herself, was excited, bouncy. The cab raced up hills and slammed to a halt at stoplights. Paula and Lexi crashed into doors, the front seat and each other. Paula screamed with delight. Lexi held on to anything she could get her hands on. She'd never met anyone as uninhibited as Paula.

Lexi wasn't sure what time it was but it was dark outside. The building looked abandoned as they pulled up to the curb. There was no sign and few streetlights as far as she could see. The fog was dense and the street deserted. Lexi's curls pulled away from her scalp and frizzed into an orange halo. They got out of the cab. As she strained to see where they were going, she thought that maybe three (or was it four?) Brandy Alexanders had been too much.

Lexi followed Paula to an unmarked door. After Paula knocked, a keyhole swished open, revealing a huge eyeball that squinted. With a click, the door slid open. They walked into a dark hallway.

At the far end, Paula pushed through dark curtains that felt damp against Lexi's hand. They walked into a cavernous room with high walls and large wooden beams crisscrossing the ceiling. Chains hung from large hooks. Pulleys and what looked to Lexi like bungee cords with curved hooks dangled from steel rods that ran across the ceiling. It smelled of sweat and perfume. Women and men were walking casually around the room, wearing only black masks covered in metal spikes with holes cut out for the eyes, nose and the mouth. A woman in black chaps was whipping a man who was kneeling over what looked like a prayer bench. The sight acted like a pot of hot coffee and Lexi sobered up in an instant, though given what she was witnessing, she wished that she could still feel the dull fog of alcohol insulating her from reality.

Paula grabbed Lexi's hand and dragged her to a bench to watch.

"You look green, Lex. There's no booze here or I'd get you a drink. Things can get out of hand when people are inebriated or use drugs, if you know what I mean." She squeezed Lexi's hand. If she hadn't had the bench to sit on, Lexi was sure she would have fallen over. It was like watching an accident. You couldn't look, but you couldn't look away. She was simultaneously awestruck, horrified and fascinated.

Several couples disappeared down halls leading from the main room. As Paula and Lexi watched the prayer-bench whipping—Lexi kept thinking of a nun spanking a child, but she had never seen a nun in chaps or a child who looked to be about 40 years old—Paula's grip tightened on Lexi's hand. Wincing, Lexi pried her fingers away.

"Geez, Paula." Lexi massaged her hand. "You squeezed the life out of my fingers. This is literally too much fun for you."

Without taking her eyes off the couple, Paula said, "Sorry."

Lexi felt ill, but it wasn't from what she was watching. She and Paula hadn't eaten except for the pretzel-and-peanut mix at The Royal Oak, and the alcohol was now turning her stomach. She abruptly stood up and announced, "I gotta go."

Lexi turned and walked quickly back to the door, through the smelly, wet curtain, and onto the street.

Paula appeared behind her. "Hey, what's wrong? Take a deep breath. This is a sex club, but you don't have to participate. We were just going to watch."

Leaning against the wall, Lexi straightened her back and inhaled deeply. "You know, I'm just feeling a little sick from the booze. Do you mind if I head home?"

She could tell Paula was disappointed, but she knew she had to get home quickly before throwing up, which Lexi was sure she'd eventually have to do. She didn't want Paula to feel judged, but all she wanted was to get home and crawl into a warm, familiar bed…with no chaps and whips and prayer benches.

Lexi's memory of the Cool Whipped Club would be the last time she gave Paula's bruises any thought.

Inside the key store, Paula continued engraving the gold metal plaque; she didn't look up or even acknowledge Lexi. Lexi often took her breaks at the shop. Paula liked Lexi's bakery stories, especially when Ben was having a bad day or when the methadone addicts lost their minds, sometimes screaming and throwing Danish and coffee.

Lexi looked distractedly at the pegboard dotted with hundreds of blank keys that hung behind the counter. The top of the counter was crowded with racks of key fobs, a carousel of Zippo lighters and another set of key chains with BMW, Porsche, Camaro, and Mercedes logos hanging from tiny hooks. A magazine rack and a newspaper stand were the only other occupants of the cramped store.

Lexi stood at the counter for what felt like several minutes when Paula finally looked up.

"Little League," Paula finally said, nodding in the direction of a pile of plaques and cheap-looking trophies sitting on the counter. The trophies were made of gold-colored plastic in the shape of a boy catching a misshapen baseball in an oversized glove held above his head.

Lexi was used to Paula's level of concentration. It often took Paula a few minutes to look up from her engraving when she was in the middle of a job. Finally feeling invited now that Paula had acknowledged her presence, Lexi sat on a stool next to the machine Paula was using.

"Is it for one of the Little League teams that McCracken's sponsors?"

"How would I know?" Paula responded, the irritation in her voice plain.

"You don't have to be a bitch about it."

Paula looked up. "Damn. I didn't mean to bust your balls, Lex. I haven't had my coffee yet. This guy's coming in any minute now to pick up the plaques for an award for every position on the damn team, and I still need to glue the nameplates on the statues. Don't want little Johnny what's-his-fuck's name-plate popping off during the ceremony."

Lexi recognized some of Ben's hot anger in Paula. She figured that was probably why Paula liked to hear stories about Ben blowing his top. She didn't recognize the behavior in herself, but laughed when hearing about other people losing their temper, often making comments such as "I can't believe that guy" without the slightest trace of irony. It was Paula's temper, as well as her lack of self-awareness, that were the main reasons why Lexi didn't let herself get too close to Paula. And, of course, the S&M sex club was another consideration.

"For the papers this week," Lexi said, reaching into her apron pocket for a dollar.

"Thanks, man." Paula finished tracing the letters on the plaque. "How 'bout that fire, huh?"

"Oh my god. It was terrible. Did you ever open the shop?"

"Nah," she unscrewed the vise and took out the metal plate. "Didn't you tell me you were going out with a fireman?" Paula cocked her head. "What was his name again?"

"Jerry." Lexi regretted mentioning to Paula that she had met someone the last time Paula had come into the bakery. Not that it mattered; Lexi preferred to keep her private life...well, private. "We haven't been going out for long." Lexi paused. "Some of the firemen came into the bakery during the fire."

"What about Jerry?"

"He didn't make it in, but that's understandable; it was a bad fire. He did wave to me from across the street." She felt as if she were defending him and suddenly realized just how hurt she was that Jerry hadn't made an appearance at the bakery. Just as suddenly, however, a feeling of guilt washed over Lexi when she thought of the gurney she had seen being loaded into an ambulance. People had died in the fire, and here she was feeling sorry for herself.

Paula looked up from rubbing the plaque with a worn rag.

"Oh," Paula gave her a wink. "I see. Well, it has been a long dry spell for you, hasn't it? I don't think you've screwed anyone since I've known you; I even thought you might be a nun. How was it?"

"Paula!" Lexi blushed a deep scarlet.

But Paula wasn't far off. Before meeting Jerry, Lexi's sexual life had been limited to a drunken grope behind her high school gym at the senior prom and, just before moving to California, she had steamed up the windows of her boyfriend's Mustang at Ward Lake. She didn't want to seem as inexperienced as she was, especially to someone with as vast a knowledge of sex as Paula appeared to have. Paula liked talking about sex, though she was secretive about her partners. But she certainly gave Lexi the impression that many of the men hanging around the magazine rack in her shop were interested in more than a key or a newspaper.

On more than one occasion, Lexi had come in to buy a newspaper or visit during a break to find Paula engraving a Zippo lighter with a man's name and the same message: "Steve, last night was tight—just right."

"The city must be littered with engraved lighters with the same message and a different name," Lexi had mused. She smiled when imagining two of the guys running into each other and seeing that each carried the very same lighter. To Lexi, Paula seemed like an exotic sea creature that had been discovered at the furthest depth of the ocean. Fascinating, foreign…and slightly off-putting.

She was relieved when Paula changed the subject.

"There was nothing in the paper about what caused the fire. Only the where and when."

Lexi nodded.

Paula picked up a bottle of glue, turned over the plaque, and squeezed a dollop onto the back, pressing it into the trophy before holding it in place to dry. Lexi noticed a yellowed spot the size of a thumbprint on Paula's wrist but, as usual, she said nothing.

Instead, she said goodbye and walked back to the bakery, thinking about how Paula never tried to cover her bruises. In a way it was refreshing. The bruises and colorful marks that Lexi had seen on Paula over time could all tell stories, but Lexi wasn't sure she was interested in hearing them.

That night, at home, Lexi didn't want to call the fire station to ask Jerry how he was doing, or anything about the fire. He was at work, and she thought he would get teased by the guys if she asked what, even to her, seemed like a dumb question, "Are you all right after that big bad fire?" Lexi's emotions bounced from anger that she hadn't heard from Jerry to feeling like a shit for not being the least bit understanding, but the least he could do was tell her he was okay.

Lexi never liked to dwell on tragedy of any kind because of what had happened to her parents. She hated answering well-intended questions about how they had died. Besides, if she showed too much curiosity about the fire, she felt like she would be what her grandmother had called a "looky-loo," someone straining to look at an accident. She even felt bad about looking at the burned-out hotel that day. Admitting any fascination with an accident, even if it were how she really felt, was out of the question. She was a Fagan and Fagans, as she had been reminded during childhood, were strong and silent in the face of tragedy.

Lexi was supposed to see Jerry tomorrow night anyway, so she put the fire out of her mind and played with Saxman until it was time for bed. After turning the lights out at midnight, she tried to force herself to sleep, but couldn't get comfortable. She tossed and turned under the covers, flipping her pillow and moving across the bed to find a restful spot. Light came in from the streetlight outside. Her front window was high enough that strangers walking up the hill couldn't look in, so Lexi hadn't bothered putting up curtains; it had never been an issue before. She blocked the light with a pillow, forcing her eyes closed, but with every tick of the clock she felt more awake.

A roaring, sputtering fire consumed her. Jerry's hand extended to pull her out, but she couldn't grab it. Fire trucks and gold plaques with names that she didn't recognize were all jumbled together.

The blare of Lexi's alarm startled her awake. She was disoriented until she realized she had been dreaming.

She then remembered that it was Wednesday. She had work and then her date with Jerry. He would finally be able to tell her about the fire.

She dragged herself out of bed, put the saucepan of water on the stove to boil for coffee and let the water from the shower revive her. Lexi rushed through her morning routine, even burning her mouth gulping down the hot coffee. Now fully awake, Lexi put a teacup saucer of food on the kitchen floor for the cat. Saxman sniffed and walked away with her tail high in the air.

"China's not good enough for you?" Lexi laughed as she bent to pet Saxman before heading for the door.

5

DECEMBER 21, 1983 – ANGER BALL

Though Lexi had gotten next to no sleep, she was buzzing with energy. She zipped around the bakery cleaning, stacking, refreshing, pouring coffee and slicing bread. She helped herself to a second cup of coffee and settled behind the counter when a scream came from the back.

"God damn! Son of a bitch mother—"

Lexi mouthed, "I'll just be a minute" to the customers at the counter staring at her.

She stepped into the warehouse. Ben was screaming at Dean who stood against a wall with a hand over his eyes. These outbursts used to terrify her, and she didn't know what to do when they happened. Victor had made it clear that Ben was untouchable and somehow managed to convince her that he was harmless. After her first year on the job she came to believe

Victor, because despite the amount of noise he generated, Ben had yet to follow through with violence. Every screaming, red-faced outburst was like a flash flood that stopped and dried up as quickly as it had started. Lexi assumed that Victor owed the guy, but she had also seen Victor employ the unemployable more than once.

Lexi recognized that Victor cared deeply for the underdog, and that maybe he only cared about things that really mattered. Like the time Victor hired Mike, a young man with cancer of the jaw. After surgery to remove the tumor, Mike had to continually wipe saliva from his open mouth. It disturbed many of the customers.

"Victor finds the bird with a broken wing," Tiny Timm had said at the time, "and nurses it back to health."

"That Mike is worse than that filthy old man in the wheelchair," tsked one of the widows.

"But that kid had a job until the cancer killed him," Beverly had replied defensively. Being new to McCracken's at the time, Lexi had only started to notice Beverly sticking up for their boss at any perceived slight or criticism.

"He's a regular St. Francis of Assisi" had been Stella's sarcastic take. "I don't buy his altar boy routine."

Lexi was jolted back to today's crisis as she watched Ben in the warehouse. "I'm going to rip your shoulders to your knees!" Ben was mid-volcanic eruption as his arm, still holding a frosting-covered spatula, crashed to the worktable.

On several occasions, Lexi had changed her mind about Ben, and then changed it back again. Despite the fact that Victor claimed Ben was harmless, Lexi wasn't entirely convinced, but it also didn't make sense that Victor would hire a guy completely off his rocker, did it?

"Are you okay?" Lexi asked Dean, who was shrinking in the corner.

Dean had only worked at the bakery for a few months, and she liked him and didn't want him to quit.

Before he could answer, Ben yelled, "O-fucking-K?"

Ben turned toward Lexi as Dean scurried out of the corner and ran into the office, slamming the door behind him in a cloud of flour dust.

"That little shit ruined my cake! Now I'm not squared away!"

"Could you tell me the problem?" Lexi wasn't feeling calm, but she spoke with an even, soft voice.

"I can't work like this!" Ben bellowed, but Lexi could tell that the volcano was already subsiding. The deep lines around his mouth softened.

Victor had always excused Ben's outbursts with a shrug.

"He can be fussy about his creations."

"Fussy?" Lexi had heard Beverly say to Victor. "You call that yelling and carrying on fussing?"

When the explanation that Ben was a perfectionist and a master baker who cared too much about his creations didn't fly, Victor shrugged and made a vague reference to the Marines and Vietnam. He told them Ben's issues stemmed from his time in the Marines. As a Marine, everything in his life was supposed to be "squared away" until he got to Vietnam and chaos ruled. At least Ben's behavior had some context, even if it didn't excuse it. He lost his temper when he felt out of control.

Lexi and Beverly assumed that Ben had a drug habit he must have picked up during the war. Victor made it clear that Ben was not a subject he wanted to talk about, and his defense of Ben's behavior was never couched as an apology.

"He cares way too much about those cakes," Beverly had said the first time he blew up in front of them both. That's when they started calling Ben's outbursts "death by spatula."

Lexi needed to get back to the front where customers would be wondering what kind of bakery they had stumbled into. Standing near Ben, who held the spatula like a knight defending himself, she looked at the half-sheet cake, chocolate with white buttercream frosting. Lexi finally saw what had set Ben off. A splotch of chocolate crumbs had somehow become embedded in the frosting along the side of the cake. It was a common enough occurrence when moving fast to frost a cake, and easy enough to fix.

Lexi said, "I know you can make this work, Ben." He raised his arm holding the spatula and passed it over the cake as if to conjure a design.

"How exactly should I do that, you dingbat?" His voice was raised, but the fire had gone out.

"You could try a bed of flowers along the bottom," Lexi said with confidence. Turning quickly, she checked on Dean. She could see him through the office window. He gave her a weak smile and a wave before sticking his head out of the door to say, "That Betty is out of her damn mind." He disappeared back inside the relative safety of the office. Lexi nodded and pushed her way through the door into the bakery.

She saw Timm pouring himself coffee. "What is going on back there? It's like a freak show, and I know what I'm talking about."

Lexi said, "Tell me about it."

That's when Lexi saw Howard.

6

DECEMBER 21, 1983 – I WANT TO LIVE!

Lexi guessed that Howard was in his early 50s and had been living on his own with cerebral palsy for a long time. His wheelchair was filthy, as was Howard. His head was shaved and covered with lesions and patches of dry flaky skin. Though he could move the lever on the arm of his wheelchair with the palm of his hand, his fingers were useless. He spoke with a heavy slur that was nearly impossible to understand, unless you listened carefully and repeated what you thought he had said. If you got it right and understood him, Howard would nod, his face breaking open with a messy smile that was almost beautiful.

"Hello, Howard" Lexi said, opening the front door all the way. "May I open the door for you?" She knew enough by now to ask Howard if he needed help instead of assuming.

Howard nodded, and the wheelchair rumbled into the bakery.

"I'll get your coffee."

Lexi leaned next to Howard, who smelled of spoiled milk and rotten food.

"Thanks for stopping by."

"You have a way with old, broken people," Stella said. Howard's head whipped around, but he was smiling.

"I was raised by old people," Lexi said. "But I wouldn't call Howard broken. He's been living on his own for longer than I've been alive. That's an accomplishment."

Most of the regular customers disliked Howard. His frequent outbursts scared them, but Lexi was patient. Not only had she been raised by her grandparents, her time working at Pioneer Home for the Aged had given her an ear for understanding the unintelligible. And when communication failed, Lexi had learned from paying attention that if you watched and listened, people would show you what they needed without having to ask. Howard's rules had been clear since the first day they met.

Howard had been Lexi's first customer at McCracken's on her first day on the job. She had just graduated from high school when she had arrived from Alaska. After a few months at San Francisco Junior College, Lexi had run out of the money she had saved from her summer job at the Pioneer Home. She hadn't gotten around to finishing unpacking; she still had boxes stacked in her apartment. She was worried sick about making her rent, and that Saxman might pull another disappearing act. The cat had jumped out an open kitchen window as soon as they'd moved in, only to reappear a few days later as if she had spent the week on cat vacation.

Determined to find a job, Lexi had hit the pavement. After filling out applications all morning, she found herself on Van Ness Boulevard, looking for a place to have lunch. Next to the restaurant, she saw McCracken's Bakery. The scent of donuts changed her mind. Forget lunch, a donut would do. There was no "Help Wanted" sign in the window, but when Lexi had walked into the bakery, Victor was at the register. Lexi took a chance and, after describing her experience working in an old folks' home, Victor hired her on the spot.

On her first day of work in the bakery, Claudia was explaining to her, in a heavy Russian accent, how they filled the cases and rotated cakes when a commotion outside caught their attention. Lexi noticed a man stumbling down the street, wearing a scraped-up leather football helmet and thick-soled shoes.

It looked as if he might tumble over with every awkward step. As he approached the bakery door, a man on the sidewalk stopped and opened the door for him. Howard started screaming incoherently and flailing his arms. He was dangerously close to falling over.

Claudia pointed and said to Lexi, "Howard. Go."

Alarmed, Lexi ran to the door, thanked the man for trying to help and reassured him that she would take it from there.

"I'm Lexi. What is it, Howard?"

"Aagh dom aks! Aagh dom aks!"

"Honey. I can't understand you. Can you speak slower?" People inside the bakery and on the sidewalk outside were staring.

"Aks! Aks! Damn Pee-pole!"

"They don't ask?" The more upset Howard got, the harder it was for her to understand him and the more frustrated he became. He nodded vigorously. The football helmet wiggled on his head and the straps swung under his chin. Lexi was holding the door open; Howard moved slowly through and sat down hard in the nearest seat.

Lexi looked helplessly at Claudia, who said, "Coffee in big cup, mostly milk, sugar."

"He's such a mean coot," Stella said to Lexi after she had given Howard a Styrofoam cup with a straw, lots of milk, a little coffee, and more sugar than was good for him.

Claudia came to his defense. "Howard's not mean. He's independent or as much as he can be with that horrible disease. That's what keeps him alive. Do you know he lives alone? That is a survivor."

Over the year that Lexi had worked at the bakery, she noticed that a lot of the customers actually drank milk and sugar with a splash of coffee. Lexi suspected the coffee and pastry was often their only meal for the day. Besides, their taste buds weren't what they used to be. Often, the older the customer, the more they turned the sugar jar over and let a stream of white powder fall freely into their cups. Then there were the Polk Street drug addicts from the methadone clinic; they craved sugar and had a terrible sweet tooth and rotting teeth. Lexi could identify the addicts because they shifted in their chairs and smoked one cigarette after another, filling the flimsy tin ashtrays with a mountain of butts.

Stella was the only one of her regulars who took her coffee black. Lexi walked to Stella's table to offer a refill.

Continuing her conversation, Stella said, "I don't mind mean, but Howard should at least be nice to you."

"Think how long it must take him just to get here."

"Oh, pooh," Stella waved her hand dismissively.

She took a sip of coffee. "I still think he's a mean, old coot. Try saying that three times fast. I can't even say it once without my voice giving out." She seemed uncharacteristically defeated. Lexi expected Stella to start swearing bitterly in anger over losing her voice, but instead she gave a hoarse, weary laugh and whispered, "There is no God. And that means there's no cosmic judgment, but that doesn't mean I can't judge. I find that comforting."

Like the rest of her favorite customers, Lexi only charged Stella at the beginning of the month, but Howard insisted on paying every time. He would ask Lexi to dig into his dirty backpack, slung over the back of his wheelchair, to pull out cash for his coffee and sugar donut. It tickled Lexi that Howard ate donuts thick with a sugar coating. The only way he could get messier was if he chose to eat powdered donuts.

Lexi knelt behind Howard's dirty wheelchair and opened his backpack. She didn't look too carefully at what was inside. Holding her breath, she dug her hand to the bottom, feeling for the rumpled envelope where Howard kept his money. She pulled out a wad of cash held together with a thick banker's rubber band, and turned her back to the room. After counting it, Lexi straightened the cash, secured it with the rubber band and put it back into the old envelope before pushing it deep into the knapsack.

The knapsack rested under a sign that read: "I am Howard Norton. I have cerebral palsy. In case of emergency, call" and then a phone number.

Stella looked over at the widows, who were nursing cups of coffee at their regular table, and said, "Where do they get those awful housedresses? I've never seen anything like them in any department store. And I've traveled."

"Ve don't have old lady dresses in Avenues," Claudia said from behind the counter with a wink, her Russian snapping her "W" into a "V."

"There are many, you say, 'housedresses' in Russia. Boat loads. They are Russian. Dreary tired blahs."

Today was Beverly's day off, and Claudia was working the afternoon shift. Between Beverly's drama with Victor and Claudia's rants about Russia, let alone Ben and whatever trip he was on, Lexi thought that as eccentric as Alaskans were, they were no match for the crowd at McCracken's. When Lexi met Claudia, she had proclaimed, "I'm a White Russian!" Her compact body quivering, her blonde hair piled high and stiff with hairspray, a yellow monolith on top of her head. It was a rare day that Claudia didn't proudly declare her heritage. A White Russian was the opposite of a Red Russian. Claudia was no communist, but she loved the service workers' union, and had supported her family by working at McCracken's for 18 years on a union salary.

Like most Russians who had moved to San Francisco, Claudia lived in the Avenues near the ocean. The community was so large that its residents filled the gold-turreted Russian Orthodox Church on Geary Boulevard. The local grocery stores were stocked with smoked fish, Russian pastrami called basturma, lebneh yogurt and sweet blintzes from the Motherland. Claudia's children attended a school that taught both Russian and English.

Claudia swept up Howard's crumbs as she told Lexi how Ben had been wielding a spatula at Dean yesterday because Dean had gotten cake crumbs on the edge of a cake Ben had been decorating. Claudia thought nothing of Ben's passionate nature. It reminded her of home, but without the tyrannical communism. "Death by spatula," Claudia whispered.

"I know," said Lexi. "I was there."

"Oh, I heard from someone else. There are no secrets here. No secret police or KGB." She tugged at her ear playfully. "Just big ears."

As Lexi began to wipe down the tables Claudia had left unfinished, she used her own ears to eavesdrop on a couple at the counter. The man was huffing at his wife, "It's foggy! We should have stayed in London!" She forced a smile. "Look at these great pastries," she said, as if talking to a child. He made a horrified grimace at the fat donuts and clunky cream-filled éclairs. Lexi's favorite moment of their exchange happened when they sat down and began to eat, their faces lighting up with each bite. The British and French tourists tended to appear less than enthused by McCracken's offerings, until they tried them. The Germans, on the other hand, were up for anything. Their curious, apple-cheeked faces examined every item they might be lucky enough to try.

After serving the Brits, Claudia fussed at the coffee stand and motioned for Lexi.

"So, did you have date vis nice fireman?" Claudia said, puffing up with pride. "He comes from where? Who are his people?"

"I don't know where his family is from." Lexi blushed. She tried to ignore the alarm going off in the back of her mind telling her that something was wrong with Jerry. She pushed the sleep button on that imaginary alarm when she saw Henry come through the front door.

On one of their first encounters, Henry had told her, "The young only talk about themselves, you know. It's the nature of youth. But you, my dear, know how to have a conversation." Lexi thought about how her grandparents would have scoffed if she had mooned over boys, or talked about what she wanted for Christmas. She had learned to keep her conversation focused on things that interested her grandparents. That left her with two categories: their health and what they'd be having for dinner. Lexi put a cream puff on a paper plate and set it on the counter in front of Henry. "Help yourself to coffee."

"Thank you, my dear," he said with a warm smile. "Do you know who you remind me of?" Both said "Susan Hayward" at the same time.

Lexi liked Henry. The first time he told her she looked like Susan Hayward her response was, "Susan who?" He told her to go to the video store and rent "I Want to Live!"

"The lovely Mrs. Hayward plays Barbara Graham, who's on death row. It's based on a true story. I remember the case."

Lexi had rented the movie from the corner video store, and she and Paula had watched it together on her tiny rabbit-eared television when they were first getting to know each other. Lying on the futon in Lexi's apartment, drinking Anchor Steam beer and eating Chinese takeout, Lexi and Paula roared with laughter over the dramatic dialogue and overacting.

Paula picked Saxman up by her scruff and asked, "Why do you call this creature Saxman Bite? Is she a vicious little thing?"

Taking Saxman from Paula and settling the cat onto her lap, Lexi replied, "Oh, no. I brought her from Alaska. She's named after Saxman, an Indian village outside my hometown, and 'Bight' is the name of the state park. It's called Totem Bight. B-I-G-H-T. It's a park full of carved totem poles."

Lexi petted Saxman. "She's my little piece of Alaska."

"Are there carvings of cats on these totem poles you're talking about?" Paula asked.

"Come to think of it, I don't think there are cats; beaver, crow, bear, eagle, but no cats. Maybe there weren't cats up there when they were carved. I don't think cats are native to Alaska. It's a good question. I'll look it up at the library."

Paula huffed dismissively. "It's a funny name." Reaching out to scratch the cat, she said, "I bet she's a biter." Saxman purred furiously. "B-I-T-E-R."

At the end of the movie they were watching the condemned Barbara Graham scream, "I want to live!" as she was led to the gas chamber.

Paula picked up the videocassette box and said, "It says here that Susan Hayward won the Academy Award for this piece of shit. Go figure."

"It was sweet of Henry to say that I look like her."

"It would have been even sweeter if he thought you looked like Rita Hayworth." Paula put down the box and looked at Lexi with a crooked smile. "But I'll give the old guy credit. He has style. Always wearing a jacket and hat, even the one hot week we get in the summer."

"I didn't know you knew Henry?"

"He comes into the store. Loses his keys a lot. I keep a spare in the back for him."

Paula stood up and stretched.

"Well, at least I know who Susan Hayward is now," she said to Lexi as she began stacking the takeout boxes scattered on the floor. "I'm flattered he thinks I look like any movie star, even one from"—she picked up the box and read the date when the film had been released—"1958."

Paula gave Lexi a sideways look and said, "Henry's blind as a bat, you know."

"He is not!" Lexi had picked up a pillow and thrown it in Paula's direction. Saxman had had enough and left the room.

7

DECEMBER 21, 1983 – IT'S RAINING GROOMS

It was close to the end of Lexi's shift, just hours before her date with Jerry. Stella was reading the paper by the window. Henry and Timm were settled with their sugary coffee and treats. Lexi was thinking about seeing Jerry in a few hours when Howard said something to her she didn't understand. Sometimes she cheated a bit and would ask if he wanted more coffee when she hadn't been listening closely to what he'd said.

"Aut my moo-nee" Howard's low growl didn't get any easier to understand, even on the fifth try.

It finally came to her. "Oh, count your money."

After counting his money, Lexi whispered, "Sixty-two dollars" into Howard's ear.

"Ank U." Howard's face cracked open with a smile. Lexi smiled back. She thought back to the people she'd cared for in Alaska. There weren't many native patients since, for the most part, their families took care of them, no matter how little they had. Many of those in the home were cranky and paranoid and some were downright nasty. They weren't nearly as together as Howard, though he had his moments and scared most people.

It had been a tiring day. The makeup Lexi had applied in the morning had faded. The energy Lexi had started the day with was gone. She'd been distracted worrying about Jerry, trying to ignore a rising panic that he might have been hurt. She kept reassuring herself that she would be with him soon, and even allowed herself to think about what she would wear. She remembered the way his warm hands had felt against her cold skin at the beach as the fog drifted in and the ocean disappeared into the horizon.

A man with short graying hair and a neat mustache came in. He ordered a two-tiered wedding cake from Lexi while Claudia helped other customers. Lexi noticed he was smartly dressed in creased jeans and a herringbone jacket.

"Buttercream filling?" asked Lexi.

"No," the man shook his head. "Whipped cream."

"Would you like a strawberry-whipped cream filling?"

"Now you're talking," he said, his face beaming. "Do you have wedding cake toppers with grooms only?"

It wasn't an everyday request but, in San Francisco, it wasn't unheard of. Victor had bought the groom toppers at a bakery convention in Las Vegas on a whim. They sat gathering flour dust at the bottom of a pile of brides and grooms in the office. Every couple of months, Lexi would sell one.

"I've got one in the back," said Lexi. The man looked at Lexi and said, "Well, can I see it, dear? I don't have all day."

Lexi was surprised at his sudden change in tone. He continued, "My friends are dying." His voice grew quiet. "I want to be even pretend-married while I still have friends to attend my wedding." His eyes welled with tears. "I'm sorry for being harsh. It's not your fault. I'm just exhausted and a little scared."

"Oh, sure." Lexi's face reddened. She had read about the deadly cancer and heard talk about a disease killing young men. She felt badly for him. He seemed healthy, but there was fear in his eyes, and when he admitted to feeling scared, she felt scared for him, too.

Lexi walked through the swinging door to the warehouse and into the office. She grabbed a stool and moved it in front of the filing cabinet. Stacked on top were small boxes. The plastic windows showed brides and grooms inside. Lexi was afraid that she might have sold the last one with two grooms. She was about to give up when she spotted a dusty box at the bottom of the pile with two men in tuxedoes standing together. She had to maneuver around Victor, who was sitting at the desk. He was focused on counting the money cashed out of the register. She took the box down, dusted it off with her apron and smoothed out the creases in the plastic window.

Back at the counter, Lexi showed the cake topper to the customer. He nodded his approval and said he'd take it home to make it look nice before the reception. Lexi rang up the purchase; they set a date to pick up the cake, and Lexi made a note to leave the top of the cake smooth. The man's mood had swung back to friendly, and he smiled and thanked her.

It was the end of Lexi's shift. She said goodbye to Claudia and went into the warehouse to tell Victor she was leaving. She stuck her head in the office. Victor stopped counting the cash. He laughed and said, "Today your drawer is over."

Lexi couldn't help but smile, too. "Today is no different than any other day. Some days I'm a little over, and some days I'm a little short. It must average out eventually."

Victor gave Lexi the once-over. "Got a date?" he said with a smile.

"Why do you say that?" Lexi pretended to be casual.

"You look different." He considered her more closely. It made Lexi squirm. "You're wearing makeup," he said triumphantly.

"I wear makeup, Victor." Lexi wanted to change the subject. "Listen, I gotta go, and not because I have a date." She sounded more irritated than she felt.

"I'm just pulling your chain." Victor half-smiled. "You're so easy, Lex." He turned and started counting again. "Have a good time."

As she walked out of the bakery, Lexi stopped to look again at the hotel across the street. There was nothing in the paper about any guests who had died yesterday in the fire, and she hoped the two people that she had read were in the hospital would be all right. The temperature was dropping as the sun settled over the ocean. It would be frigid at the beach. She shivered, but not just from the cold.

Once at home, Lexi fretted over what to wear and finally decided on a thick sweater over a T-shirt, a scarf and blue jeans. Easy to slip into and out of, she thought with a smile. Six p.m. came and went. Seven. Eight. Miffed but resigned that Jerry must have been called to work, Lexi put her feet up and turned on the television.

She considered calling the fire station but remembered how much ribbing he had gotten from his coworkers and didn't want to be the cause of teasing about his girlfriend checking up on him. As the television droned on, she drifted off.

Lexi woke to the sound of hissing. The electronic snow on the television screen flickered in the room. The clock read 3:17 a.m. She turned the television off and, without changing, curled up into a ball, pulled a blanket over herself and fell back to sleep.

Fire tore through the bakery, incinerating the warehouse. Life-size plastic brides and grooms melted, their mouths open in silent screams, their bodies merging into grotesque puddles.

Lexi woke startled, her hair matted, the blanket wet with sweat. She stumbled into the kitchen, filled a pan with water and set it on the stove. She stared at the flame. She hadn't heard from Jerry. She had hoped to get the story of how the fire had started from him before reading it in the newspaper. But if she were being honest, she was devastated that he hadn't even bothered to call to cancel their date.

Once dressed and still warm from her cup of tea, Lexi walked fast down Larkin and cut across to Polk Street. The morning was foggy, and the dampness was starting to sink into her bones. If a bus came by, she'd take it, but waiting on the deserted street made her nervous, especially this morning. Yesterday had been a long day, and the stress of the fire and confusion about Jerry was getting to her. At 6:00 a.m. it was too late in the morning for the Polk Street prostitutes to be out, though sometimes she had seen women leaning into car windows or screaming at each other in territorial fights over customers on holiday weekends. But today it was dead quiet. As Lexi walked, her muscles started to loosen and unclench.

There was a noise behind her. She turned and saw a man one block away. She didn't get a good look, but she wasn't going to wait to find out if he was somebody she should worry about. Despite the chill from the fog, sweat formed on her face and under her arms as she ran to Broadway. By the time she reached Van Ness, she was out of breath, holding a stitch in her side. It was another 15 blocks to the bakery, but even that early in the morning there were cars and delivery trucks driving on Van Ness. Running might have been an overreaction to guy who was probably coming home from a night shift, but Lexi could hear her grandmother's voice in her head: "You could be kidnapped. Raped. Murdered. There are bad people in the lower 48 looking for girls like you." She mentally apologized to the guy. *Unless you are a rapist and a kidnapper; then screw you, Mister.*

Adrenaline coursed through her. Lexi felt ashamed that she had been dumped by a guy she had seriously fallen for. Welcome to the big city, she thought bitterly.

She was damp with sweat from running when she slipped the key into the lock of the bakery. Relieved, she let herself in, and then made sure to double-check that she had locked the door behind her. Daylight was filtering through the fog. Lexi didn't turn on the lights, but walked into the back to organize the cash drawer in the office. She unlocked the safe, counting out 20s, 10s, 5s and 1s, then cracked the change, still wrapped in its paper casings from the bank, into the drawer. She was grateful for the routine.

She took a deep breath. The smell of hot bread, cake dough, fried grease and cinnamon calmed her and made her hungry. Ben and Dean would be mid-way through their shift by the time the doors opened at 7:00 a.m. She had forty minutes to fill the counters. As she walked out of the office, she saw Ben at the cake table. She didn't see a cake or bowl of frosting. In fact, the table was empty. Ben was leaning over the table with something in his hand. His eyes were expressionless. He swept a small pile of what looked to Lexi like flour from the table onto the floor. Something was off. She wasn't up for asking if everything was okay or trying to figure it out. Not this morning. She turned and walked back into the bakery.

Standing by the register, Lexi pieced together what she'd seen. Was it a straw? Ben drank soda all day, so having straws around was normal. Her thoughts were interrupted when Dean backed into the room, wheeling a rack filled with éclairs and gooey tarts in front of the cold counter. He stopped moving the rack so fast that a few pastries slid to the edge of the baker's sheets. Lexi pulled a tray and set it on the counter as they both began unloading the treats.

"I think I saw Ben acting strange."

Dean laughed, "That's like calling a 'kettle beige.' He's all drugged up."

"What?"

"Oh, Alaska. You little mountain goat. It's from *The Boys in the Band*."

"I don't know what you're talking about. What boys in what band?"

"It was a play that was made into a movie." Lexi stared at Dean. "You're hopeless, Alaska."

Lexi said, "Well, you have a point there. So, what did I just see?"

"Oh, honey, Ben has a raging coke habit. Please pretend that you knew that."

Lexi played along. "Alright, so he has a drug habit. That explains his outbursts, right?"

"You are adorably virginal, doll cakes. Maybe the drugs have turned him into a rage machine, but I know the make and model of that cocaine and it doesn't make me cranky in the least." He pulled a cream puff with strawberry filling out of the counter and blew the powdered sugar on the top toward Lexi before taking a bite. She laughed and continued placing the racks of pastries under the counter.

"How do you think he gets so much work done?" Dean asked. "He's higher than the space shuttle zipping around up there." Dean pointed toward the ceiling.

Lexi looked around the room and lowered her voice. "Does Victor know about this?"

"It may not be the swinging sixties, my dear-ling, but it is 1983. We're all doing it, except you, apparently. I think Victor knows, but Ben must have something on him. Why else would he keep not-squared-away Rambo First Blood working and all of us in danger of being murdered every day."

"Beverly and I call his outbursts 'death by spatula' after you ruined his cake." Lexi gave Dean a friendly nudge.

"Easy for you to say. You're not staring at the business end of that spatula." Dean walked to the swinging door, turned and said, "'A drowning man takes down those nearest.'" He looked at Lexi, exasperated that she didn't recognize the quote. "Nothing?"

Lexi looked blank. "I can't keep up with your movie references."

Pushing the door, Dean said, "It's from *Who's Afraid of Virginia Woolf.* Liz Taylor and Richard Burton. Get ye to the video store!" The door swung closed behind him as Dean disappeared into the warehouse.

At 11:30 a.m., just before the lunch rush at the end of Ben and Dean's shift, Lexi cashed out her drawer and left it on the desk in the office before pushing the last of the baker's racks out front. She stopped to check in on the guys. Anything to distract her from thinking about Jerry and how wrong she had been about him. She didn't want to feel, and the only way she knew to stop crying was to stay busy and embrace the ongoing drama of the bakery.

Dean was prepping cakes to be filled. Cutting through the middle of one, he moved the cake knife carefully, his eyes focused on the blade. She stopped to admire his precision after such a short time on the job and remembered that he might be high too.

Dean looked up, saw Lexi and stopped. He put the knife down and tapped the side of his nose with his finger. He nodded his head in Ben's direction and snorted loudly.

"Aren't you close to being done for the day?" Lexi said quickly to divert the attention from Dean.

"We're not done and we'll never be done. We're not casseroles." A menacing rumbling sound came from deep in Ben's throat. Lexi was alarmed. Flour in Ben's hair and mustache puffed around his shaking body. Lexi realized that Ben was laughing. *There's a first*, she thought. Relieved, she walked back to the front.

A man with neat salt-and-pepper hair walked in a few minutes later. Lexi watched him check out the Styrofoam cake near the front door. His mustache was more pepper than salt. His tight T-shirt, creased jeans and sports coat screamed neat and tidy. He looked at the faded pink roses, then down at a chunk of plastic cake missing out of the bottom tier. Though the bride and groom on the top of the cake grinned obliviously, the dusty display had seen better days. *I've got to tell Victor to get rid of that thing*, Lexi thought.

The man circled the case before making his way to the counter. His brows squeezed together and his mouth turned down in a questioning frown.

"Can I get you something?" Lexi asked.

The man leaned over the counter. Lexi could see the skin under his thin mustache and smell his musky cologne.

"Do you have wedding cake toppers?"

"Of course."

"Do you have specialized tops?" He drew out the word special-ized.

Lexi took a chance. "Do you mean two grooms? Yes, we carry those."

"I do, young lady. I heard that McCracken's might carry wedding cake toppers with two grooms and I'm not disappointed." The man smiled with straight white teeth, his eyes wide with delight. "Put one aside for me, honey, and I'll come back later."

Lexi was proud to be the number one seller of groom cake toppers. Two orders in as many days had to be some kind of record.

"Do you want to order a cake to go with the grooms?"

"No," he said, looking at the dilapidated Styrofoam cake at the front of the store. "I wouldn't order a cake from here." The sad cake didn't deter any brides from ordering their wedding cakes from McCracken's, at least none that Lexi could remember, but this guy clearly wasn't interested. She smiled at Timm as she noticed him watching them. She hadn't seen him come in and sit down.

"Your name?" She turned her attention back to her customer.

"Jamie." His green scarf set off his eyes that were framed by thick dark eyelashes. Lexi wrote down the order, and Jamie left. Hopefully, there would be another groom cake topper in the office. At this rate, she'd need Victor to order more.

She took a damp towel and wiped the tables. When she got close to Timm he said, "Why do all cops look like gay men?"

"You have it backward. Gay men look like cops, not the other way around. It's something about the mustaches and the worked-out bodies."

"You do know that wasn't a cop, right?" Timm said.

"Of course," Lexi snapped the towel lightly in his direction. "I'm not that naïve."

8

DECEMBER 22, 1983 – WOMEN ARE LIKE THAT (COSI FAN TUTTE)

During its heyday in the late 1940s and '50s, McCracken's had dozens of stores, with Van Ness being the main store and production facility. The McCracken family started the business in 1945. Their bakery empire had shrunk over the years to the two satellites: one on Kearny Street in the Financial District, and the other on Geary Boulevard, near the ocean. The McCracken's were an old San Francisco family. Victor McCracken's parents still lived in Pacific Heights, where he grew up. As a young man, Victor had held a variety of jobs at McCracken's, until his father retired and Victor became manager. McCracken's was the only work environment Victor had ever experienced, and none of the business classes in college seemed to have had any effect on his laid-back management style.

Lexi was friendly to Victor but kept her distance. Everyone knew he had a girlfriend but was also having an affair with Beverly. The situation had "disaster" written all over it. Lexi only allowed herself to be pulled into Victor's messy personal life when she needed a car. Victor often loaned his girlfriend's VW bug to anyone who needed it. It had no first gear but, for the most part, was reliable. He said his girlfriend only kept it for sentimental reasons, and that she usually drove her BMW. Lexi suspected that she didn't even know the VW was gone when Victor handed out the keys.

To Lexi, Victor was a big-hearted guy, but a total dog when it came to women. She didn't know his girlfriend's name and had only seen her at the bakery once. A sensuous blonde with blue eyes and round cheeks, she was the opposite of Beverly, who was six feet tall, dark and intense with black hair that, even braided, hung past her waist. While they made a striking couple, Lexi thought that Beverly was much better suited to Victor than the blonde. Victor was tall and thick as an old tree and lumbered around like a bear in the forest. Beverly was willowy and moved with the grace of a dancer. Her delicate hands had a light touch. Lexi suspected she would make a good surgeon once she had graduated from medical school.

Timm was long gone when Victor came into the front of the bakery and motioned for Lexi to follow him into the office. He sat down and put his foot on one of the drawers that was half open, overflowing with files. There was no other chair in the office, so Lexi leaned on the door jam.

"I have a proposition to make," he said.

"That sounds provocative."

"I have tickets to the opera, and I want you to go with me."

"That's rich." Lexi was incredulous. "What about Beverly?"

"My relationship with Beverly is complicated and, frankly, I'm not going to get into it with you."

"What would she think?"

"Beverly hates the opera. I think she'll be happy that I'm not taking my girlfriend." Victor sat up. "Listen, it's my favorite opera, and I have tickets. Do you want to go or not?"

Lexi knew she'd be a heel for accepting, but she had been obsessing over being stood up by Jerry, besides, she had never been to an opera. On the other hand, Beverly might be hurt despite Victor's objections to the idea. It was tempting. How many times had she walked by the Opera House, imagining herself in the audience?

She intended to say "no" but instead found herself saying "yes." Beverly would have to accept the truth that her friend had no designs on her lover, and Lexi would have to live knowing that her loyalty was for sale for the price of an opera ticket.

"It's *Cosi fan Tutte,* and it's tonight. I hope you have something nice to wear." They made arrangements that Victor would pick up Lexi at her apartment. She spent the remainder of her shift considering her wardrobe, and wishing it was Jerry who was taking her to her first opera.

On her way home from work, Lexi decided to stop by Tower Records to pick up a recording of the opera, even though she couldn't remember the name clearly. She caught the 47 Bus and got off at Bay Street. Fisherman's Wharf stretched before her along the water. The boats bobbed gently as seagulls circled overhead; the smell of sea air and fish a reminder of her hometown.

Inside Tower Records, Lexi passed the checkout counter lined with clerks and walked back to the tape department. The rows of cassettes blended together as she searched for classical music. She was about to give up when a store employee approached.

"You in the weeds?" The clerk's long hair was matted into dreadlocks and tied with a loose bandana. Her T-shirt read "Okeh Records." A riot of colorful braided bracelets crowded her wrists. "Looking for something in particular?"

"Did I look that lost?" Lexi laughed and said, "It's an opera. Costa futti or something."

She looked at Lexi and said, "Mozart. In the opera room."

Lexi followed the clerk's paint-spattered Doc Martens to the glass room at the end of the tape aisles. She opened the door.

"There's a whole room for opera?" marveled Lexi.

"This is San Francisco," she said and addressed a guy behind the counter. "Take care of my friend here. She needs the best recording of *Cosi*." Before leaving, she roused the clerk behind the counter with his nose in a magazine by saying, "Opera was the Disco of its day!"

The classical-department clerk looked up, annoyed to be disturbed. His T-shirt had a silkscreen of a cat-eyed bouffant beauty with the name "Maria Callas" written above the image. He spoke slowly, as if underwater.

"The 1935 live recording of the Glyndebourne Festival Opera House in East Sussex is my favorite." He pulled down a cassette and handed it to Lexi.

She bought the tape and left the store, walking first from the quiet stillness of the classical room through the main room with punk rock pounding on the speakers, and out the front door. Once on Columbus Avenue, she opened her Walkman, took out a Talking Heads tape and popped in the Mozart. Lexi pressed Play. As the opera slowly began playing, it seemed to transform the sweeping bay in the distance into a scene other than the one she'd been watching earlier. It was as if she had been transported to a different, more beautiful world. Her mind wandered as she walked to the pier, the waves ebbing and flowing along with the music.

Lexi owned exactly one black dress. It had a full skirt that stopped just below her knees, a tight bodice and a velvet belt that flattered her figure. She wished she were dressing for a date with Jerry. After trying on everything else she owned, Lexi decided to pair the dress with a men's jacket she'd picked up at a thrift shop, black pantyhose and high heels. Walking in the heels proved to be a bit of a challenge, she teetered when she walked, but decided to stick with them. They looked great with her outfit, and it wasn't like she would be running to the opera.

By 5:00 p.m. Lexi was dressed and ready to go. Victor was picking her up in an hour and a half for the 8:00 p.m. performance. She kicked off her shoes, slipped the recording she'd bought earlier into her cassette player and tidied up a bit, distracted by the beautiful melodies of the opera. She folded the futon back into a couch, threw away cartons of take out, emptied ashtrays and, not wanting to get hair on her dress, used a long stick with a feather tied to the end to play with Saxman. After turning the cassette over, she pressed Play and sat down, tucking her knees under the jacket, its silky lining cold on her legs. Saxman curled up nearby. As the light turned a dusky blue, she lit a cigarette and stared out the window. A black Mercedes pulled up in front of the apartment, and Victor got out. Lexi had never seen this car and realized with embarrassment she had expected the orange VW to pull up. He never handed over the keys to this car, and she could see why. Putting out her cigarette, she grabbed her handbag, locked the apartment door and met Victor on the street.

After an awkward hello, she got in the car.

"It feels weird sitting in Beverly's seat. Or is it your other girlfriend's seat?"

"You look nice." Victor said, ignoring her remark.

"Thank you. I've never seen you in anything but chinos and T-shirts." She couldn't quite give him a compliment even though he looked great in a tuxedo. His frame seemed to fill the suit perfectly.

Victor turned onto Union, but instead of making a left toward the opera house, he continued toward the Marina. They passed jewelry stores, clothes boutiques, Perry's Bar and a disco.

"Where are we going?" Lexi asked.

"I need to pick up the tickets at my parents' place."

It seemed strange that he hadn't picked up the tickets before the night of the performance, but Lexi was curious to see where Victor had grown up. He turned on Fillmore and drove up the hill, the Mercedes engine straining against the steep incline. She couldn't imagine the VW making it up this hill. As they reached the top, elegant apartment buildings with picture windows gave way to larger and larger houses. Victor pulled in front of what could only be described as a mansion. Columns on either side of the front door supported a second-story balcony. On the landing was a wind-swept tree in a ceramic pot.

Lexi wanted to stay in the car. She was already feeling intimidated.

"Come on," Victor winked. "You must be curious about where the rich kid grew up." She got out of the car.

To her amazement, the front door wasn't locked, and they walked into a large hall. Marble stairs swept around to the right, and a hallway disappeared into the back on the left. With his hand on her back, Victor guided Lexi to a sitting room across from the stairs. There was a large picture window with views of the Golden Gate Bridge and Marin Headlands that was so perfect a scene that it looked like a painting. She had never seen anything like it before. As if showing off, the last of the sunlight faded as the bridge's lights turned on. The churning ocean turned from dark blue to black, the whitecaps bursting to the surface. Victor nudged Lexi forward. Returning her attention to the room, Lexi looked around. The windows were bordered by long, heavy curtains drawn back by thick ropes ending in fist-sized tassels. Stripes and flowers patterned every cushion and chair. A large portrait in a heavy, gilded frame above the couch depicted a young woman holding a bow and arrow. She was standing in a green wood. Her red hair flowed over her shoulders; a deer in the distance scampered behind the trees. Under the portrait was a long couch decorated in a bold print, and sitting on it was a large man with graying hair. Lexi guessed this was Victor's father. The flowers seemed to shrink around him. He had a book open on his lap, but his eyes were closed.

Across from the couch, in a wingback chair, sat a woman whose red hair was streaked with white—Victor's mother. She had been thumbing through an *Architectural Digest* magazine, but as Lexi and Victor approached she stood up and, giving Lexi a discreet once-over, extended her hand. "Celia McCracken."

Lexi recognized the face as an older version of the woman in the portrait. She took the proffered hand and said, "Nice to meet you."

"This is my husband, Victor McCracken Senior." Victor's father opened his eyes. He stood up towering over them. His hand was warm and dry as he gave Lexi's a gentle shake. He and his son were both what Victor called "Black Irish." They had wild, thick hair, pallid skin and dark blue eyes that looked black in the right light.

"How old are you?" Mrs. McCracken was talking to Lexi but looking at her son. "Sixteen?"

"Nineteen." Said Lexi.

Ignoring her son, Mrs. McCracken said, "We wanted to meet you before giving Victor the tickets to the opera tonight."

Mr. McCracken chimed in, "Our son has a tendency to be very generous with our season tickets." Lexi looked at Victor, whose eyes were on his mother with an expression of bemused detachment. *Do they know about Beverly? Do they disapprove of the girlfriend?* Lexi felt this might be a set up on Victor's part, but she wasn't sure what game he was playing. She suspected it had to do with fooling his parents, his live-in girlfriend and his lover. Adding one more lady to the mix seemed the wrong way to go, but she was just happy to see an opera and pretend that she wasn't heartbroken.

"Dad, we need to get a move on," Victor grumbled. "It starts at eight."

"Very well." Mr. McCracken sat down and waved vaguely to his wife. "Celia, the tickets."

She glided towards a delicate desk set nearby; the chair looked as if it would break if anyone in the family but Mrs. McCracken sat on it. Lexi noticed a gold frame on the desk with a tintype of a worn looking couple. Their thin, unsmiling faces looked straight into the camera. The man bore a resemblance to both Victors, his face being almost identical to theirs; however, even though he shared the same large body frame, he was very thin. His cheekbones and chin stuck out, and his eyes were sunken. The woman sitting next to him appeared tiny in comparison. Her hair was pulled back under a scarf and, even though the picture was deteriorating, Lexi could see that the woman's face was covered in freckles. There was such a difference in their sizes that Lexi thought giving birth to Victor's dad must have killed her. Celia noticed Lexi looking at the photograph.

"Those are Victor's grandparents." She opened the center drawer, took out two tickets and handed them to her son. She pressed his arm and said, "Have a good time with—"

"Lexi," Victor smiled warmly, but quickly pulled his arm away from his mother's hand. "Lexi Fagan."

"Can I have a glass of water?" Lexi asked, smiling at Victor. She was intimidated by Victor's mother, but wanted to see more of the house. She was sure this would be the last time she would be in the mansion, and maybe there was another amazing view in the kitchen. Victor's eyes widened, but he followed Lexi, trailing behind Mrs. McCracken, down the hall toward the kitchen as she murmured about the maid's day off.

Lining the walls of the long hallway heading towards the back of the house were photographs of Victor at school, and a young girl who must have been his sister. Both children held various trophies and wore different uniforms throughout the series of photos. Lexi lingered in the hall, looking at the various pictures of Victor playing football in mud-spattered jerseys while his sister hit tennis balls in pleated white skirts, her long tan limbs glowing with sweat. The girl's photos were placed above and below the pictures of Victor and his teammates at eye level, indicating the family hierarchy. The picture in the center of the display showed a group of boys crowded around a table full of trophies, a large banner above their heads stating: "St. Andrew's Catholic Preparatory School." Lexi looked at the victorious faces of the young men. Victor's thick hair stuck out in all directions. His smile was so wide that his eyes appeared almost closed. His left arm was draped around the neck of the boy next to him, who was also beaming a winning smile.

It was Jerry.

She turned around to Victor who had been trailing behind her. "That's Jerry."

Victor's forced smile disappeared. He rushed forward, pushed her toward a doorway and whispered, "Get your water and let's get out of here." Lexi stumbled into an enormous kitchen. Mrs. McCracken stood near the sink with a juice glass of water extended in Lexi's direction. The large countertops and enormous stove reminded Lexi of a restaurant kitchen. The butcher-block island with two built-in sinks in the center of the room was more like a continent than an island.

Lexi downed the water and ran to catch up to Victor, who was already at the front door. She wanted to stop in the hall to get a better look at the picture, but Mrs. McCracken was right behind her. Maybe it wasn't Jerry. Maybe she was trying so hard not to think about him she was starting to imagine him into pictures. As she passed the photographs, all she saw was a blur of school uniforms. "You mustn't be late," Mrs. McCracken said near her ear.

Victor echoed the same sentiment at the front door. “We really need to be going.”

Once outside, Victor opened the passenger door, and Lexi sat down. Victor hurried around to the driver’s side, slid into the seat and pulled away before his seat belt was fastened. As they drove toward the opera house, Lexi said, “That kid in the football photograph looked like Jerry Stevens.” When there was no response from Victor, she continued. “You know, the fireman I’m dating.“ She paused before correcting herself. “I was dating.”

“That’s impossible. Those are school photos and I didn’t go to school with a Jerry—what was his last name? Stevens?”

She must have been seeing things. *Get a grip.* She changed the subject. “Do your parents know I work at the bakery?”

“Yes.”

“I know it’s none of my business, but do they know about Beverly?”

“You’re right. It’s none of your business.”

They drove in silence until Victor pulled in front of the opera house. A valet opened the door and helped Lexi to her feet. Victor handed the keys to the valet, and the car disappeared around the corner.

Lexi had walked by the opera house many times on her way to the bank to make McCracken’s daily deposit. She had always liked the building with its old-world architecture, carriage lights and thick stone walls. The columns and arches seemed to go on forever. During the opening of the opera season, Lexi liked to scan the newspaper for pictures of society women in couture dresses and men in crisp tuxedos. They looked grand; a world away from Lexi's experience. She couldn't believe she was actually here. As Victor put away the parking receipt he'd gotten from the valet, Lexi took a moment to look around and soak in the scenery, watching people as they made their way up the stairs. Lexi noticed Victor staring at her. She already felt out of place, and Victor's bemused look wasn't helping.

The balcony on the second floor was crowded, slightly less so than outside the lobby. Women with hair piled high, their long ball gowns peeking from beneath thick fur coats, stood next to men wearing tuxedos with wide collars and the occasional cashmere scarf. Everyone seemed to be holding a drink and surveying the competition.

As they climbed the stairs, Lexi said, "Did you know the opera house is actually also a war memorial and was built in 1932?" Victor was silent. Undaunted, she continued. "It is a classic example of Beaux-Arts architecture." She hoped she didn't sound like an overbearing teacher, though she was showing off what she'd recently read at the library.

"No, but thanks for sharing." Victor smiled.

Lexi couldn't help herself. "Outside of New York, San Francisco has the largest opera company in the United States."

"Where do you get this stuff?"

"I read it somewhere," she said casually.

Lexi noticed that, on the corner opposite the opera house, the Davies Symphony Hall was lit up as well. That building was only three years old. It somewhat resembled a spaceship, and Lexi thought it looked as if the building wanted to separate from its moorings and fly back home. To her it appeared cold and forbidding. Lexi preferred the classic high-arched doorways and set-back windows of the opera house; its warm light spilling out through the open doors seemed to invite patrons inside.

Lexi and Victor continued up the stone stairs towards the main entrance. Lexi could barely contain her excitement. She marveled to herself that she was actually in the opera hall, and tonight she would see her very first opera. She sighed with delight. The people around her were glancing her way. She realized with embarrassment that her sigh had been loud enough to draw attention, and that she had a stupid grin on her face.

As they approached the entrance, Lexi saw stone faces carved above the arches of the doors to the theater. Moving indoors, she was surprised to see columns inside the entry hall. The ceiling was bathed in light and dotted with octagonal cutouts, creating the effect of a golden quilt hanging high above them. The lobby was noisy and crowded, and they slowly made their way up the side staircase. Lexi let Victor guide her to the bar on the second floor, his hand pressing into the small of her back. She wondered if he ushered Beverly around like this.

"What's your pleasure?" he asked Lexi.

Before she could answer, he turned to the bartender and asked for two glasses of champagne.

"I'll have champagne!" Lexi said more loudly and sarcastically than she meant to. She took the bubbling flute the bartender offered. Victor laughed at her, and she relaxed. She saw an usher handing out programs, but asked Victor to buy one of the detailed programs she'd noticed were being sold. Whatever game he was playing introducing her to his parents was going to cost him. She was starting to put together that Victor wanted to introduce her to his parents to complicate things with Jennifer, the woman he lived with, but why? She couldn't understand, but she felt she was being used to make a point. The free program wouldn't cut it; besides, she wanted a better memento of her first opera.

Victor led Lexi to a chair with a fleur-de-lis border carved into the high wooden back that sat near the bar. She felt silly sitting there alone. Victor had disappeared back into crowd in search of a program. Lexi watched as he stopped to talk to different couples, and marveled to herself how relaxed he seemed in this sea of tuxedos and designer dresses. How different he was here than at the bakery, where he avoided the world by burying himself in his messy office and ignoring almost every issue or question. While she was thinking about these two faces of Victor, a man approached Lexi and asked, "Aren't you the girl from that bakery?" He looked familiar, but she couldn't place him.

"The grooms," he reminded her.

Now Lexi remembered the mustache, the slim figure and the green eyes. "Oh, the cake topper."

"I'm Jamie," he reminded her.

"How was the wedding?"

"We're not married yet." A handsome man with a smooth face and blond hair was carrying two wine glasses as he walked up to them. He handed a glass to Jamie and extended his free hand to Lexi.

"This is the redhead I told you about from the bakery."

"Hello. I'm Matt. I'm the bride."

"Pleasure."

"So, you're an opera fan?"

"Well, I think I am," answered Lexi. "This is my first."

"A virgin," said Jamie breathlessly. "You couldn't have chosen a better composer for your first than Mozart."

"*The Magic Flute* would have been a better cherry popper," said Matt with a wide grin.

"What do you know about popping cherries? You must have meant 'The Magic Fruit.'"

Lexi laughed.

When Victor returned, program in hand, she introduced him to Matt and Jamie. Victor and Lexi excused themselves and opened the program. She read that there would be supertitles for this performance and couldn't believe her good luck. It was the first time the San Francisco Opera would be using supertitles.

"Supertitles are for amateurs." Victor huffed. "It's ridiculous. The subscribers won't put up with it. It's a passing fad."

"Amateurs? It says here that they're a big hit at other opera houses," Lexi said helpfully. "Besides, I don't speak German. How am I supposed to know what's happening?"

Victor wasn't swayed. He frowned and said, "You don't need to make opera popular. If people can't appreciate good music, leave them to their discos."

"You can like more than one kind of music, Victor." Lexi wanted to show off what she'd picked up from the clerk in the Tower Record's classical music department. "Opera was the Disco of its day," she teased. "What a snob you are, Victor."

A chime rang. Victor took Lexi's arm and escorted her to a door hidden behind a red curtain. He pulled it aside and stopped, turning to look at Lexi.

"You're pretty, in an off-kilter kind of way."

"Shut up!" Lexi said, socking Victor in the arm. She hoped he was just making fun of her, and that he wasn't really interested in her. They walked through the doorway and onto a small terrace. There were four seats in the box overlooking the stage, but they seemed to be only ones there.

Victor had been attending the opera since he was young, and was very blasé about the whole thing, but Lexi still couldn't believe that she was here. There had been only one music group who performed in Ketchikan, the Irish Rovers. Her grandparents had been excited to see them, but Lexi had to stay home, she'd been too little to go. *I bet Mr. and Mrs. McCracken would have liked that Irish group, too,* thought Lexi sarcastically.

Victor barely fit into the velvet-covered chair; his knees touched the front edge of the balcony. They were so close to the stage that Lexi could see the threads unraveling on the red and gold curtain covering the stage.

Lexi handed Victor the program.

"Read it to me." She was feeling the champagne.

"You urchin. I'm not reading to you."

"Please."

"I'm never taking you to the opera again." Victor said, his grin taking the sting out of the remark. He started reading. "It says that Mozart wrote the opera in 1789 for Austria's Emperor Joseph II, who famously said of the opera, quote, 'Too beautiful for our ears and monstrous many notes, my dear Mozart.' Mozart reportedly replied, 'Exactly as many as necessary, your majesty.'"

"Wow. That takes balls."

Victor looked around the room and said, "Don't believe everything you read in the program. I've seen this quote linked to every opera Mozart wrote, but I believe it refers to '*Die Entführung aus dem Serail*.'"

Lexi felt light-headed. "Stop showing off," Lexi said, laughing. "English, please."

"*The Abduction from the Seraglio*."

"It's still a great line," Lexi said. "Monstrous many notes."

Victor nodded.

The setting was majestic. The chandeliers gleamed. The arch atop the stage was decorated with gilded sculptures. Every seat was filled except the seats next to them. Victor explained his parents had tickets for the entire box, but his mother didn't like Mozart.

"Who wouldn't like this?"

Victor nodded that it was absurd.

Lexi couldn't wait to read Herb Caen's column about the opera in *The Chronicle* the next morning. This was just what she needed, an experience so outside her normal life that she could push Jerry from her mind, at least for a little while. When she thought of the photograph at the McCracken's, she no longer saw Jerry's face on the young football player. She had imagined him because she was suffering from Jerry on her mind.

The lights dimmed. The curtain rose, and the music that she had heard on her cassette player earlier filled the air. On stage, the brothers pretended to be other men in order to trick their fiancés, also sisters. As Lexi watched the sisters being fooled by the waving brothers, she remembered Jerry waving to her from the burning hotel.

It seemed as though hardly any time had passed when the music ended.

"Lexi!" Victor was motioning to her from the entrance to the box. "Let's go! Intermission."

Victor walked Lexi to the outdoor balcony. It was a clear night with bright stars overhead. The sharp, frigid air cooled her face. She took a deep breath, pulling her jacket around her savoring the beauty of the lights glowed on the tarnished green dome of City Hall across the street. The cold air seemed to rouse Victor, who had been yawning from the warm theater and the champagne.

The rest of the opera flew by in a whir of double crosses and loves lost and then found. When the curtain fell after the final encore, Lexi was completely and blissfully satisfied.

Victor was a gentleman when he dropped her off an hour later. He said goodnight and didn't object when she opened the car door and left with a quick thank you. As she slipped the key into the front-door lock, she thought briefly that she could get used to going to the opera with Victor. Unfortunately, Lexi knew it would be difficult, maybe impossible for Beverly to wrap her mind around the idea that Lexi had no designs on Victor. Being Victor's regular escort to the opera didn't sound on the up and up. Lexi decided that this would be the only time she would accept an invitation from her boss, and that she would keep it a secret from Beverly. At least for now. She wouldn't be able to keep it a secret forever, but when she did fess up, she hoped Beverly would understand how important it was to her and how little Victor factored into it.

Once inside, the apartment was cold. Saxman rubbed against her legs, leaving short tan hairs around the ankles on her tights. There were no messages on her phone. She turned on the heat, slipped off her shoes, rubbed her feet, and collapsed onto the futon, snuggling with her cat under a blanket. She wondered if Jerry liked opera, or if it even mattered since he clearly had no interest in continuing to date Lexi. She wanted to cry but wouldn't let herself fall apart over a guy.

9

DECEMBER 23, 1983 – THE FIREHOUSE

The next day at the bakery, Timm was the first to ask how "their" date had gone.

"How was our date, *ma cherie*?"

Lexi first thought that Timm was asking about Victor but realized he meant the date she was supposed to have had with Jerry a few nights ago.

"If it was 'our' date, we would have had one. Jerry never showed up."

"He stood you up?" Timm was indignant. "That bastard!"

"I'm sure it had something to do with work." Lexi hoped, more than knew, that to be the case. "Maybe he was hurt in the fire? I haven't seen anything about injuries to firefighters on the news or in the paper. Have you?"

Timm shook his head and gave Lexi a reassuring smile. "He had better broken a leg to miss a date with my Lexi."

Paula had come in for a quick cup of coffee and a chocolate chip cookie. She wasn't as regular a customer as the retirees, since she was the only person working at her key store—or with a job, for that matter —compared with most bakery customers, but when she did come in, she sat with the widows.

"Why do you always sit with them?" Lexi asked Paula, refilling her cup with coffee.

"Because they're into security."

Lexi looked puzzled.

"You forget I'm in the security business. Those ladies are afraid of their own shadows. I've added locks to the doors in all their apartments. You'd think we lived in New York."

Lexi pictured the widows spending their golden years behind doors lined with locks and a chair wedged under the doorknob; the image Paula brought up reminded her of the New York apartments she'd seen depicted in movies.

Surprising herself, Lexi felt sorry for the widows.

The rest of the morning was uneventful. During her afternoon break, Lexi couldn't stop thinking of Jerry. There was nothing for it. Her anger at being stood up dissolved. The opera faded, and the family intrigue with Victor seemed a distant memory. There was only Jerry at Manka's. Jerry at the beach. Jerry the rescuer of damsels with nosebleeds. She had to know if he was okay. Even if it meant a humiliating call to someone no longer interested in her. She decided to call the firehouse. Teasing be damned. If she was in luck, she could ask whoever answered the phone if he was all right and avoid talking to Jerry. Victor was sitting at the desk when she walked into the office to use the phone. He didn't look up from his invoice, so she picked up the phone and dialed the fire station.

Trevor answered, and after Lexi identified herself, he replied, "Hello, love, sorry about the news."

"What news?"

"Jerry."

Lexi sat on the end of the desk, her heart pounding. "What about Jerry? Did he get hurt in the fire?" she asked. "Is he in the hospital?"

"Sweetheart, I thought you'd heard by now. I'm sorry to be the one to tell you. He's dead, I'm afraid," Trevor's voice was casual. His accent lessened the gravity of the words.

Lexi clutched the phone and tried to breath, unable to speak.

Trevor said, "Lexi. Are you there, love?"

Victor looked up, concern etched on his face. Lexi could only concentrate on a spot on the wall in front of her. She must have heard wrong.

"You can't be talking about Jerry Stevens," she stammered. "Oh my god. What happened? How?"

Trevor explained that Jerry had gone into the hotel by the Franklin Street entrance. He was in the south wing of the hotel, where they now believe the fire had started. A pipe exploded and knocked his mask off. Overcome with smoke, he passed out. It wasn't until the clean up after putting out the fire that they found his body.

"But I've been reading the papers and watching the news. There were two people hurt, but they were guests staying at the hotel, and they're in the hospital."

"I'm sorry to tell you, they've died too."

Lexi was trying to comprehend what he was saying. This wasn't the first time that death had touched her life. Her parents had died when she was a baby, but she hadn't known them. Her grandparents had made her feel loved her whole life, so the loss of her parents, while tragic, never deeply affected Lexi's childhood, except when people would whisper, "That's the little girl whose parents died. Poor thing." This was different. Jerry had begun to be important to Lexi; he simply couldn't be dead.

"But, why haven't they reported anything about Jerry in the paper?"

Trevor slowed his words as if talking to a child. He told her that there hadn't been any news coverage yet, because the fire department had asked the local news stations and the papers to wait until Jerry's family had been notified of his death.

"Prepare yourself, Lexi. The news is going to be released when *The Examiner* comes out tonight."

"What will it say?" She immediately regretted asking.

"That he was burned, Lexi."

Lexi doubled over, the phone still pressed to her ear. Victor looked up, alarmed, but remained quiet.

"Is Ralph there? Do you think I could talk to him?"

"Sure." Lexi heard Trevor yell for Ralph. A moment later he picked up the phone. During the firehouse date, Lexi had liked Jerry's friend Ralph the most.

"Lexi, I'm so sorry. I didn't think to call you. We're all so upset."

"Oh, no. I get it. Please don't feel bad. I wouldn't be bothering you, but it wasn't in the papers. I didn't know."

Ralph sighed. "You're right, of course. I shouldn't be telling you this, but the real reason they withheld information about Jerry is that the Chief asked that the papers keep the news quiet."

Lexi held her breath.

"That's all I know, Lexi."

"I don't understand. Trevor said it was until his family was told. Is there something else?"

Ralph said, "I don't know anything more. Listen Lexi, I have to run. I'm so sorry." He said goodbye and hung up. The dial tone buzzed in Lexi's ear.

An image entered her mind. Jerry engulfed in flames, his flesh burning. She let the phone drift away. Victor stood up, gently took the phone from her hand and hung up. He put his arm around her, lifted her until she was standing. Her face sank into his chest, and she started to cry.

Beverly walked into the back. Lexi opened her eyes and saw Beverly give Victor a wicked look before slamming a loaf of bread into the slicer. The blades clacked loudly as the bread moved through the machine. Lexi knew her friend was upset and had misinterpreted why she was crying in a room with Victor, but at the moment she didn't care. Not now. Beverly bagged the bread and stomped out front, pushing the swinging door so hard it bounced off the wall and nearly hit her.

Victor told Lexi to go home. She grabbed her things and left. She couldn't deal with Beverly thinking Victor had been the reason for her tears, not right now, and it was definitely no time to tell her about the opera; besides telling Beverly about Jerry's death was out of the question. It would not be a short conversation, and she didn't want to break down. She just wanted to get home where she could curl up with Saxman.

On her way out, Lexi stopped by Henry's table to say goodbye. She returned his concerned look with a weak smile. For some reason, it was less painful to tell Henry, and she managed to keep it together. He gave her a pat on the hand when she explained what had happened. *How could Jerry be dead?*

Lexi didn't want to take the bus home. She walked down the street, the misty wetness so different than the torrential soaking she was used to growing up in Ketchikan. For the first time since leaving home, she wanted to go back to Alaska. Or better yet, she wished she were a child again, jumping in puddles without a care in the world. Her grandmother always had a cup of hot chocolate topped with whipped cream ready for Lexi when she came inside. She wanted to be someplace else, at another time, to feel anything but this oppressive sadness.

As she cut down the alley to Polk Street, zigzagging her way between buildings, she didn't feel the cold against her skin. It was as if the wet damp air were touching someone else. Without knowing how she got there, Lexi stood at the front stoop of her apartment building. She wanted to call Paula but realized she didn't have her number. Every time they had seen each other outside of work, they had planned it at work.

Her grandparents would be no help since she hadn't told them about Jerry to begin with. Explaining everything would be harder now than not telling them. She didn't talk to them often. It was expensive to call Alaska, and conversations with them were difficult since they refused to wear their hearing aids. But mostly she didn't call because she didn't have the energy to start from the beginning. There were too many things she hadn't told them.

Her list of people to call was shockingly small. The only other person whose shoulder she would have wanted to cry on was Beverly, but Beverly had clearly misunderstood the scene in the office.

At home, Lexi didn't know what to do. She ended up staring out the bay window at Larkin Street, but after sitting for a long while with Saxman purring nearby, her restlessness took hold. Walking to the kitchen, she put the pot of water on for tea.

Back at the window, cradling her mug, she watched as cars drove by. People walked along the street with purpose. Even though it was cold and foggy out, there were people eating ice cream at Swensen's around the corner on Hyde Street. Her eyes turned to the spot on the landing in front of the apartment building where she and Jerry had kissed when he dropped her off after their night at Tomales Bay. She was numb from cold and light-headed with hunger when she finally went to bed and let herself drift into a fitful sleep.

She woke and gathered the quilt around her. After a few days of trying to push Jerry out of her mind, assuming he had rejected her, she now wanted to remember every detail of their time together and replayed their first date in her mind.

A week had gone by since her gusher of a nosebleed without a word from her "knight in shining scarlet armor," as Beverly had called him. She and Lexi had been talking when Lexi saw Timm near the front door. She ran to open it before he had to struggle with his crutches.

"Let me help you."

"Lexi, *ma cherie*!" Timm's diaphragm was compressed, and his voice was high and fluttery. "I'm not like Howard. You can always help me, and you don't even have to ask permission." Since he was small, Timm's head reached the bear-claw level near the second shelf of the donut case.

"Come with me to ze Kasbah!"

"Maybe tomorrow," said Lexi. "Can I get you your usual?" Lexi waved him to his regular seat before she brought a Russian teacake and coffee to the counter.

It had been slow; the only customers were Timm, Stella and a group of Japanese tourists. Beverly had been cleaning tables. She tapped Lexi on the shoulder and mouthed wordlessly, "Jerry," pointing to a table off to the side, and then she started humming the wedding march. "Dah da da da..."

As Lexi turned to look, Jerry walked over to her. He was wearing a dark blue uniform with deep creases running through the pockets and down the front of his shirt. She noticed the snug fit over his muscular frame.

"How about I take you to ze Kasbah?" he said with a wink.

Lexi smiled and said, "I'd consider it."

"How about tonight? I can pick you up after work."

"That sounds great, but I'll have to go home and change first." Lexi stared at Jerry's dark blue eyes. They reminded her of fresh blueberries. Bear food. She hesitated before adding, "But what makes you think I'm free?"

"Nothing. I was just hoping."

She scribbled her address and phone number on an order form and handed it to him. "Lexi Fagan." He read the name slowly as if tasting the words. He looked up, took the paper from her hand and let his fingers linger where they touched hers.

"Jerry Stevens."

"I remember," said Lexi.

"Until tonight then."

Lexi blushed and smiled, not taking her eyes off his.

"Oh, I'm taking you to the firehouse for dinner. I'm on call tonight."

"Then we're going to need dessert. What would the guys like?" Lexi motioned to the cake counter with German chocolate cakes, cheesecakes and whipped-cream cakes with strawberry filling. Jerry selected a cheesecake, and Lexi boxed it up for him.

"Until tonight, then."

"I'm looking forward to it."

After Jerry walked out of the bakery with the cake, Stella motioned for Lexi to come to her table.

"That's trouble on two legs," she said.

"Why do you say that?"

"Anyone that good looking has to be trouble."

At her apartment before her date with Jerry, Lexi paced in front of the window.

Unable to remain still, Lexi walked down the hall and into the kitchen. There was a life-sized paper skeleton hanging next to the bathroom, a present from Beverly that showed her med-student humor.

The kitchen wasn't any better than the living room, so she walked back to the window, past the skeleton, this time grabbing its bone hand as she danced around the hall. Saxman woke at the commotion. Opening a sleepy eye, she stretched from head to tail, then curled into a ball and went back to sleep.

Lexi was surprised that Jerry wanted to introduce her to his co-workers on their first date. She was nervous and didn't want to be too dressy or too casual, so she'd decided on black jeans and a nice sweater. She left the clothes she had rejected on the unmade bed. Her futon was almost always pulled flat because she rarely had anyone over and never bothered to make it into a couch.

Even though her front window looked out onto the street, Lexi was too excited to wait inside another minute, so she went outside and sat on the steps of the apartment. She thought about having her emergency cigarette but changed her mind. *Firemen probably don't like smokers.* After a good twenty minutes, a long fire truck drove up and double-parked. Jerry got out and walked to where Lexi was sitting on the stairs. He was dressed in the blue uniform he had on earlier.

"Hello," he said with a wide grin. "May I?"

He held out his hand. It was warm and rough. Lexi squeezed it as she rose from the stairs to stand up. They walked to the passenger side of the fire truck. Lexi was going to let go of his hand, but Jerry firmly held hers until she climbed into the cab. The air was cold, but Lexi didn't notice. Her skin was radiating heat, and she couldn't look at Jerry when he got into the truck.

"Do you always drive a fire truck on dates?"

"I'm a fireman. How do you think we get around? Haven't you ever seen firemen shopping for groceries?" Jerry reached over the seat and touched Lexi's face. She turned toward him. He smiled and said, "It leaves an impression."

"Oh, I'm impressed."

Jerry held his hand to her face for a moment before letting go and starting the engine.

It was too early for dinner, and Lexi didn't know or care where they were going. Her nervousness evaporated into something new: pure happiness.

"I'm taking you to the Palace of the Legion of Honor before we have dinner."

As they drove, Lexi started to relax. It was a cloudless windy day. The Golden Gate Bridge came into view.

"Will they be open?" Lexi asked, noticing the empty parking lot.

"No. I come here for the view."

"I bet you take all your dates in a fire truck to this make-out spot."

Jerry looked hurt. "No." His sincerity touched her.

"I'm sorry. I was just teasing." She said in a nervous rush of words.

"I wanted to show you my favorite view of the Golden Gate." He kept his eyes on the road leading up to a fountain across the street from the museum.

Lexi realized that she hoped to share her favorite views—Alcatraz from Russian Hill, the Transamerica Pyramid building from Columbus Avenue, and Coit Tower from almost any street in North Beach—with him as well, unless she'd already blown it.

Jerry smiled, brushing it off. "It's a private tour."

He pulled into the empty parking lot that surrounded the fountain and turned off the engine.

"Let's walk," he said, opening his door and jumping to the pavement.

Lexi's heart was beating fast. She started to unlatch her door but realized Jerry was already at her door, so she stopped. He opened the door. He reached for her hand but didn't let go even when her feet touched the ground.

They walked to the cliff's edge. The Golden Gate Bridge stretched across the choppy Pacific Ocean on one side, while sailboats strained against the wind in the Bay on the other. Scrubby trees that had been battling against the wind their entire lives cast cold shadows as Lexi and Jerry walked to a bench and sat down. They sat in silence, the wind blowing a in circles around them. Lexi didn't want to say another stupid thing that might hurt his feelings.

"So, what do you think?"

"I've only seen this view in postcards. It's so beautiful. Thank you for bringing me here."

He leaned in front of her, blocking the wind that had been biting her face, and kissed her. When he released her with what Lexi thought was reluctance, Jerry looked at his watch.

"We don't want to be late for dinner." Jerry stood and Lexi joined him. He took her hand and, with one last look at the bridge, they walked back to the truck.

The fire station was at 2nd and Townsend Street near the train station. Jerry pulled the truck into the garage, parked and got out. He walked to the passenger side, opened the door and helped her down. Heavy yellow fire jackets hung from hooks along the walls of the garage, with a short bench underneath them and black boots lined neatly on the ground. There was just enough room to walk around the trucks to the metal stairs in the back of the garage. It smelled of oil and exhaust and an unfamiliar musky scent.

Jerry motioned for Lexi to follow him upstairs. She didn't know what to expect. She could handle any street bum, drug addict or prostitute that came into the bakery, but somehow a room full of men in uniform made her nervous. If she said the wrong thing or wasn't up to snuff with one of them, she was sure she'd disappoint Jerry.

At the top of the stairs, Lexi saw the lights blazing in the kitchen and dining room ahead. She guessed there were 15 men in blue uniforms sitting at two tables in the front of the kitchen as she walked into the room. The tables were crowded with plates and bottles of Coke. The noisy room went dead quiet as Lexi and Jerry walked in. All eyes turned to the couple. The firemen sat straighter in their chairs. One of the men jumped up and rushed up to Lexi.

"I'm Ralph Murphy." He took Lexi's hand and kissed it. She turned red. Ralph's light hazel-colored eyes crinkled as he smiled, his crooked teeth and short, unruly hair make his boyish face look even younger.

A chorus of ribbing filled the room.

"You've got some competition there, Jerry."

"You loser. You can't stay away from this place."

"Too cheap to take your lady to a real restaurant."

"Where did this dunderhead find a girl like you?"

"Everybody," Jerry said to the room. "This is Lexi Fagan."

A cacophony of "Hello red" greeted her. Half the men pulled out their own chairs and offered them to Lexi. Jerry steered her to an empty seat near a young man wearing a large white apron folded around his waist. He jumped up, extended a large hand and introduced himself as Trevor Hayes.

"You hoodlums," Trevor roared. "Lexi is here for dinner at the finest establishment in town." There was a lilt in his voice, an accent that she couldn't put her finger on.

Trevor turned to the stove and threw a handful of mushrooms in butter as the guys scooted their chairs closer to the table and raised their forks straight up as if in a cartoon, cracking each other up until they finally settled down. They peppered Lexi with questions. She was overwhelmed with the attention and looked to Jerry for help, but he said, "You're on your own."

She told them she was raised in a small town in Alaska where it rained all the time, and how rivers of rain flowed back into the ocean once it hit the ancient lava rock of Deer Mountain.

"It rains so much no one bothers to carry an umbrella. Everyone wears rain slickers and shoepacs."

"Shoepacks?" Ralph asked.

"Rain boots." Lexi was puzzled. "Don't you call rubber boots 'shoepacs?'"

The men laughed and unanimously decided Alaska was a firemen's paradise. It rained all the time, so nature did most of the work putting out fires. They would be going to Ketchikan on their next vacation. They asked about her family. She said she was an only child raised by her grandparents. Luckily, they didn't press her about where her parents were, so she didn't have to tell them. The guys agreed that her grandparents would love them to visit. The next group decision was that Lexi should join the fire department and everyone volunteered to be her big brother.

The radio crackled, and everyone went silent. Lexi looked at the frozen faces around the table and thought they looked as if they were posing, in mid-sentence, perhaps for a painting or photograph. The static on the radio disappeared. Ralph nodded, and the kitchen exploded with noise again.

"Being a firemen is like being a soldier." Ralph yelled to Lexi over the many conversations around them. "There's a ton of preparation, a lot of waiting, and then all hell breaks loose when there's a fire."

They offered her a Coke, which she accepted. Five bottles were set on the table, and everyone laughed when she accepted each with a cordial "Thank you, kind sir." Trevor brought a huge skillet with steak smothered in mushrooms to the table.

"Shut up, you boobs. Why are you grilling this lady? I'm doing the cooking here." Trevor gave Lexi a wink.

The skillet came close to Jerry's head, and he moved quickly to avoid being hit. *It's even dangerous* inside *the firehouse,* Lexi thought.

The steak was delicious. Once everyone had sopped up the last of the bloody juice with bread, Lexi turned the conversation away from her and to the latest *Star Wars* film, and who was married and who had a girlfriend. She knew if she got them to talk about themselves, they'd soon stop focusing on her. As excited as she was to be on a date with Jerry, she was getting tired. Her day had started early, as usual, she had the opening shift at the bakery, and she was beginning to fade.

"I've heard of firehouse food being gourmet-quality," she said to Trevor. "Now I know why."

"Thanks, love." Trevor beamed. He turned to the guys and said, "That's what gratitude sounds like, mates." A shower of napkins floated his way. Several men stood up to clear the dishes and wash up. Lexi resisted the urge to help. Trevor disappeared with a quick, "Nice to meet you, Lexi."

Jerry sat back, looking at her.

"What?" she asked.

"I'm just admiring a beautiful Irish girl. You know what they say? The best way to a woman's heart is through her stomach. Especially an Irish girl. I'd better be careful or Trevor will cook his way into your heart."

"I don't think so." Lexi gave a sheepish smile. "Although he does have a cute accent. They all seem like great guys, Jerry."

"Yeah, we're like brothers. It's like a fraternity at each firehouse. We live together and play together, but you don't necessarily feel the same about all the guys."

Jerry moved his chair closer to Lexi.

"Where is Trevor from anyway? I bet he's closer to being Irish than I am." His accent sounded English to her, but Lexi had plenty of experience with tourists and knew that he could be Scottish or Irish, or even

Australian. She had learned not to guess out loud. If she guessed the wrong country, it would invariably insult someone.

"Scotland." Jerry leaned in and kissed her on the cheek. "I know it's a surprise because he's actually a decent cook."

Lexi gave him a stern look that was just pretend.

"I'm just teasing." Jerry leaned back in his chair. He noticed Lexi trying to stop a yawn. "Come on. I'll take you home."

Lexi said goodbye to the firemen cleaning up. Jerry's hand rested on the small of her back as he led her to the garage and into the truck.

As they drove to her apartment, Lexi was thinking to herself that the dinner must be what it's like to come from a big family, everyone talking over each other with a lot of teasing and vying for attention. Even though she was uncomfortable being the focus of so much attention, it had been the most fun she'd had with other people since moving to town.

They pulled up to the apartment, and Jerry turned the key to off. The cab where they sat was so high that Lexi could see inside her bay window. Her apartment was a mess. She had been distracted and nervous about the date and hadn't thought about coming back to her place when it was over. There were piles of clothes spilling out of the closet and onto the futon. Saxman was still curled up on one of the piles. An open carton of Chinese food sat on its side next to the bed. Saxman had probably knocked it over, trying to get to the stray noodles at the bottom.

Lexi waited for Jerry to say something, but instead he leaned in and kissed her. She slid across the seat until their bodies touched. Jerry's hands were on her face, caressing her skin. He kissed her, his mouth and tongue exploring hers. Heat rose between them. Things were moving fast, Lexi didn't want to stop. Though she wasn't sexually experienced, her doubts and insecurities faded as their kisses grew even more passionate. It felt natural and right. Jerry's hand moved down her neck and under her sweater. There was no space between them now. She pressed her hands on top of his, which were pressed on her breasts. His fingers cradled her nipples.

When he pulled away, he looked into her eyes with new intensity.

"Lexi, I want to continue this, but we can't go back to the firehouse. I sleep with a room full of guys."

Lexi caught her breath. She wanted Jerry to stay. The way he looked at her, and the way she responded, made her feel something new, something forbidden, something she didn't want to stop.

She opened the truck door motioning for him to follow. They raced up the stairs and to the front door. She fumbled with her keys as Jerry pressed his body into her back. They managed to get inside the apartment and fall onto the bed in a tangle of arms and wet kisses. Saxman barely made it off the clothes pile and onto the floor before they landed. The messy apartment was forgotten as night turned to morning.

The morning light woke Lexi. She felt Saxman's tail on her face. Opening her eyes, Lexi stroked the cat with one hand. She moved her other hand to where Jerry would have been if he had stayed. The sheets were empty and cold. He had left after about an hour, explaining that he didn't want to continue past a certain point. He told her their first time together should be something more special. She had reluctantly agreed. Besides, he had been on duty and needed to head back to the firehouse. They made a date for the weekend. He didn't tell her where they would be going, only to dress warm.

If things went well, she hoped to show Jerry her favorite places in San Francisco, perhaps on their third date or the one after that. She smiled thinking of it. She would take him to Tosca Cafe in North Beach, and they would drink cappuccinos spiked with Brandy as opera played on the jukebox. She wanted to show him the view of the bay from Larkin Street at the top of the stairs leading to Fisherman's Wharf. The future seemed full of possibilities. She rolled around in the sheets laughing. Joy coursed through her like a drug. Saxman jumped off the bed in disgust at Lexi's behavior, licking her paw calmly as soon as she landed as if she had always meant to make a quick exit from the bed.

10

DECEMBER 23, 1983 – ST. ANDREW'S CATHOLIC PREPARATORY SCHOOL

Lexi sat at her kitchen table, her coffee growing cold as she tried to believe that Jerry was dead. She had watched the fire blazing while she was working across the street. Had she been watching while Jerry was dying? If she had only run across the street to see him, to talk to him that morning, would that have changed the course of his day somehow, would he still be alive? Lexi snapped out of her reverie when the phone rang. Patting around with her hand, she found it, picked it up and answered with a rough, "Hello."

A man's voice came through the receiver, "Hi Lexi. It's Ralph Murphy."

"Ralph." Lexi said with relief.

"Sorry I had to rush you off the phone earlier. We had a call that turned out to be a false alarm. I hope you don't mind that I called. I found your number in Jerry's phone book."

"Of course not."

"The guys at the station and I just thought you'd like to know about the memorial service, in case you want to come."

Lexi was unable to speak.

"He was a great guy," Ralph said, filling the painful silence. "The memorial will be just after Christmas, the 27th, Tuesday, at Saint Peter and Paul Church in North Beach. It's kind of a strange situation for a lot of reasons." Ralph was clearly uncomfortable. He was talking fast. "Jerry's family wanted the service to be as soon as possible, so Saint Peter's rearranged their schedule even though it's so close to the holidays."

Lexi hugged her knees to her chest.

"Remember I told you the Chief kept information about Jerry out of the news? It's because the fire is being investigated by the fire marshal. It's completely standard when anyone in the department dies, but it could take a while to wrap things up. So even though Jerry's body won't be released from the coroner's office until a full report is filed, the family wants to have the memorial anyway. They've worked it out with the church."

Lexi rocked gently back and forth. Her mind was foggy. She wasn't taking in half of what Ralph was telling her. Should she go to Jerry's memorial? See his family? Lexi didn't want to let go of him yet, but she didn't know if his family even knew about her. Who would she be to them? An acquaintance? A guest of the fire station? His girlfriend? What did it matter? He was gone.

"Of course, I'll be there," she stammered.

"Your boss Victor will be there too."

Lexi stopped rocking. "Victor?"

"We all went to school together."

She repeated, "Jerry went to school with Victor."

"Didn't you know? St. Andrew's. We were all there. Class of '72." He was trying to keep things light, but his voice was sad. "Go Fighting Irish."

"Thank you for letting me know about the memorial." Lexi hung up. Great gasping sobs overwhelmed her. After what felt like a long time, the storm of tears subsided. She dried her eyes and remembered the photo in the McCracken's home. Victor and Jerry posing with the high school football team. She was right; it had been Jerry in the picture. Not only that, but Ralph was probably somewhere on the wall of pictures as well.

She looked around at her apartment. All of her things looked different. Even the futon seemed like someone else's bed. It was no longer the apartment where she had started a new life in a new city, or the place where she had spent time with Jerry. Now it was a place of loss. Lexi heard loud meowing from the kitchen. It was only ten past two, too early for Saxman's dinner, but she was a sensitive cat and must have picked up on Lexi's feelings. She cried until Lexi picked her up and cradled her in her arms.

Lexi couldn't sit in her apartment any longer. She'd been puzzling over Victor's denial that it was Jerry in the photo on his parent's wall, and she decided to find Jerry's high school, St. Andrew's. There must be someone there who remembered the class of 1972. She showered and put on fresh clothes, then fed Saxman. Lexi looked at her watch. It was 3:15pm. Opening the phone book, she found the address for St. Andrew's Catholic Preparatory School and wrote it on the back of an envelope. In a junk drawer near the sink, she found her stained and ragged map of San Francisco. As she spread the map on the table, she discovered that the folded edges had frayed and become holes. Small sections of San Francisco had been obliterated. She found St. Andrew's and thought that Jerry's school must have been old, because the building and the name of the school were printed on the map. It was in Pacific Heights on Pierce Street.

Wrapping herself in a coat, she stuffed the envelope with the address in her pocket, folding the map carefully so as not to tear any more of the city away, and put it neatly in her purse. Locking the door behind her, she walked down Larkin to Pacific Avenue. It was a beautiful day, clear and windy. The sun was low in the late-afternoon sky. She was thinking about how little she knew of Jerry Stevens, and of her boss as well. In fact, how well did she know anyone in her life? Victor had told her that he didn't know Jerry; yet barely an hour ago, Ralph had told her that they had all gone to school together. Maybe they had simply lost touch; Jerry hadn't mentioned that he knew Victor either, yet Jerry was at McCracken's when they had met. As far as she knew, there was only one McCracken family in San Francisco. Jerry must have known Victor ran the bakery. So why would Victor bother to lie? And why hadn't Jerry mentioned he went to school with her boss Victor? Lexi was determined to find out. The walk was easygoing at first. Lexi breezed down Pacific Avenue until the streets got steeper. When she reached Alta Plaza Park at the top of a large hill twenty minutes later, she was winded and hot. She cut through the park, stopping to take off her coat and unbutton her sweater.

Lexi crossed Clay Street and saw a small church. Walking toward it, she admired its red brick façade outlined with sandstone. The metal roof had a green patina gutter that reminded Lexi of the house in *Peter Pan*. "St. Andrew's Catholic Preparatory School, 1916" was etched into the stone above the front door to the right of the church doors.

The church was sandwiched between the high school and an apartment building. Lexi walked up the steps of the church to the large wooden doors and pulled on the handle. To her surprise, the door opened easily. She walked in and stood still for a moment until her eyes adjusted to the dim light. The small entry room had wood- paneled wainscoting and a few benches between two ceramic statues, one of the Virgin Mary with a snake at her sandaled feet and the other of Joseph holding the baby Jesus with one hand. Lexi walked to the corkboard on the wall and read the flyers. There were announcements, a schedule of church service hours and a sports calendar neatly tacked in place with pushpins. Lexi tried to imagine Jerry in high school, standing in the same spot looking at the football schedule. She opened the heavy doors leading into the main church and walked inside, the door closed slowly behind her. The room was larger than it looked from the outside. The walls seemed to expand to accommodate the long wooden benches separated by a wide center aisle.

Lexi faced the altar. The tabernacle looked like a miniature golden cathedral crowded with ornate towers reaching to the ceiling. Walking to the front of the church, she admired the statue of Jesus. He wore simple robes. A half shell formed a crown around his head. His index and middle finger extended upward, pointing towards heaven. As many times as Lexi had seen that sign, she still didn't know what it stood for. *Peace?* There was no one in the church, so Lexi sat in the second pew and closed her eyes.

The sweat she'd worked up on her walk started to evaporate in the cool air. She shivered and pulled her coat around her. What was she doing here? Did she think she would suddenly know something more about Jerry than when she had talked to Trevor or Ralph? What she did realize, sitting in the silence of the church, was how deeply she had fallen in love with him. She felt as if she were filling with sadness. She was about to stand up to leave when a door opened to the right of the altar. A priest in black robes walked into the room, stopped and looked at Lexi. He was tall and slender with thinning hair and a sad face. Lexi guessed that he was in his early 40s.

"Hello," he said as if he'd been expecting her. "I'm Father Doyle."

"Lexi." She stood to greet him, extending her hand. "Fagan." Father Doyle walked in front of the pew where Lexi was standing and shook her hand.

"Fagan," Father Doyle smiled. "That's an Irish name, I think."

"Right" Lexi pointed awkwardly to her red hair. He motioned for her to sit.

"Now what can I do for you, Miss Fagan?"

"I'm not sure." Lexi looked at Father Doyle's face. His skin was smooth, with deep creases around his eyes and mouth. "I lost someone." She stopped and took a shallow breath. "Someone I thought was going to be special in my life." Father Doyle motioned for Lexi to sit in the pew next to him.

"Why don't you start at the beginning," he said.

Lexi explained that she had dated someone who had been a student at St. Andrew's and that he had died in a fire.

"Who was this friend?" Father Doyle asked.

"His name was Jerry Stevens."

Father Doyle's face drained of color.

"Oh, no. I knew Jerry, of course." He put his hand to his heart. "His poor family."

"I'm so sorry to be the one who told you. I didn't even think—but of course you could have known him." Lexi felt terrible. She hadn't planned any further than getting to the school, and had not thought that she might be breaking the bad news to anyone.

"No. No. I was informed of Jerry's passing. This is still the family's parish, but there weren't many details. His mother didn't say there was a fire. Only that an accident of some kind took her son. She was so upset. It's just such a shock. Was it the hotel fire?" Father Doyle asked in a whisper.

"Yes." Lexi told him how she had watched the fire from the bakery across the street, but that she didn't know Jerry had died until she called the firehouse looking for him. Doyle asked compassionately, "Were you two close?"

"Yes. Though I didn't know Jerry for very long, we were close, but there's so much I don't know about him. I came today to try and learn something.

I know he went to school here. I'm sorry, I didn't mean to upset you." Lexi couldn't think of what to do or what else to say. She stood up, but Father Doyle stopped her.

"No, please stay." He had recovered his composure and his strong sermon voice returned. "Maybe I can help."

Lexi sat back down and said, "Can you tell me anything about Jerry when he was a student?"

Father Doyle was silent for a long time before speaking.

"I was, gosh, just out of seminary school back then. I was a bit older than Jerry is now—was." His mind seemed to drift. "Those boys were quite something. Jerry was the star of the football team and a high achiever. The Fighting Irish won the state championship the year they graduated in '72."

Father Doyle seemed to anticipate Lexi's follow up question and said, "We're known as the Notre Dame of the West. Jerry was the quarterback and his buddy Victor McCracken was the wide receiver. Jerry was a great quarterback, and he and Victor were unbeatable on the field." Father Doyle kept talking about football but Lexi had stopped listening. Jerry and Victor hadn't just gone to the same school, they had played football together. Maybe they had had a falling out? She felt as if she hadn't taken a breath since Father Doyle started speaking. She filled her lungs with air, reviving her and bringing her attention back to the cold church.

"I'm sorry to interrupt, Father Doyle, but can you tell me anything about Jerry—I don't know—something personal?"

"Oh, of course, dear. Sorry. We just haven't had a championship team since they graduated." Father Doyle looked at his hands resting on his knees. "The boys got into some trouble, I remember. There was an unfortunate incident with a classmate, but nothing to do directly with Jerry or Ben, mind you."

"Ben? You mean Victor."

"Oh, yeah. Victor, of course."

"What was the incident you mentioned? What happened?"

"Nothing, really." Father Doyle stood up. "I'd love to talk with you more, Miss Fagan, but I have a lot of things to take care of, including comforting the Stevens family now that I know the extent of what happened." His voice grew distant. "I have you to thank for that."

"Of course." Lexi stood up as well. "Thank you for your time, Father."

Father Doyle shook her hand. Even though his smile was the same as when he met her, something had visibly shifted inside him. This was his game face.

Lexi turned quickly and fled from the church and into the night.

When she finally reached home, Lexi couldn't shake the feeling that something had been off with Father Doyle. Tomorrow was Christmas Eve. She wasn't sure if Victor would be at work but she wanted answers.

11

DECEMBER 24, 1983 – CHRISTMAS EVE

Lexi often thought that she could set her watch by bakery time. The donuts came out the first thing in the morning and were replenished throughout the day. The cookies, hamantaschen and Tiny Timm's favorite, the Russian teacakes, were made twice a week.

It was brisk business at the bakery on Christmas Eve. There were vacationers, neighborhood families out for a treat, and the regulars without families, those who called the bakery home. Claudia would be working. Overtime was overtime. Lexi and Beverly didn't mind working Christmas Eve. Beverly was Hindu—another reason that Victor would be afraid to tell his parents about her—so working the holiday wasn't a problem for her. Lexi told herself that she wanted the time and a half, but the truth was she wanted to keep busy. It was easy to slip into a funk around the holidays when you had no family nearby to celebrate with. Lexi was finding it difficult to keep her mind off Jerry, and didn't want to be alone with her thoughts, even though Saxman was good company. Though she had agreed to let Claudia work her Christmas shift, Lexi would deal with what could turn into a very lonely Christmas tomorrow.

While Beverly was in the warehouse sorting out cake orders, Lexi replenished the refrigerated counter with fresh cakes. Henry walked up to the counter. He seemed to time his visits to the arrival of the cream-filled puff pastries from the warehouse.

Lexi had a knot in her stomach since talking to Father Doyle yesterday, but it disappeared when she saw Henry. He reminded her of her grandfather. She kept the refrigerator doors open and took out his favorite pastry. The powdered sugar hadn't settled yet, and some of it floated off onto her arm as she placed the dish on the counter.

The cataracts on his eyes created a light blue circle around his irises. Lexi wasn't sure why he didn't have them operated on, but perhaps he was worried that there would be a mistake and he'd lose what little sight he had left. Medical horror stories were circulated by the older crowd at the bakery on a daily basis, most of them coming from the widows. Stella refused to participate in their talk and dismissed most of it as hooey, but Henry always looked worried when one of the widows told a story of a cousin who had suffered from a botched operation, or how a brother had died of a misdiagnosed something-or-other. Henry didn't actually participate, he usually hid behind the newspaper, but Lexi suspected he was listening to every breathy detail.

"Help yourself to coffee," Lexi said, waving his money away. "You are too kind," Henry replied. Though she didn't always charge her regulars, the widows were a different story. She happily took their money, even though they complained loudly about being broke and living on fixed incomes. Lexi hated the condescending way they called her an angel when she helped Howard.

"They have little charity in their own hearts," Henry had counseled. "But best not to judge others so harshly. You don't know what their lives have been like."

Lexi was mortified that Henry had noticed how she felt about the widows. It had dawned on her that she wasn't as subtle as she imagined. Her thoughts weren't just taking place inside her head but being expressed to the wider world.

A bus filled with German tourists pulled up, and they streamed inside. One after the other, they ordered chocolate-covered custard donuts and tea. Claudia filled up the pot with hot water three times. They dipped the same Lipton tea bag into fresh cups of hot water even though Lexi and Claudia offered them fresh tea bags.

Being open on Christmas Eve was always a relief to the regulars and especially to tourists. They would have gone on strike in Hamburg or wherever they called home in Europe over working on holidays, but you could see the delight in their eyes when they saw the neon "Open" sign in the window of the bakery on Christmas Day.

One of the Germans asked Claudia if she was afraid of earthquakes.

"Earthquakes!" she huffed. "Try living through Stalin!"

Lexi heard a commotion at the door as Howard pressed his wheelchair against the glass. She ran to open the door.

"What's the matter?"

Lexi could see Howard scowled as his electric wheelchair sped into the bakery. He was talking too fast for Lexi to understand, and seemed to be in no mood to be misunderstood. She knelt to get closer to his face and watched his mouth to better understand him.

"Far!"

"Fire?"

Howard nodded in a rough jerk toward the door.

"Is there a fire?" Lexi asked.

"NO!" he screamed. The other customers were watching them. Henry asked if everything was okay, and Lexi nodded yes.

"Howard, slow down. I'll get it."

He pointed across the street.

"The fire at the hotel?" she tried.

Howard nodded.

"Die," he said.

After some back and forth, she pieced together that he was talking about Jerry's death. He was trying to tell her that people had died in the fire. She started to tear up again, but forced herself to keep it together. At this point, everyone that worked at the bakery and most of the customers had heard that two guests and a fireman had died in the blaze. When she thought of Jerry now, she tried to focus on the time they'd had together and not to imagine his charred body. She pushed the image out of her mind and pictured his face just before he kissed her on their first date.

As Lexi brought Howard his coffee and a sugar donut, she noticed that Stella and Henry were sitting at the same table. They were whispering and glancing at a table where three men were drinking coffee and eating donuts. Lexi had served the men, but hadn't recognized them. They didn't look like tourists with their long-sleeved polo shirts and khaki pants; they looked like guys working at the new computer store down the street. As if on cue, they stood, walked briskly to the front door and were gone. Lexi picked up a towel and walked over to clean the now vacant table.

Stella caught her eye. "Those pigs were suspicious," she croaked. "Talking about investigations in the middle of the bakery. Anyone could have heard them."

"And I did hear them," said Henry. "They were fire marshals, beginning their investigation." Stella and Lexi looked at Henry.

"It's my eyes that give me trouble, not my ears," he said. "I overheard their conversation."

"What were they investigating?" asked Lexi.

"The fire, obviously. They wanted to know if any of us had seen anything the morning of the fire." Before Lexi could ask why the men hadn't bothered to ask any questions, Henry continued, "They think the fire might have been deliberately set."

"Now doesn't that just beat all." Stella sat up and slapped the table. "Arson."

"They didn't want to call it an arson investigation," said Henry. "They were adamant about that. In fact, they went out of their way to make it seem like standard procedure, but I could tell by their tone there was more to it. They whispered, almost as if they were trying not to be overheard."

Lexi waved to Claudia to get her attention and mouthed, "I'm going on a break" before sitting down to join the others. "I got a call from one of the firemen I met the night Jerry took me to dinner at the firehouse. He said something about an investigation, but he didn't mention anything about arson." said Lexi. "It would be awful if Jerry and the others had died in an accident, but if it were arson. That's murder." She tried to think if she had seen anything suspicious the morning of the fire, but nothing came to mind.

Henry looked at Lexi. "This chap called to tell you about an investigation?"

"Oh, sorry. No. He called to tell me about the memorial service, and suggested I might want to be there. He also said that the fire department is investigating the fire."

Stella piped up and said, "That's why those pigs were here."

"Did you hear what they were talking about specifically?" Lexi asked.

Henry leaned across the table and said, "They said something about how the Stevens boy died, but I couldn't make it out." Henry patted Lexi's hand. "I only heard clearly that they don't want to call it an arson investigation. And then they said that they wanted to get the report completed so his body could be released as soon as possible."

Claudia was wiping down a nearby table and interrupted them. "You know who they should look to with arson? Ben. He was in Vietnam. You know Agent Orange rots the brain."

Lexi, Stella and Henry stared at Claudia.

Lexi piped up, "That's not fair. He may be Mr. Squared Away. And he's angry a lot and can come at you with a knife sometimes, but I can't imagine he'd set fire to anything on purpose." Then again, she thought, maybe she could picture it. She was protecting him against the allegations of her regulars because she felt that she was the only one who could call him a lunatic.

Henry said, "He did act strange the day of the fire. I remember that he ran outside and seemed a bit wild."

"Well, I say it's about time we had some action around here." Stella was excited and spoke louder than her vocal cords usually allowed. "This provincial town can be dull as dishwater." Henry gave her a look. "Oh, right. I'm sorry about your beau, Lexi." She gave Lexi's arm a quick pat with her small dry hand.

Lexi didn't like where this was leading. They didn't know how quickly things had developed in such a short time, only that she and Jerry had had a few dates. The talk about arson and Jerry's death was hitting her hard. She supposed she should just tell them she had been, and still was, in love with him, but felt shy and protective of what she and Jerry had shared.

Henry looked from Stella to Lexi. "When a first responder is killed, they always investigate, but it sounds as if they don't expect to find anything sinister. Nothing as dramatic as arson, anyway."

"It doesn't make sense for those guys to come in and leave without asking anyone a question, though," Lexi mused.

"I don't see too clearly, but I can see better than him." Stella pointed to Henry. Lexi could tell she didn't intend for it to sound as mean is it did. Luckily, Henry wasn't offended. He smiled and winked in Stella's direction. She continued, "One of those guys looked across the street at the burned-out hotel and those pigs were outta here like they'd seen something." She made a face.

"Again," Henry corrected, "they were fire marshals."

Lexi looked at Henry. He still had his hat on, but he had pushed it high onto his forehead and she could see the thin gray hair under the hat.

"You don't know this about me, young lady, but I was a private investigator for Melvin Belli before I retired in 1968."

Timm had been quietly eating his tea cookie when he turned around, looked at the group with a conspiratorial smile and exclaimed, "A private dick! What do ya know. You sly old fox. Working for the King of Torts, ey. What are his offices really like?"

Henry smiled, "As crazy as they look from the windows. There's a mannequin in full knight's armor next to a couple of life-size shadow puppets from Indonesia. He has a huge saddle in the corner. Stuff everywhere." He shook his head. "There was no place to work. Every surface was covered with stacks of magazines with Belli's mug on the cover, or a miniature statute of David, apothecary jars filled with snake skins, and God knows what."

"Where is this?" asked Lexi. Timm and Henry laughed at Lexi's puzzled face.

Timm said, "You have a lot to learn about San Francisco. It may be provincial in its way, but it's still that gold-rush town with dreamers and beatniks alongside crazy lawyers and a thriving Financial District. It's a city of one-of-a-kind self-starters like Belli."

"Belli's office is in the Bell Building on Montgomery Street. If you walk down Columbus from North Beach toward the Financial District, you can't miss it."

"Why did you call Mr. Belli the King of Torts?"

Timm said, "He wins every case."

Stella piped up. "I'll always hate him for defending Jack Ruby."

"Well, he wins almost every case. At least he lost that one, Stella," Timm said. "I'll give him this. He's even famous for his losses."

"Why do you hate him for that?" Lexi asked Stella, who was squirming in her chair with agitation.

"The truth died with Oswald, didn't it?" Stella's thin arms jutted above her head. "We'll never know why that bastard killed Kennedy." Stella was getting increasingly agitated, and the other customers were staring at their table.

"What does that have to do with his attorney? The deed was already done. Oswald was gone," said Timm.

"We're getting far afield now," Henry said with a firm but calm tone. "I didn't work on the Ruby case, if that makes you feel any better about me."

Stella shook her head, "You're okay in my book. Actually, I used to like old Belli, before he became a pompous ass."

Lexi wanted to get back to their pre-Belli conversation. "Why didn't the fire marshals just ask us whatever they wanted to know when they first came in?

"I think they planned to," said Henry.

"Yeah, but they're no different than cops," Stella said with a twinkle in her eyes. "They don't do anything without coffee and a donut first."

An hour later, Stella and Henry were on their third and fourth cups of coffee but now were sitting at separate tables, reading sections of the paper. Howard and Timm had gone home, and the tourists had cleared out. Beverly had started her shift and given Lexi the cold shoulder. Lexi walked over and sat next to Henry. He put down the newspaper and smiled.

"I've been thinking about your problem," said Henry. His eyes seemed less cloudy and more focused as he talked.

"Which of my many problems would that be?" Lexi teased. "My tiny apartment, lack of friends or my dead boyfriend?"

"You don't have to pretend this doesn't hurt." Henry said in a low, tender voice.

Lexi swallowed the lump in her throat. "It's the only way I can get through the day."

"I understand." Henry nodded. "Is it too painful to discuss the Cathedral Hill Hotel Fire case?"

"So, now it's a 'case.' I thought you said it was normal to investigate when a firefighter dies in a fire."

Claudia came to the table to tell Lexi that she had a phone call in the office. Lexi excused herself and went into the back. She picked up the phone.

"Hello. Lexi Fagan speaking."

"Ms. Fagan, my name is Detective Robert Reiger with the police."

She didn't know what to say, so she used her receptionist voice. "What can I do for you, Detective?"

"I'm hoping to come down and ask you a few questions about the Cathedral Hill fire."

"Ok," Lexi stammered. "What would you need to ask me about?"

"I understand that you were working the morning of the fire, and I want to know what you observed that morning."

"Are you working with the fire department? We had a few of their guys in here today. It must be investigation day." Lexi didn't mean to sound flip. It was getting harder to distance herself from her feelings about Jerry's death when everyone wanted to talk about the fire. It already seemed needless that he died, and it terrified her to think that the fire might have been set. But would it really make a difference if a cigarette started the fire, or if someone had intentionally started it? The end result was the same, Jerry was lost to his family and friends, and whatever future she might have had with him was gone.

"Really?" Reiger paused. He seemed irritated. "Will you be at work on Tuesday? I'd like to come in and talk to you for a few minutes."

"I'll be here." Lexi hung up and took a couple of deep breaths. *What is this all about?* She went back out front and Claudia took her break. Victor came out of the back and took the cash from the register. "He likes you," Stella whispered pointing to Victor as Lexi wiped down the tables.

"You know he has a girlfriend, right?" Lexi looked into Stella's magnified eyes. The memorial was on her mind, and Lexi wanted to talk about something other than the fire, the investigation or Jerry. She certainly didn't want to talk about the call from Detective Reiger, but Victor was also not an area she wanted to get into.

Stella continued. "A girlfriend doesn't make any difference to a guy like that. He has a wandering eye."

Lexi hadn't realized even customers knew about Victor's personal life. Now Stella thought he was after her.

"There is nothing between us." This was not the change of subject Lexi had in mind, especially with Beverly behind the counter.

Stella looked as if she didn't believe her. "When is the funeral of your other boyfriend?"

"It's a memorial service. This Tuesday, after Christmas. I'm still on the fence about going. It'll be hard to make it. I managed to get Christmas Day off but not the Tuesday after, and Claudia has some

Russian holiday thing to do, so I can't switch with her. Even if the buses are on schedule, I wouldn't make it to North Beach in time. It's at Saints Peter and Paul across from Washington Square."

"Make Victor drive you." Stella took a drink of her lukewarm coffee, the paper cone soggy with lipstick. "He does so much for every stray urchin and ragamuffin that wanders across his path. He could do something for you. Besides," Stella said with a wry smile, "he would love for you to be beholden to him."

Stella saw the world as a register of checks and balances. Since she lived off her wits and marijuana that her nephew supplied, help from friends was a necessary check in a world out of balance. It was the only way to make it beyond the basics of survival.

She admired Stella for choosing an independent life; a gypsy existence full of blues, jazz and travel. Stella didn't have any more money than the widows, in fact she probably had less, but chose to live a life of adventure instead of timidly counting her pennies. She liked to say, "I was often broke, but never bored and always brave." Lexi's deep fear was that she was too cautious and would end up more like the widows, alone, broke and bitter.

One of Stella's stories was of singing for free in the cellar of The Purple Onion jazz club on Columbus Avenue in North Beach in the late 1950s. The owner had tried to "have one off," as she put it, so she told him to keep his money and walked on stage, sang her set and left empty-handed.

"There he is," hissed Stella, staring in Victor's direction. "Go ask him to give you a ride." They stood up together. Stella gave Lexi a push that had more force than Lexi would have guessed could come from such a tiny arm. Lexi really didn't want to ask Victor for any favors. She was concerned how it might look to Beverly, but she just might make it to the memorial on time if she left a little early on Tuesday and drove. She wanted to ask Victor why he had lied about knowing Jerry, but that was conversation for another time and place. Lexi walked up to Victor, grabbed a cookie from the counter and asked, "Can I ask you a question?"

"Sure. Let's go into the office."

Once in the small room, Victor took a seat and leaned back. His sleepy eyes looked up at her.

Lexi stammered, "I'd like to borrow the VW on Tuesday. I'm going to Jerry's memorial. If I take the bus after my shift, I'll be late."

Victor sat up. "I'm surprised. You only had a date or two, isn't that right?"

Lexi blanched. Would it look as if she were trying to make herself more important in Jerry's life than she actually had been?

"Not that you shouldn't go, Lex. I only meant that you've only known him for a little while, and I didn't think you'd even met his family yet."

Lexi was angry. "The guys from the firehouse invited me. Well, invited is the wrong word. They asked—encouraged—I'm not crashing the memorial, Victor."

"Oh, you know what I mean. That came out wrong." Victor stood and scooted his large frame around Lexi to get to the office door. "You can take the VW. I'll leave it out back with the keys in the ignition." With that, he turned around and disappeared into the warehouse.

Lexi wondered what it was to him? Why had he given her such a bad time?

12

DECEMBER 24, 1983 – CHINATOWN

Lexi had gotten off work at 3:00 p.m. Since it was Christmas Eve, she had made arrangements to meet her bakery regulars in Chinatown for an early dinner. Until then, she had a few hours to fill. She called her grandparents to wish them a Merry Christmas, and filled them in on the lighter things in her life. She wasn't sure if she would ever tell them about Jerry, but she certainly wasn't in the mood to get into it today.

At 5:00 p.m., Lexi met Timm, Stella and Henry at the corner of Stockton and California where two cable car lines met. As they walked up Stockton into the heart of Chinatown, they discussed where they should eat.

"I know where to go, *ma cherie*," said Timm, winking at Lexi.

"Sam Wo's," said Stella and Henry at the same time.

"Okay." Lexi was surprised they all had the same place in mind, especially when there seemed to be hundreds of restaurants in Chinatown. For the three of them to agree on a restaurant, on anything, really, was remarkable.

They passed shops with gold and red lanterns hanging from their ceilings, tasseled fans, animals carved from jade inside their stores, and bamboo furniture and giant wooden dragons on the sidewalks outside.

"I would imagine Chinatown looked just like this 100 years ago," said Henry, peering into a shop window crammed with tiny carved fortresses and small fist-sized dragons baring their teeth. They stopped at a table on the sidewalk filled with dolls in silk pajamas, colorful paper umbrellas and cloisonné bowls filled with jade bracelets. Henry stopped to read a plaque on the side of a building. His nose almost touched the wall. "Established in the 1850s, San Francisco's Chinatown is the largest Chinatown in the U.S."

Stella lost patience. "What are you talking about?" She croaked, "Let's make tracks."

Lexi and Stella made a path for Timm as they pushed their way through the crowded sidewalks. They passed butcher shops with chickens and ducks hanging above counters that were filled with baskets of noodles, beans and dried peppers. Chinese shoppers blocked their way. Timm stopped and moved his left crutch to his right side. He picked up a fat baby doll with a smiling porcelain face and said, "Look, made in China." Lexi couldn't help herself and laughed along with Timm.

Lexi was only 5'7", but she towered over her three companions, one shorter than the next. They walked past a crowded bus stop with a sea of people pushing to get on the 30 Stockton. An older man leaned into the street and blew his nose into the gutter before stepping on board.

Timm shook his head and said, "Chinatown."

They wove their way through the crowded sidewalks to Washington Street.

"There it is," Timm pointed to the dingy yellow sign that read "Sam Wo's" in faded neon above a small doorway. It didn't look like a restaurant to Lexi, and it was the most unusual set up she had ever seen.

They walked down two steps into the kitchen. Cooks in front of a flaming stove along the wall were throwing handfuls of meat and vegetables into woks, followed by a distracted flip of water and oil tossed with a long-handled spoon. A crescendo of hissing steam and smoke exploded into the air. The smell of soy sauce and ginger followed them as they maneuvered up the stairs on the far side of the kitchen. Timm handed Lexi his crutches, turned around and pushed himself backward up the steps, using the banister to steady him on the narrow staircase.

"This railing is disgusting," Timm said.

"I bet the stairs are worse," Stella said. "They probably haven't been cleaned since they opened—"

"In 1912," added Henry.

At the top of the stairs, Timm took back his crutches. Henry read from a faded sign attached with yellowing tape, "All Foods—capital 'F'—then there's a period and 7-up, Coke & Pepsi only. No booze. No B.S. No jive. No coffee, milk, fortune cookies."

"No fortune cookies?" Timm feigned offense. "What kind of Chinese place is this, anyway?"

From deep inside the dining room, they heard Ford Fong yelling, "Cripple in the house!"

The waiter patted Timm on the back, smiling broadly.

"Fong, you nasty devil," Timm cried. "Give me a good table or it's a 10 percent tip for you." Fong's smile disappeared and turned into a frown. He motioned them to an empty table in the center of the room and walked away.

"What was that about?" asked Lexi.

"Oh, that's right. You've never been here before," Stella explained with a wave of her hand. "Sam's is famous for their great food and rude service. People come from all over the world to be abused by Edsel Ford Fong."

"I don't understand."

"You will. Sit and watch."

They took off their coats, draping them on the backs of their chairs, and sat down. They picked up the sticky menus Fong had flung onto the table before walking away.

Lexi looked around the dim room. Sam's was a small restaurant crowded with Chinese families. They sat elbow to elbow at tables of steaming food and bowls of rice, chopsticks flying.

"Be prepared, *ma cherie.* You can order anything off the menu," said Timm, "but Fong will serve whatever he thinks you should have."

"This is the strangest place I've ever been—" Lexi cut herself short, remembering the club Paula had dragged her to when they first got to know each other.

"Welcome to San Francisco!" Timm laughed.

After they decided what they would attempt to order, a round man with bushy eyebrows came to the table. He was wearing a bow tie. He waved to Timm and said, "I know what you want." Then he walked away. They laughed at the absurdity of a restaurant that ordered for you and, even though you would get the dishes Fong decided you wanted, it was part of the fun to order anyway.

After a waitress had served hot tea and they were alone, Lexi told them she'd gotten a call from a Detective Reiger, who wanted to see her and question her about the morning of the fire.

"A detective from the police?"

"That's what he said."

"Now this is getting truly exciting," said Stella in a raspy whisper.

Henry nodded.

"Aren't they rushing a funeral with so much up in the air?" Stella asked.

"Memorial," Lexi corrected before continuing. "Yeah, one of the guys at the firehouse called to let me know that the family wants a service sooner rather than later. They invited me."

"To a funeral?" Timm asked.

Everyone stopped drinking tea and playing with their chopsticks to look at Timm, even Stella.

"Oh, it's a memorial service because there's no body," said Timm, mostly to himself.

Stella explained to the group that she had encouraged Lexi to go to the service and to at least use Victor's car so she could make it on time.

Henry turned his kind eyes to Lexi. "You should go. He meant something to you. You'll regret it if you don't go." A string of busboys appeared with plates of pot stickers, beef with Chinese broccoli, chicken and bell peppers, a whole fish with bulging eyes and a stiff tail, followed by a large bowl filled with rice. The food crowded the table.

Henry resumed talking. "Just so you're prepared, Lexi. There might be a casket, even if it's empty.

"Back to my question." Stella poured herself tea. "Why rush a service when they don't know what happened?"

"I understand the family wants to mourn their son," Lexi said. "People grieve in different ways. Why should they wait through an investigation that could take a long time? Ralph said Jerry's family wanted the service to happen before Christmas, but the church couldn't make that work, so they picked the Tuesday after. It doesn't feel that rushed to me." She could tell that Stella was skeptical, but thought she was making something out of nothing.

Looking around the table at her friends, Lexi asked, "What should I say to his family?"

"Since they must be Catholic, tell them that you never went to the Kasbah with Jerry."

"Shut up!" Stella punched Timm in the arm. "You have a dirty mind, little man." She wasn't really upset and gave Timm an attaboy smile. Henry frowned, obviously displeased with Timm's innuendo.

"I was just trying to make Lexi smile," Timm protested to Henry.

"It's okay." Lexi rested her hand on Timm's arm where Stella had punched it.

"She's got quite a punch for a small person," Timm said, smiling at Stella.

"Who's calling who small?" They laughed and started serving themselves and pouring tea from the chipped teapot.

Timm was well into his second helping of chicken, and Henry was struggling with his chopsticks but knew better than to ask Fong for a fork. Stella picked at a pot sticker and nursed her tea. Lexi munched on a slice of bell pepper.

"Why don't you come with me to the service?" Lexi knew it was unlikely, but she wanted backup. They stopped eating and looked at her.

Stella looked stern and said, "Don't be a wimp, Lexi. You've got to face this thing. Get in there and find out what's going on. Ask that what's-his-name, Ralph, and the other fire guy what happened. There's something more to it. I feel it in my bones. Dig!"

"Besides," said Timm, "You can't bring a date to a memorial, *ma cherie.* Talk about drawing attention to yourself. I'm not exactly inconspicuous."

"Oh, Timm," she said.

"Not to worry. That's how I like it. My parents got me into a special school for handicapped kids, and I hated it. I'm not one to blend in, ever."

"I don't understand." Henry picked up the pot and motioned to Lexi if she wanted tea. She nodded. He poured.

"I'm used to being the special one," Timm explained. "It's like a brilliant kid getting into Harvard or Yale. They might be used to being a star in high school, but suddenly they're one of a class of brilliant kids in college. It's a shock." Timm looked from one to another to make sure they understood.

"I agree with Timm," said Henry. "You need to go by yourself and try and blend in to gather information on the case."

"Please don't call it a case," Lexi said.

"Why not." Timm made his case for calling it a "case." "Your boyfriend died in a fire. The police and fire departments are looking into it. I'd call that a case.

There's definitely funny business going on." Timm was proud of his conclusion.

"I didn't really believe the fire could have been deliberately set before, but now I have to know." Lexi hadn't realized how helpless she'd been feeling. Focusing her energy and doing a little investigating of her own would allow her some control over the situation.

Henry said, "Remember, Lexi, listen and observe. That's the key to an investigation. Don't draw conclusions without checking your facts. That's why you should go to the memorial. Not just to say goodbye to someone you obviously cared about, but also to watch how people act. Arsonists and killers often show up at funerals and memorial services."

"That's awful!" Lexi felt sick. "Jerry was a fireman, which is a dangerous job already; but for him to have died in a fire that might have been set, well that's just terrible. His poor family." Lexi paused for a moment, lost in thought. "It's not just that, though. I've never been to a memorial or a funeral before. No one I know has died. Well, other than my parents, but I was a baby when it happened. Their deaths didn't have much of an emotional impact for me, it was more like I grew up with ghosts."

Stella looked out the window. "Honey, you're lucky. When you walk in on a guy with a needle in his arm and his eyes are staring at you stone cold dead, that's the shit." They looked on in silence. She continued,

"Some of those musicians could play all night high as flag poles. And they were good. That's what gets you. Those cats could blow the roof off. And sometimes, after the greatest set of their lives, they'd just slump in their chairs and die."

Timm's eyes widened. "Did you ever try it?"

"No. I saw what it did to people. To their families. To their careers. To me, the high from heroin was never worth the risk. Pot's my game. It doesn't kill you. And it makes me hungry."

"Well, that's unexpected," said Henry, looking at her nearly-full plate.

"I'm not always high!"

Lexi couldn't tell what Stella was thinking behind her big glasses, but she imagined she was pretending to be angry. Henry took it in his stride.

"Let's examine the facts as we know them," said Henry, taking out a reporter's notebook and pen from his coat pocket. "Tell us about the guys at the firehouse."

Lexi told them she really didn't know much. Trevor was the cook. He'd come in the day of the fire and was the one who told her Jerry had died. She'd talked to Ralph that day as well and he was the one who called to tell her about the memorial, she'd met both of them at the dinner date at the firehouse. She couldn't remember many details about the others.

"Lexi, what is this Trevor like?" Timm asked.

She felt bad admitting that she didn't like him. "It's nothing I can put my finger on. Trevor's always nice and polite to me, but there's something forced about him. I don't know. He has a great Scottish accent though."

"He sounds like a fake, like the widows." Stella added.

"How about Ralph?"

"He is very nice. Kind."

Henry wrote: "Trevor—cook" and "Ralph—good to Lexi"

"You know," Lexi remembered the photo at the McCracken home. "There was a weird thing I haven't told you yet." She squirmed in her chair. "Victor, Ralph and Jerry all went to high school at St. Andrew's."

"That's not weird," said Henry. "San Francisco is a pretty small town. If you were a Catholic boy, odds are you went to St. Andrew's."

"There's something else. I saw a photo of Victor's high school football team." She could see the questions forming in her friends' heads but didn't want to explain how, or where, she had seen the photo. Going to the opera with Victor seemed disloyal to Jerry and kind of a dumb thing to do knowing Victor's history with women. He was cheating on two women and it might look odd if she was with him outside of work.

"The point is that Jerry was in that photo, and Victor said it wasn't him. He made a big deal that he didn't go to school with 'a Jerry' is how he put it."

"Are you sure it was him? You didn't know Jerry for long. Well, you hardly knew the guy." Timm picked up a pot sticker.

That stung. Beverly was the only person Lexi had told about her weekend with Jerry, so she couldn't be angry with Timm. With a sudden clarity, Lexi realized that she hadn't told Beverly that Jerry had died.

Several busboys descended on the table clearing dishes. As they were boxing up the food, one of them asked in typical Sam Wo's style after the fact, "To go?"

Stella grabbed her cup. "Leave the tea!"

Once they were gone, Henry said, "Can you find out why Victor's distancing himself from Jerry?"

"I can. And I will." Lexi felt good saying it.

"So, you think they were still friends? Victor and Jerry?" asked Henry.

Lexi poured another cup of tea. "I don't know." She was about to tell them about her conversation with Father Doyle when Timm said, "It'll be a closed casket for sure." He meant it to be funny and was trying to lighten the mood, but when he saw the look on Lexi's face, he started babbling. "But maybe you'll feel something at the service. Sometimes you need to put a period at the end of . . . you know, what could have been a relationship. Get some closure or a sense of peace?"

Henry said, "It's a good idea. It will give you a chance to say goodbye."

Lexi smiled weakly as Fong came to the table to give them the check.

"Usually, no fortune cookies." Fong scowled at them. "But these fell off truck so good fortunes for you," he said, handing fortune cookies to Lexi, Stella and Henry. "But you, little Timm, no good fortune today." He grimaced at Timm, who couldn't help but giggle. Before walking away, Fong reached in his pocket and handed Timm a cookie.

They opened their cookies and, sure enough, there were no fortunes inside. Everyone laughed. Timm said, "No kidding, these cookies fell off a truck. They were rejects from the fortune cookie factory!"

Tourists at the next table were watching the exchange, poised for an onslaught of harsh words from Fong. Lexi suspected that they had read about Fong's reputation in a guidebook. Then he walked over to their table. As they ordered, Fong scribbled on his pad and nodded politely. Everyone looked disappointed until his sharp voice pierced the air. "You no want wor wonton soup. You get sizzling rice!"

Lexi and Timm watched as the patrons' perplexed looks turned into nervous smiles. Timm leaned over and whispered, "You never expect the Spanish Inquisition, or Ford Fong." Lexi smiled as she recognized the Monty Python reference.

"In this case, they do expect Fong to give them a tongue lashing," Henry said. "They come here to have something to write about on their postcards home."

They split the bill, over-tipped Fong and handed the cash and the check to a passing waiter.

Lexi couldn't help but smile. She was once again delighted with the character of San Francisco. She picked up her coat as they stood to leave.

Once they were standing on Stockton Street, Timm turned to the group and said, "I have an idea. I know that fire station, Jerry's fire station. Maybe six years ago, they rescued me when the power went out in my building, and I tried to climb 15 stories up to my apartment. I made it two flights before collapsing. A neighbor heard me banging my crutches on the stairs and called the fire department. There might be different guys working now, but what if we cut the power to the elevator and I call for help getting to my apartment again. Let's see who shows up."

Henry said, "That's a crazy idea. Why would we want to do that?"

Stella interrupted, "It's freezing. Let's get a move on." They walked up the street as vendors pulled their wares from the sidewalk and closed their doors for the night.

Timm continued, "The fire marshal thinks there's something fishy about Jerry's death. Now there's a detective from the police involved. Why don't I ask the firemen who show up for the call about the hotel fire and see what they say?" Timm looked at the stunned faces staring back at him. "People tell me all kinds of things. They open up to me. You'd be surprised." Henry looked at Lexi.

She said, "Having any information about the fire from firemen who knew Jerry could move the case forward."

Henry smiled and said, "You're finally thinking of Jerry's death as a case."

"Sure, even if this is a dumb idea, and I think we all agree it is, we might rattle some cages." Lexi was glad they were doing something, anything, to get to the truth about Jerry's death.

Henry nodded.

Stella whispered, "I'm in."

The next day was Christmas, and the bakery was open but, luckily, Lexi hadn't signed up for more overtime. It would be her first day off in ages. Since none of the group had plans for the holiday, they decided to call the fire department to Timm's apartment the next day. Lexi was relieved. She didn't want to be alone on Christmas Day.

13

DECEMBER 25, 1983 – CHRISTMAS

Christmas morning, Lexi woke with Saxman's butt in her face. She pushed the cat's rear end off the pillow and reached for her alarm clock. It was already 11:00 a.m. Leaping out of bed, Lexi felt the sting of cold as she walked to the kitchen to feed the cat.

"Sax," Lexi said opening a can of tuna. "It's Christmas and I'm late with your breakfast, so how about a special treat?" Saxman meowed loudly, jumping onto the table and watching Lexi's every move.

Earlier in the year, Lexi had decided to stay in San Francisco for the holidays because a plane ticket to Seattle and the ferryboat to Ketchikan would run her almost a thousand dollars. Now she was even more grateful to be staying. She wouldn't have to hide her sadness from her grandparents. They worried about the danger of the city, so Lexi always kept their conversations light. To them, Alaska was the only safe place to live, and any reports of run-ins with a homeless person or unpleasant bus rides validated that opinion in their eyes. Their righteousness overshadowed any concern they might have for Lexi's feelings. There was no way she was going to tell them about Jerry. She didn't want to give them any reason to push her to move back home.

That afternoon the group met in Timm's apartment and formulated their plan. It seemed like less of a solid plan in the light of day. Luring firemen to Timm's apartment on the pretense that he needed help so Timm could ask them for details about the hotel fire. Why would they tell Timm anything that wouldn't already be reported in the newspapers?

The idea was for Lexi and Henry to locate the building's circuit breakers in the basement of Timm's apartment building, next to the laundry room, and trip the elevator. Stella and Timm would go to the laundromat across the street from Timm's building and wait for Lexi and Henry to join them. Then Timm would call the fire station from the phone booth on the corner. He would explain to the fire station operator that the elevator in his building on Sutter was out, that he was disabled, and that he couldn't make it to his apartment on the 15th floor. Once that was done, Timm would go into the lobby to wait for the fire truck to arrive at his building.

With the elevator disabled, Lexi and Henry met Stella at the laundromat across the street from Timm's building. Lexi was surprised it was open since it was Christmas, but she thought that was one of the many advantages of living in a big city.

Stella was happy because she had laundry to do.

"Nothing's sacred in this unholy place. And thank God for it," said Stella before disappearing into the mouth of a large dryer.

After the call, Timm gave them the thumbs up and made his way to the front of his apartment building. About 10 minutes later, a fire truck pulled up to the curb. The lights were flashing, but the siren was silent. Lexi recognized Trevor and Ralph as they hopped out of the back of the cab, but she didn't recognize the driver who stayed with the truck.

"I met both of those firemen at the firehouse," Lexi said to Henry and Stella, amazed at their luck. "I know they were at the fire." The fire truck wasn't completely blocking the front door to Timm's building, so they could see what was going on. They had propped open the door to the laundromat in case they could hear what was going on.

The firemen swung from the truck to the street. Towering over Timm, Trevor asked, "Are you Mr. Davidson?"

"I am."

"Do you mind if I lift you?"

"By all means." As Trevor lifted Timm like a rag doll, Timm handed the keys to Ralph, who held Timm's crutches in his other hand. "I'm on the 15th floor, but at least I weigh less than your average man."

"Lucky us," said Ralph with a smile as they disappeared into the lobby of the building.

In the laundromat, a man in his 40s who looked the worse for wear pulled the door shut, grumbling under his breath about cold weather and idiot people.

When Timm turned on the light in his kitchen, the agreed-upon sign, Henry and Lexi went outside to the pay phone to wait for Timm's call. The cold wind had driven Henry into the phone booth. He pulled the collar of his suit coat around his ears. There wasn't room for Lexi, but she told Henry her heavy overcoat and boots protected her.

The phone booth door was broken and wouldn't shut. Lexi said, "I almost forgot that we stopped the elevator. I was feeling sorry for Timm."

Henry smiled and patted her arm, "You'd make a good P.I."

Lexi laughed. "I just forgot our plan."

"I wasn't being sarcastic. You were showing empathy, something you need to make a good private eye. Put yourself in someone else's shoes, so to speak."

Lexi smiled and turned her attention to the apartment building entrance as Trevor and Ralph came outside and walked up toward Polk Street, leaving their truck on the street.

The phone rang. Henry picked up. Lexi signaled to Henry that she was going, and walked back to the laundromat to wait with Stella.

Lexi asked her, "The firemen disappeared around the corner. Where could they be going?"

"Where do you think? Honey." Stella peered over her glasses at Lexi. "The bar. It is Christmas. Give the guys a break."

Lexi thought about this as Henry walked in.

"Well, Detective?" Lexi asked.

Henry nodded, clearly enjoying being called a detective again. "Timm's going to join us after we get the elevator working again."

Stella had her dry clothes in a laundry bag slung over her shoulder. She, Lexi and Henry headed towards the basement of Tiny Timm's building to turn the circuit breaker back on. After joining them in the lobby, Timm admitted that his studio apartment wasn't the best place for four people to fit and, though Timm lived around the corner from the bakery, they didn't want to be overheard. Timm suggested they debrief in a nearby park on O'Farrell Street. The light bulbs above the strip club on Larkin sputtered on, and the sunlight faded to dusk as they reached the park.

The wind rushed up the street. Now that she didn't have to observe anything, Lexi pulled her hood over her head and hugged her coat more tightly around her.

"Did Trevor make a pass at you?" Stella teased.

"Behave." Henry gave Stella a friendly nudge.

Lexi said, "He's definitely not gay if that's what you're getting at. He kept asking if I had a girlfriend to date. And made some pretty salty remarks about female anatomy."

"So, what did they say about the fire?" asked Henry.

"They were open about the investigation but played it off as standard procedure. They said the same thing would happen after any fire when there's a death. Ralph said Jerry's body wasn't completely burned." He looked at Lexi before continuing. "He also said there was a beam that must have knocked him unconscious. Then Trevor started talking. He said they didn't expect to find anything suspicious, and that the fire marshal was playing it by the book."

"Why do you think they told you so much?" asked Henry.

Timm smiled. "People tell me all kinds of things. If I ask a question, I get a straight answer, probably because people feel sorry for me. It's been like this my whole life."

"Well," Henry said, "we know something knocked poor Jerry out, and that's why he didn't make it out."

Those talkative firemen are like a Christmas gift to us," said Timm. "Just like McCracken's and Sam Wo's being open around the holidays."

"And that laundromat," added Stella, patting her clothes on the bench next to her. "It is disappointing though. That's all they said? Not much juice there." Stella's shoulders slumped. "Did anything else happen?"

"Not really. Ralph was nice. Normal. Trevor was very charming, if a bit crude, but he did give me an Artful Dodger vibe." Timm looked at everyone hunched against the cold on the bench next to him. "You know, from *Oliver Twist*."

Stella said, "We know who the Artful Dodger is. Are you saying he's a pickpocket?"

Lexi had her hood on, so Timm's voice was muffled. She leaned closer and said, "What do you mean?"

"Well, they came into the apartment and before they left, Trevor picked up a statute of the Infant of Prague that my mother had left me."

"The what?" asked Lexi.

"Infant of Prague. Jesus. It's from the old country. One of the few things my parents took when they left Czechoslovakia, running from the Nazis. My family was one of the few Jewish refugees accepted into the U.S. during the war."

"Why did they have a statue of Jesus?" asked Stella.

"Someone slipped it to them as they boarded the train. Even if they didn't use it to hide their identities, the gold on the statue is pure gold, so they could have used it to bribe a station agent or a passenger who might get suspicious and threaten to call the authorities. It saved their lives, the border guards suspected my parents of being Jewish because they had no papers—"

"Or couldn't show them the ones they had, more likely," added Henry.

"That's right," Timm nodded before continuing. "They were about to be taken from the train by the SS when one of the officers found the statue wrapped in clothes at the bottom of my mother's bag. She didn't know if it would work, but without it..." He stopped talking and bowed his head.

Lexi put her hand on his. "You must miss her very much."

Just then, a disheveled drug addict Lexi recognized from the bakery staggered into the park and glared at them.

"Don't worry," said Timm. "He won't bother us. These homeless guys feel sorry for me, which is sad since I'm the one with the apartment." Timm lifted his crutch resting next to him on the bench. "Alms for the poor?"

Ignoring Timm's joke, Stella said, "So what if the guy—what's his name, Trevor?—fondled your statue?"

"Well, it was odd how Ralph rushed him out of there saying they had another call, because I didn't hear his radio go off. What happened when they left the building?"

"Straight to the bar," Stella said proudly. She appreciated naught over nice.

"Why are you sure that they went to a bar, Stella?" Lexi asked, seesawing her legs to keep warm.

Henry pointed to the truck across the street. "Where else would they go around here without their truck?"

"Well, comrades, I have to get my ass someplace warm." Stella's voice cracked. "I may join the fire department for a hot brandy."

Henry stood. "Yes, it's getting dark out, we should think of getting home."

"God bless us, everyone," said Timm, laughing as he grabbed his crutches.

Lexi left her friends and headed home to spend Christmas night watching "A Christmas Carol" on her tiny television with Saxman. Their caper hadn't yielded much information, but at least they'd done something. Tomorrow she would dig for information. Only this time she'd pursue it alone.

14

DECEMBER 26, 1983 – THE LIBRARY

With two days off in a row, Christmas and now the day after, Lexi felt as if she were on vacation. She had spent Christmas playing detective with her bakery friends, but this morning had been devoted to catching up on laundry and shopping. Once she was done with her chores, Lexi planned to go to the library. She wanted to look up any stories about St. Andrew's dating back to when Victor and Jerry and, apparently, half the firemen in San Francisco, had gone to school there. Maybe the incident Father Doyle had mentioned was big enough to be newsworthy and made it into the paper. In their conversation, Father Doyle had said that Victor and Jerry had won the championship the year they graduated in 1972, 11 years ago. She decided to look for anything newsworthy relating to St. Andrew's from their sophomore to senior years.

In the late afternoon, Lexi finally started walking to the library. Since it was cold out, she moved fast and made good time. There weren't many people on the street, but the few lingering around the liquor stores in the Tenderloin looked as if they had left their Christmas spirit somewhere in the 1960s.

The library was at one end of a large square opposite of City Hall. A federal building and some kind of meeting hall completed the square. The library was a classical building with pillars and latticed windows. It was a beautiful building, but City Hall was so lavish it made the library look like something out of the Soviet Union.

The library's hours were posted on a brass plaque next to the large wooden doors: 9:00 a.m.–9:00 p.m. She walked inside, found the reference librarian and asked how she could find newspapers from 1969 to 1972. The librarian suggested that Lexi limit her search to *The Chronicle,* that way if she found anything in the morning paper she could start looking at the afternoon *Examiner* for follow up stories. She pointed Lexi to the microfiche files and showed her how to look up a newspaper page. Then she patiently showed Lexi how to pull the microfiche, load it onto the machine, enlarge the type and move the page around using the lever in the front.

Three hours passed. Lexi was getting discouraged. Her neck ached, and she decided to give up for the day. She looked at her watch. It was close to 8:00 p.m. No wonder she was hungry, she'd worked through dinner. She took one last flip through the file, put the next slide into the reader and stopped short. The headline at the bottom of the front page for Wednesday, September 13, 1972 read:

> Possible Teen Suicide Linked to Hazing at St. Andrew's School
>
> WEDNESDAY. The body of a St. Andrew's junior was discovered hanging from the rafters in the church vestibule on Sunday morning. Sixteen-year-old Stuart Ferguson's parents informed the police that Ferguson, an altar boy, had walked to the school church an hour before the service. The boy's mother, Wallace Ferguson, insists that her son would not have committed suicide and requested a full investigation into her son's death. Mrs. Ferguson reported to the school administration that her son had written a diary entry about a hazing incident before his death and has turned the diary over to the police.

Lexi read the article again. A suspicious death at St. Andrew's the year Victor and Jerry graduated was more than just an incident. She wondered if Victor had been worried that Jerry might have told Lexi about Stuart's death, and if that was why he had asked her what she and Jerry had talked about on their date. She had thought it was a strange question at the time. Still, why would he care if she knew about Stuart Ferguson's suicide, unless he was involved in the hazing incident, and that hazing was a direct cause of Stuart's suicide?

She wanted to know more about what happened before the library closed. It was getting close to 9:00 p.m. After searching frantically for twenty minutes through both *The Chronicle* and *Examiner* files for a follow-up story, Lexi came across another article buried on page 4A of the *Examiner* from September 15, 1972.

> FRIDAY. The funeral for Stuart Ferguson, a St. Andrew Preparatory High School altar boy, and beloved son of Mack and Wallace Ferguson, will be held at the Old Saint Mary's Church on California Street on Saturday. The death was ruled a suicide by the County Coroner, Dr. Edward Yu.

Lexi put the microfiche back in the file box and sat down, contemplating what she knew. There had been a hazing incident involving Stuart. She suspected

Victor and Jerry were involved, based on her conversation with Father Doyle. Since the article said that the coroner had declared Stuart's death was a suicide, there must have been an investigation. Lexi knew she was getting close to something, but in order to get the information she wanted, she needed to talk to Victor.

By the time she packed up and left the library, they were closing the door behind her. She heard the heavy lock click as she ran down the stairs to the street. She decided to walk home along Van Ness where there were more cars; the Tenderloin section of Polk Street would be sketchy this late at night. If a bus came, she'd take it. She realized that she was starving and stopped at the liquor store to pick up a frozen burrito and a beer. It was going to be a long night.

15

DECEMBER 27, 1983 – DETECTIVE ROBERT REIGER

Lexi woke on Tuesday dreading the day. This was the day of Jerry's memorial. After giving it a lot of thought, she realized Henry had been right, it would give her a sense of closure to be there, but she was not looking forward to meeting Jerry's parents and explaining to them who she had been to their son. Before that though, Detective Reiger was going to show up at the bakery to question her about the fire. Even though she didn't know anything, she was still nervous about being questioned by the police.

In a fog, Lexi got herself ready and to the bakery. In the afternoon, Beverly came in for her shift. She walked past Lexi, who had been replenishing trays of cookies, and into the warehouse. Lexi decided it was time to set things straight and followed her into the back.

Hearing the swinging door behind her, Beverly turned around, her expression stern. Lexi said, "Jerry died in the hotel fire." Her voice cracked.

Beverly's face transformed from anger to compassion. Her brows softened, her eyes welled with tears as Lexi started to cry. They hugged and cried together.

When they finally let go of each other, Beverly took a quick peak through the glass window of the swinging doors to see if any customers were waiting, and returned to Lexi.

"I'm so sorry," she said in a low voice.

"And I'm sorry I didn't tell you that's why I was upset in the office with Victor."

Beverly smoothed a few pieces of loose hair back into her braid. "We'd better get out there. I'm sure my mascara is running down my face."

"You clean up," Lexi said, moving toward the front. "I'll hold down the fort."

As the day passed, Lexi was thinking about what she'd learned yesterday at the library and how Victor had lied to her about knowing Jerry. She was boxing a cake when a commotion from near the cash register snapped her attention back. A disheveled man with wild eyes said in a loud voice, "Give me a muffin."

"What kind would you like, sir," Lexi asked, keeping an eye on his movements.

She could see Howard's wheelchair coming down Van Ness. The man asking for the muffin paced in front of the counter. He stopped short and rocked back and forth, mumbling incoherently. Lexi wanted to get to the front door to open it before a well-meaning patron tried to help Howard. But the muffin guy was getting more agitated. She needed to get him served and out the door before she could get Howard inside the bakery, and she needed to do this quickly so that she could take care of both men without either of them having a meltdown.

"That one." Lexi looked at where the man was pointing. His fingers were swollen; the skin stretching over his knuckles was pink and raw. She had seen this before on drug addicts. There was a methadone clinic in the neighborhood, and she guessed he was somewhere in the cycle of addiction and recovery.

Lexi took the prune muffin out of the case and put it on the counter. His hand was shaking as he snatched it up. With his free hand, he dug in his jeans pocket and dumped a pile of change, mostly pennies, onto the counter. Howard was getting closer to the door, and one of the tourists sitting at a table with his family stood up to open it. Lexi grabbed the change on the counter and tossed it into the register, even though it wasn't nearly enough. She took a step toward the door. But before she could take a second step, something smashed into her face, and she tasted prune.

"That's it, I'm calling the pol—" Before Lexi could finish her sentence, she heard Howard screaming at the tourist's presumption that he needed help. In the middle of all the ruckus, Ben appeared. He grabbed the muffin guy by the collar and walked him past the bewildered tourist still standing at the door, past Howard yelling incoherently from his wheelchair, and dumped the guy onto the street. The customers clapped and cheered. As he walked back in, he opened the door wide and motioned for Howard to enter.

"Not a word out of you, old man," Ben said to Howard. "You let people help you. They don't understand a word you say, so let them be decent human beings!"

Howard stopped yelling and pressed the lever on the wheelchair forward, maneuvering through the open door.

As Beverly took over the register, Lexi brushed the muffin off her face, thanked Ben for helping her with the muffin man, and then prepared Howard's coffee. She told Beverly she was on break and brought it over to him.

"You can't yell at all the customers," Lexi said with a smile as she placed Howard's coffee in front of him and moved the straw near his mouth. "We need a few to pay our salaries." Howard grinned and sipped his coffee. Then Lexi excused herself and walked over to sit with Henry. Stella joined them, and Lexi motioned for Timm to sit at their table as well. Henry looked at Lexi with kind eyes and said, "The memorial is today. How are you feeling?"

"I haven't had time to think about it, which is a good thing. Let's just say the day has been full of distractions." She told them Detective Reiger was coming in to talk to her about the fire.

"I'm nervous. Why would a detective want to talk to me?"

Henry said, "They must know that you went out with Jerry, though there's no way the police are working with the fire department. There's a long-standing rivalry between the departments. They're just like fraternities, loyal only to their own. But don't get them started on each other's departments and how they're run. Fire and police don't mix."

"I guess that explains why Jerry wanted our first date to be at the firehouse," said Lexi. "I had to pass muster with his brothers in arms or whatever."

Stella said, "A trial by fire, so to speak."

"Ouch!" said Timm. "It's a good one, but too soon, Stella." He looked at Lexi and shrugged his shoulder. "Right?"

Lexi smiled. "It's okay. Humor helps."

Things had finally slowed down. Lexi was getting nervous about the time. The memorial was only hours away. She would see Jerry's family for the first time and firefighters she had met during their date. She wasn't sure she was up for it.

Lexi saw an African American man standing at the counter, struggling to get his wallet back into his back pocket after paying Beverly for a tea and pastry. His suit jacket was tight and the buttons strained against their holes. Lexi had noticed his thick-soled shoes when he came in and thought he must have bad feet. He looked up, saw Lexi standing at the end of the counter and said, "Are you Lexi Fagan? I'm Detective Robert Reiger." He showed her his badge. "May I ask you a few questions regarding the Cathedral Hill Hotel fire?"

"Sure." Lexi asked Beverly to take over while she took a break, and walked over to join Detective Reiger at a table near the front window, away from the other customers. Reiger set down his tea and bear claw and motioned Lexi to take the seat across from him.

Lexi asked, "Is this part of the fire department's investigation?"

"I don't know what the fire marshal's office take is yet. I'm investigating the death of the fireman, Jerry Stevens."

Lexi put her hand to her heart. She stared at Reiger's eyes, deep brown with gold flecks. He had a salt-and-pepper mustache, and his graying hair was cropped short; his skin the color of toasted almonds.

"His death. Why?" She had assumed there was nothing to investigate, but there must be more to it if two agencies were investigating what appeared to be an accidental fire. Detective Reiger noticed Lexi shudder. She said, "Someone must have walked over my grave."

He raised an eyebrow. "There are a few loose ends I'm trying to tie up."

"I don't understand." Lexi wasn't sure what loose ends there could be.

"This is just standard procedure. Any time someone dies in a fire—accident or not—it's looked into. I have a few questions about the timeline. I can probably close the books on this case pretty soon." Reiger paused. "Definitely sooner than Fire Marshal Berry will wrap this thing up."

Lexi asked, "So you *don't* think it was arson?"

Reiger ignored the question, took a notebook out of his breast pocket and said, "Shall we?"

"Okay." Lexi said. "The police and the fire department are investigating the non-suspicious death of a fireman in a fire." Lexi looked at Reiger. His lips curled into a faint smile that made Lexi smile, too. She started to relax.

"How well did you know Jerry Stevens?"

"We hadn't known each other for very long, but we were close." Detective Reiger was silent, so she continued. "I met him here at the bakery." Reiger seemed to be waiting for something worth writing in his notebook. Lexi blurted out, "I have to know. Was Jerry's death an accident? Doesn't the arson investigation confirm that it wasn't?"

"Arson investigation?" Detective Reiger looked up. "Lexi, I need your full cooperation. If you know anything about arson or about Jerry's death you need to tell me. Take a deep breath, and let's start over. Why don't you just tell me everything you know, starting with the day of the fire."

Lexi told him everything she could remember about that morning. Detective Reiger took notes and didn't interrupt. He nodded encouragingly when she paused. She told him that there were a lot of people on the scene, but she hadn't noticed anyone who didn't look like a fireman or paramedic. There were reporters too, but she had been busy and wasn't watching the whole time.

"Firemen were in and out of here all day. The cook that I met on my date at the firehouse, Trevor, came in, but he was the only one that I recognized."

Detective Reiger looked up from taking notes.

"What about Jerry? Did he come in to see you?"

"No. But I think he waved to me." Lexi was getting upset thinking about it. "From across the street." Her eyes welled with tears. Reiger took one of his napkins and handed it to Lexi. She wiped her face.

"Why would you doubt it was him?" Reiger asked.

"He was in full gear with an oxygen mask, so I couldn't see his face."

"And he didn't come into the bakery?"

"No."

"I had hoped it wouldn't come to this," Reiger said, referring to the lump of disintegrated napkin in Lexi's hand. He smiled as he took a handkerchief from the breast pocket of his coat and handed it to Lexi.

Detective Reiger sat back and said, "I'm going to tell you something, and then you're going to tell me everything you know about the arson investigation."

Lexi looked at Reiger's kind face.

"The fire department thinks there's something fishy about the fire, and questions have been raised about Jerry's death."

Lexi felt as if she'd been punched in the stomach.

"Did you see anything suspicious? Anybody odd hanging around the bakery? It's not unusual for arsonists to watch their handiwork."

Lexi blew her nose in the handkerchief. "I really can't say. There were a lot of people in and out all day, but I don't remember anyone in particular who didn't look like a tourist or one of my regulars."

Reiger looked closely at Lexi. "There's going to be an autopsy." She felt ill, and Reiger gave her a moment to digest what he'd just said.

"Now, what do you know about the arson investigation?"

Lexi composed herself and said, "Not much. A group of fire marshals came in yesterday. I waited on them. They sat at the table in the corner eating donuts and talking about the fire."

"How many of them were here, and what did they ask you?"

"There were three of them. They didn't ask me anything. One minute they were talking and eating—a chocolate-cake donut and two glazed donuts—sorry, I always remember what people order. They talked for about twenty minutes until something made them get up and leave in a hurry, but I don't know what.

They weren't wearing uniforms. I only knew they were fire marshals, because Henry overheard them talking about the fire."

"Slow down," Detective Reiger looked puzzled. "Who's this Henry person?"

"Henry's a friend, one of my regular customers. He comes in almost every morning. He used to be a private investigator. His eyesight is bad, but his hearing is excellent."

"What did Henry tell you the marshals talked about?"

"Henry said they avoided all mention of the word arson, and they didn't say outright that there was any suspicion around Jerry's death, but Henry could tell it wasn't a run-of-the-mill case. They talked about Jerry's body, but he couldn't hear what they said. They also said they wanted to wrap things up quickly so that it didn't interfere with the service today."

"Wrap things up by today?" Detective Reiger was incredulous. "We don't even know what the cause of death is yet."

Lexi was stunned. "I thought Jerry died in the fire. The cause of the fire might be arson, but wouldn't that still mean he died from fire and smoke inhalation? Even if he'd been knocked out by a falling beam."

"What beam?"

"We—" Lexi paused. She didn't want to tell Detective Reiger about how the fire department was called to Timm's apartment on Christmas when they had learned of the beam that might have knocked Jerry out. "I mean, Henry overheard the fire marshals say there might have been a beam that fell and trapped Jerry in the hotel."

"That's interesting. So why do you think they didn't talk to you or anyone else who had front-row seats to the fire?"

"I don't know. But Stella—" Reiger put his hand up to stop her from going on. "Not *another* private investigator customer of yours?"

"No. She's not a PI, but she is a customer. She was talking to Henry that day and saw one of the fire marshals look at the hotel, something seemed to interest them, and they got up and left. She tried to make out what they saw, but she couldn't see anything going on across the street. It seemed to Henry and Stella that something had spooked the marshals."

"Well," Reiger said with interest, "is there anything else you can tell me? Did Jerry mention having problems with anyone? Was he upset about anything? Problems at work?"

"He didn't mention anything like that to me. He seemed happy, and he told me that he loved his job." Lexi paused. "There is something else." Lexi decided to tell Reiger about Victor's connection to Jerry. If it had been arson and the fire was what killed Jerry, the arsonist wouldn't have known who, if anyone, had died in the fire. But she wanted to help any way that she could. Detective Reiger could decide if something was relevant.

Reiger took a drink of tea, set the cup down and picked up his pencil. "Tell me."

"I don't know if this has any significance to anything but my boss, Victor McCracken, went to high school with Jerry and another fireman who works"—Lexi stopped herself—"worked, with Jerry." But when I asked Victor about it, he said he didn't know Jerry, but then he asked me a lot of questions about what we talked about after Jerry and I went on a date. It just seemed odd." She left out the part about seeing the photo of Jerry with Victor at his parent's house.

She suddenly felt that she was betraying Victor, so she started to backtrack. "I think Victor may have been playing the protective big brother." She decided to leave out what she had learned from Father Doyle at St. Andrew's and what she had discovered at the library. She thought she should give Victor a chance to explain what had happened before putting him in the middle of the investigation.

Reiger leaned in and pursed his lips expecting more.

"Jerry and Victor went to high school together."

Reiger made a note. "Were they still in contact?"

"I don't think so," said Lexi. "Jerry never mentioned Victor, but I think he would have since we met at McCracken's."

Reiger ate the last bite of bear claw before asking, "What's the history of McCracken's Bakery? I'm just curious. I drive by here all the time."

"Victor's grandparents came from Ireland and opened the bakery sometime in the early 1930s. Victor took over when his father retired just before I started working here about a year ago."

Reiger looked through his notes. "Back to the case. So, Jerry attended St. Andrew's Catholic School for Boys in Pacific Heights." He looked up. "And your boss went to school with him."

"Yes, they were in the same class. They graduated in '72."

Detective Reiger folded his notebook and put it in the pocket of his herringbone jacket. He reminded Lexi of a professor.

"So, to recap, you didn't know Mr. Stevens for very long." Lexi nodded before Reiger continued, "You seem pretty upset by his death for such a short relationship, but it sounds as if you might have been one of the last people who isn't a fireman to see him alive, and then you watched the place where he died go up in flames." He paused. "I think that's all for now."

He stood up from the table. Lexi tried to hand him back the soggy handkerchief. "Keep it." He waived her off with a sympathetic smile. "Will you be at the memorial service?"

Lexi nodded again.

"Then I'll see you there." Detective Reiger threw away his trash and replaced the empty cup holder. Before leaving, he turned to Lexi, handed her his card and said, "Call me if you think of anything else."

Lexi decided that she liked this San Francisco "Columbo." It was the way he had fumbled with his wallet when he paid, dropping it on the counter, a wad of cash spilling out and the rumpled jacket and nurses shoes. He seemed like a nice guy with a sense of humor.

Lexi watched Reiger walk outside and disappear down the street. She felt as if she had already had a full day. It was getting close to the time she had to leave, and there was still no sign of Victor or the VW.

Lexi was slicing bread in the warehouse when Beverly came into the office.

"There's a Mr. Berry here to see you."

Lexi sighed and followed Beverly into the bakery. She recognized the man as one of the group of fire inspectors. She was irritated that he wanted to interview her now and wondered if the timing had anything to do with the visit from Detective Reiger. She needed to hit the road soon or she would be late for the service.

"Lexi Fagan?" He extended his hand. It was clammy and soft.

"Inspector Berry."

"What can I do for you?" she asked.

"I have questions about the fire. Standard stuff but we need to ask."

"Let's sit. Can I get you some coffee or a donut? You and your buddies left without finishing the other day."

He gave Lexi a sidewise look but ignored her comment. They sat down near the front window. Lexi glanced across the street at the charred, empty hotel.

"What did you want to know?" she asked.

Inspector Berry's face was blank. His puffy white face looked even pastier against his jet-black toupee.

"When did you notice the fire?"

"Notice? The fire started at eight o'clock. We had been open for about an hour. I heard a—"

"And when did the fire trucks arrive?" Berry cut her off.

"I'm sure you can get that information from your own men," Lexi answered curtly.

"I'm just confirming everything for my report."

"I'd say the fire trucks arrived at ten after eight, and the ambulance came right after—" She got the last part in about the ambulance before he interrupted her again.

"When did the power go out?"

"The clock stopped at 8:12."

"So that's when you think the power went out?"

"I'm pretty sure it's a fact." She waited for him to speak, but when he didn't she continued. "The clock stopped when the power went off. Speaking of time, I have to go."

"I have a few more questions. How long had you been going out with Jerry Stevens?"

Lexi looked at Inspector Berry's little eyes. "Not long. Why?"

Sweat beaded along his upper lip and appeared around his artificial hairline. Without acknowledging Lexi's question, he continued. "Just curious. And who came into the bakery during the fire?"

"I don't know, lots of people. Do you mean which firemen came in?"

There was a long pause before Berry said, "Of course. Firemen."

"We were busy, I really don't remember how many came in. I only recognized Trevor Hayes."

Inspector Berry paused when he should have been asking questions and asked questions when he should have been listening.

"Do you like fire?"

The question was so out of the blue, Lexi was taken aback. She wondered why he hadn't asked how she knew Trevor Hayes. She said, "Really? What kind of question is that? Listen, I've never dated a fireman before Jerry Stevens asked me out. We dated a few times, and then he died. End of story." Lexi stood up, turned away from Inspector Berry and started walking away.

"Well," Berry harrumphed as he stood up. "That will be all. This fire investigation is officially closed." Before Lexi could turn back to face Berry and pepper him with questions about how that was possible after such an inconsequential interview, Inspector Berry was out the door.

16

DECEMBER 27, 1983 – IN MEMORIAM

Lexi had read in *The Chronicle* that as dangerous as firefighting could be, it was rare for a fireman to die on duty. Because it was unusual, and firefighters were a tight fraternity, Saints Peter and Paul Catholic Church at Washington Square would be filled to capacity. Firefighters from all over San Francisco would be there and, of course, Jerry's family and friends. If she'd felt awkward at one time about her relationship with Jerry, she didn't feel that way anymore. So what if they'd only had two dates, she knew she loved him. She remembered the gurney covered with the white sheet, and how it could have been the one carrying Jerry's body. Something had happened to him that day, and she needed to know what.

Victor walked into the bakery and gave Lexi the thumbs up. They had arranged for him to leave the keys in the ignition.

Since Mr. Berry had made her be so late, Lexi rushed from the bakery without saying goodbye to anyone. She grabbed her coat and jumped into the orange VW bug that Victor had parked in the alley behind McCracken's while Berry had been questioning Lexi. She drove down Van Ness to the Broadway Tunnel. The bug's engine worked hard to make it up Columbus Avenue to Saints Peter and Paul. The noise was so loud it drowned out Metro Dave, who was giving a traffic report on the radio.

The memorial was scheduled to start at 3:00 p.m., and it was three now. Columbus Avenue was still decorated with Christmas wreaths on lampposts, and the shops and restaurant windows were painted with holly leaves, red berries and the occasional Christmas tree. The winter sun was blindingly bright.

Lexi turned right on Filbert. She saw people filing into the church. Unfortunately, as she suspected, there was no parking in the immediate area. It was 3:10. Lexi turned left at Grant Avenue, heading away from the commercial district. There was no way she would find a spot closer to North Beach where the Savoy Tivoli and Café Trieste were big draws for locals and tourists, even in winter. Every spot on the narrow street was filled as she passed tightly-packed apartment buildings.

Lexi spotted someone leaving an apartment on the corner of Grant and Lombard. She slowed down when she saw car keys come out of the guy's pocket. She was frantic and unsure how many blocks she'd driven away from the church. As soon as his Renault pulled out of the spot, Lexi parked and walked as fast as she could down Grant toward Filbert, while struggling to get her arms through the sleeves of her coat. She had forgotten her high heels at work but was grateful when she started jogging toward Washington Square in her work shoes. She turned down Filbert and headed toward the twin steeples of the church. Lexi was relieved to see a few stragglers walking up the stairs, and a man in uniform she recognized.

"Ralph!"

Ralph turned and waited for Lexi to catch up with him. His young face looked older than she had remembered. She noticed creases around his mouth and hazel eyes. He was older than she had originally thought. Maybe it was the dress hat covering his unkempt hair. He gave her a big hug that she wasn't prepared for, and when he released her, she nearly stumbled over. Flashing her a big smile, Ralph said, "I'm so glad you came." She steadied herself on his arm and smiled, saying, "It was good of you to let me know about the memorial service. I want to be here with people that loved Jerry."

"Better get inside," Ralph said. "It's already started."

Horrified, Lexi realized that she was still wearing her apron. Her coat was already unbuttoned, so she quickly slipped it off before ripping the apron off and stuffed it into her purse as she walked behind Ralph into the church. She had been tugging at her black cocktail dress under her uniform all day at work. Now she thought it might not be appropriate for a memorial, but it was the only black dress she owned. It was also too late to worry about it.

The newspaper had been correct. The pews were packed. Ralph disappeared into a sea of blue uniforms. Most of the benches were filled with firefighters in crisp dress blues, their hats in their laps. Lexi assumed the people sitting in the first two pews were members of Jerry's family. She went to sit in the last row in the back of the church when she spotted Trevor standing near the front. He saw her and waved for her to join him. She shook her head, but he kept motioning for her to come to the front. Realizing he wasn't going to sit down, Lexi relented. She walked down the aisle past rows of stone-faced firemen until she reached Trevor's pew, just behind the family. She tried not to look directly at the casket in the space between pews and the steps to the altar. Father Doyle was standing at the head of the closed casket, intoning, "We are all children of God, but what we are to be in the future has not yet been revealed."

When she had finally excused herself past mourners and squeezed in next to Trevor, she looked up. Father Doyle was looking at her.

He kept talking, his hands in front of him, palms up. "Those are the words of John. I would like to remember Gerald as a child of God."

She flushed and looked anywhere but at Father Doyle or the casket.

Gerald? It hadn't occurred to her that Jerry had been short for something, and it filled her with sorrow. She and Jerry would never have the chance to share more of themselves. Love had opened her heart and was now causing it to shatter.

Lexi brought her attention back to her surroundings. Something about the church seemed familiar, the smoky incense, the diffused light from the stained-glass windows, the rhythm of the priest's voice. It was like looking into the distance at someone she knew; out of focus at first. She was filled with a sense of longing. But it wasn't Jerry she was thinking of this time; to her shock and disbelief, it was her parents. She remembered someone telling her once that loss resounded in loss, but at the time she hadn't understood what it meant. To stop herself from dwelling on her feelings, Lexi concentrated on the tabernacle gleaming against the gray-veined marble wall. Tiny gold statues of saints were molded into the doorframe. Lexi strained to make out every figure.

Since it was Christmas week, scarlet poinsettias were arrayed on the stairs, and velvet ribbons tied into giant pinecone-studded bows draped the altar. Father Doyle turned, walking up the steps to the podium. Hanging on the front of the podium was a tapestry that extended down the stairs and onto the floor.

Father Doyle looked pale. Lexi let her eyes rest on the casket. It seemed large and imposing and was draped in purple and gold. Lexi recognized the school colors of St. Andrew's from the pictures in the McCracken home.

Father Doyle prayed, "I am the way, the truth and the life."

Lexi repeated the lines along with the congregation, the memory of the call and response flooding back from her childhood at church with her grandparents. She must have been at her parents' memorial. There were no bodies in their service since they had disintegrated along with the plane. She was a baby when they died, so she had no memories, only an unspoken longing for them. Warm tears ran down her cheeks. This time she didn't try and stop them. Her thoughts shifted from her parents back to Jerry. Her eyes closed, she pictured the fire that killed Jerry and felt as if she were watching him die. Father Doyle's voice washed over her.

There was a hush, and Lexi opened her eyes. Ralph was at the podium.

"We remember Gerald Alden Stevens III. The football star. The living example of the fellowship, leadership, scholarship and service that Kappa Sigma represents. And of those ideals, service was what spoke to Jerry, and that's what made him a great fireman. He was a true servant of the people." Ralph's voice was even and strong, as if he were used to speaking in public.

As Ralph continued, Lexi could only think of the many things she didn't know about Jerry. His favorite color, or what he liked to watch on television. That he was Gerald Alden Stevens III. She tried to remember what she did know about him. That he liked the Eagles and Led Zeppelin. How he had shuddered at her love for Earth Wind and Fire. There were so few things she knew about his history. It made her question the sense of connection she had felt with him. Was she exaggerating his importance to her in her mind? Was he just someone to fill the void of her loneliness? No. There had been a real spark between them. She gave herself permission to miss him and even yearn for what could have been.

Ralph's voice broke through her musings, "There isn't one of his fellow firefighters who wouldn't put himself in Jerry's shoes so that Jerry could be standing here today."

A sob rose from a woman in the first row. She slumped in her seat, her hat dipping out of view. Lexi looked at the people around her. The firefighters were dabbing their eyes and shifting in their seats.

Lexi noticed an imposing man whose head was covered in unruly thick black hair, sitting in one of the family pews. It was Victor. Even though Ralph had told her he would be here, she was a surprised to see him. He was sitting next to his girlfriend, the blonde. If Victor was still in touch with Jerry, why hadn't he mentioned it to Lexi?

Ralph finished his eulogy, and Father Doyle returned to the dais and began talking. As if a cosmic force had turned down the volume in the church, Father Doyle stopped mid-sentence as he stared into the distance. A murmur went through the crowd as heads turned to where Father Doyle's eyes were fixed at the back of the church. A woman wearing a black dress with a heavy veil covering her face walked slowly down the aisle. The low murmur turned into rumblings and outright conversations. Lexi caught the words "Stuart," "St. Andrew's" and, finally, "The mother." Obviously, this was the mother of Stuart Ferguson, the boy who committed suicide after the hazing incident at St. Andrew's.

Lexi turned back to the front to look at Victor. His face was contorted in pain. She turned again and thought she saw Ben standing at the back wall before a black wide-brimmed hat blocked her view. When she managed to maneuver her body to see around the hat, he was gone. Maybe she had been mistaken.

Stuart's mother was seated. The rumbling in the pews became murmurs and then turned to silence.

When the final prayer was over, Father Doyle thanked everyone for coming. The honor guard that had been standing at attention along the outside walls of the church started to file out. Everyone sat silently until the last of the guard was gone. Then the room erupted as hundreds of people rose from their seats. The front row filed into the center aisle first. Jerry's family walked to the back of the church, nodding solemnly to familiar faces as they passed. As their row filed out, Trevor stuck close to Lexi, and when they had crowded in the entry hall he gave her his handkerchief, even though she didn't need it anymore. She was looking for Victor, but she couldn't shake Trevor.

He moved even closer to her and said near her ear, "What did you see?"

"What do you mean?" Lexi tried to step back, but there was a column behind her.

"The morning of the fire. What did you see?"

"Nothing really. I heard glass breaking and saw smoke coming out of the window. Why do you ask?"

"What window?"

"The second story window on the left," she looked at Trevor, intently trying to figure out why he was questioning her. His face was serious. A group of firefighters surged into the hall from the church, and soon they were surrounded.

"What time was that?" Trevor ignored that his buddies were trying to get his attention.

Ralph appeared and asked, "What time was what?"

"The fire," Trevor turned to Ralph.

Lexi's head filled with questions about Stuart's mother, about Victor...had she seen Ben at the service?

"You know what time the fire started, Trevor. Does this have to do with the arson investigation? I already told the police investigator, Detective Reiger, that I didn't see anything suspicious. Why all the questions?"

Trevor ignored her question, but his eyes widened when Lexi mentioned Detective Reiger. "Who came into the bakery the day of the fire?" he asked with a softer voice.

"Well, you did."

Ralph gave Trevor a funny look and said, "No need to interrogate the poor girl. The department's investigation is complete. There was no arson, so that's that."

Trevor smiled and winked at Lexi. "Quite so."

Lexi looked at Ralph and said, "How is it that the fire investigation is over, but the police are still investigating? I don't think they've even finished cleaning up the hotel yet. It's still a mess over there."

The fire fighters standing around them were talking about the gathering they had arranged at the Gold Spike on Columbus Avenue. It was getting too crowded in the church entryway, and Lexi was starting to feel pinned in. One of the guys she recognized from the dinner at the firehouse asked Lexi how she was holding up. Several of them complained that the post-memorial reception was at an Italian bar and not an Irish pub, as it should be.

"We picked Jerry's favorite spot, not yours," said Ralph before he and Trevor disappeared into the swelling crowd. Trevor said over his shoulder, "I'll catch up with you later." *I hope not,* thought Lexi.

Once Ralph and Trevor were gone, Lexi took a deep breath and moved toward the exit when a small, thin woman, whose face was covered in a dark veil, appeared in front of her. Lexi was about to move out of the way when, without a word, the woman took Lexi's hand and squeezed something into it. She closed Lexi's fingers around the round object, looking as if she wanted to say something, but instead she turned and walked away. Lexi quickly lost sight of her as a crush of blue uniformed men moved out of the nave and into the lobby.

Opening her hand, Lexi looked down at a silver badge. She turned it over. There was an eagle at the top, "firefighter" printed on a scroll underneath, and a ladder crossed with two brass hoses in the middle. She wondered if the woman had been Jerry's mother. Who else could it be? But even if his mother had known about Lexi, how would she have recognized her? Lexi's tears dropped onto the badge and into her palm like raindrops on the pavement.

She squeezed the badge to her heart before putting it into her coat pocket, more determined than ever to find out what had happened to Jerry. A few firemen gathered around her, so she pulled herself together and made small talk for a while before excusing herself. She maneuvered her way down the church steps to the sidewalk; the cold air on her face a bracing relief from the perfumed and incense-heavy air of the church.

She recognized Detective Reiger's gray hair and dark mustache in the crowd. She was glad to see him. He wore the same tight suit jacket he'd had on earlier. Lexi made her way through the crowd until she reached him and said, "I thought your investigation would be wrapped up well before the fire marshal's report was finished." She enjoyed teasing him. "I just heard straight from the horse's mouth that their report is complete."

"From Inspector Berry? Well, what do ya know?" Reiger gave her a strange smile. "A few more questions and we'll close the books and let Jerry rest in peace." But there was something in his eyes that made Lexi think he was saying that for the benefit of the people around them.

"I hope you'll stick around for the reception at the Gold Spike," Reiger said to Lexi as his eyes followed Jerry's family walking by. "Some firemen and a few friends will be there. The family's having a private reception at the Stevens's home."

Just then, Lexi saw Victor holding Jennifer's elbow. Lexi excused herself. She wanted to tell Reiger about the hazing and the suicide, but that would have to wait until after she confronted Victor. She was suddenly filled with anger. How could Victor treat the women who loved him so poorly?

"Victor!" A lot of heads turned, and Victor waved when he saw that it was Lexi who had called out to him. He excused himself to Jennifer, who gave Lexi a dirty look as Victor made his way through the sea of people. She didn't know how to act when he gave her a quick hug. She just stood there with her arms at her sides. She could feel the hair escaping from her ponytail in what she imagined were wild Medusa-like tendrils.

Lexi felt out of control, anger welled inside her, and she said too loudly, "You never told me his name was Gerald!"

Victor pulled her away from the crowd, looking around for Jennifer.

"Calm down. What are you talking about?"

Lexi lowered her voice to a whispered shout. "You never told me Jerry was short for Gerald. And you have to choose between Beverly and what's her name." The words were gushing from her in a torrent of mixed-up thoughts.

"And…and"—she slowed down—"and what are you doing here? Are you and Jerry still friends?" she stammered. "And are you marrying Jennifer and just jerking Beverly around?" Lexi looked at the blonde keeping a watchful eye on them from across the room.

Victor laughed. "I'll take those one at a time if that's ok with you. You know Jerry and I went to school together. St. Andrew's Catholic Asylum."

"You lied to me at your parents' house. You told me you didn't know him. Not only did you know Jerry, you were friends."

"We weren't friends. Besides, we haven't talked since high school. Our parents are neighbors; I came for the family." Victor stared down at Lexi.

"And to address your second concern, my love life is none of your business."

"Don't mess with people who love you, Victor. My folks died when I was a baby, so I never got to love them while they were alive. That's an awful feeling. Do you understand what I'm saying? Now Jerry's gone and no one will ever get to love him again. You have to be good to the living. It's no fun loving dead people, Victor."

Victor looked like he had taken a punch. A few firemen across the hall were calling Victor's name and waving to him. He waved back with a weak smile. Lexi thought he must have known them from school as well. San Francisco was starting to feel more like the small town she had moved away from, rather than the big city she thought she had found.

"That's not all." Lexi was furious. She touched his arm and said, "I know about the hazing at St. Andrew's."

A shadow crossed Victor's face. His eyes focused on her.

"I was afraid of that." Victor put his arm around Lexi's shoulders and pulled her back up the stairs to the church. Inside, he moved her to the edge of the entry hall. He manhandled her between two pillars and loomed in front of her blocking her view. He whispered, "What do you know?"

Lexi was trying to be calm, but this was a side of Victor she'd never seen before. *At least there are still people around,* she thought. She took a deep breath before answering, not wanting to seem shaken. She looked up at Victor towering over her, met his gaze and said, "Just what I read in an old *Chronicle* from 1972."

"Whatever that article said isn't true. The reporter tried to make a sensation out of something tragic."

"Then you tell me what happened." She met his gaze.

"Hazing didn't cause Stuart Ferguson to kill himself." Victor's eyes darkened. "No matter what the Fergusons said and keep saying about what happened. I do understand why they don't want to let it go. He was their son."

Victor's shoulders slumped, and he looked even more like a bear, but some of the fierceness had evaporated. He sighed heavily and said; "Listen, I can't talk to you here. Jennifer and my parents are waiting for me. We're expected at the Stevens family for the reception at their house."

Lexi was surprised at the distress in Victor's face. She decided not to press the conversation. "Ok. But you have to promise that you'll tell me tomorrow. I have to know what happened."

"I promise." He stepped back. "I'll tell you everything. Please don't bring this up to anyone else." Victor's eyes softened. "It would destroy Stu's family to dredge this up again."

"I won't say anything until we talk." Lexi felt her stomach unclench.

Victor looked relieved. "You surprise me, Lexi Fagan," he said before lumbering away.

Lexi's head was swimming. It seemed that there were never answers, only more questions. Out of the corner of her eye, Lexi saw Detective Reiger talking to Trevor near the door. She had picked up on the detective's not-so-subtle hint that she should follow him to the firemen's event. After talking to Victor, Lexi was no longer sure what, if anything, she wanted to tell Reiger about Victor or Stuart Ferguson's death. Yet, how could Jerry's murder and the eleven-year-old death of their classmate be connected?

Lexi was never happier to leave a church, but before she could get very far, she heard someone calling her name.

"Miss Fagan!" Lexi turned and saw Inspector Berry. She stopped and let him catch up to her. He wore a black uniform with brass buttons pulling at the seams, and gold stripes at the cuffs. The badge over his breast pocket gleamed. She was irritated that he wanted to talk to her now and decided to start talking before he had a chance to ask questions whose answers apparently didn't interest him.

"Why did you bother talking to me when the investigation was over by the time you came into the bakery?"

Berry pulled a Berry and ignored Lexi's question. He looked uncomfortable in his too-tight dress uniform. "I'm curious that you're here. You told me that you didn't know Jerry for long."

Lexi fidgeted and looked around for an escape. She wanted to be as far away from Inspector Berry as she could.

"Listen, ask your own men about why I'm here." Before Berry could respond, she turned and walked away.

17

DECEMBER 27, 1983 – THE GOLD SPIKE

The Gold Spike saloon was packed, and the beer and whiskey were flowing. A silver plaque at the door read: "A San Francisco Landmark since 1920." Though she had passed the bar while walking around North Beach, Lexi had never been inside. The ceiling was covered with smoke-stained dollar bills and business cards that dated from the early 1950s. The antlers from a dusty stuffed moose head jutted into the room with dollar bills pierced onto its antlers. Silver tinsel hung from the animal heads, and a garland of popcorn and cranberry hung on a small tree in the corner. Colored lights were strewn across the mirror behind the bar. Hundreds of faded Polaroids of customers were pinned on top of older photos and cluttered every wall. The ancient cash register was the shiniest item in the room, the brass polished to a warm gold, glowing under a green banker's lamp trained on the keys.

Lexi felt out of place. It suddenly seemed like a terrible idea to have come. There were no wives or girlfriends among the sea of men in uniform. She didn't want to stay long. She pushed her way to the bar and ordered a drink. The air was thick with smoke that burned her eyes. Realizing how hungry she was, Lexi scooped up a handful of peanuts from one of the bowls on the bar.

Lexi was relieved that Inspector Berry was nowhere in sight. All she needed was for him to think she was scoping out another firefighter to date and set fires with. She decided to finish her drink, say goodbye to Reiger and go home when she heard Ralph Murphy and Trevor Hayes talking behind her.

"What gives?" Ralph said, "How is your new lady?"

"I told you. I don't have one." Trevor's voice was light and casual.

"I heard you on the phone." Ralph paused. "Listen, buddy, if you don't hang with girls, I'm cool with that."

"You imbecile."

Lexi turned around and saw Trevor take Ralph's head in his hands and rub it with his knuckles in a friendly noogie. They were having a good time, and the mood was light. They were blowing off steam.

"It was me mum I was talking to, you nit." Trevor let him go, and they laughed and smacked each other on the back before heading to a table in the corner.

Trevor looked over his shoulder and spotted Lexi. He and Ralph changed direction and came over to where she sat at the bar. Trevor offered to buy her a drink. She was already lightheaded from the martini she was gulping fast. Trevor reached for her hand.

"Come on." He said. "You look like you need another."

Lexi looked down and saw a bad burn on Trevor's hand. He noticed her looking and said, "Cooking is more dangerous than fighting fires in my case. Unfortunately, not for poor Jerry."

There were more firemen pushing their way towards the bar in an effort to catch the bartender's attention. Trevor let go of Lexi's hand and started talking to other people, leaving Ralph and Lexi to stare into their drinks at a loss for words.

"That looks like a nasty burn on Trevor's hand," Lexi said.

"I love him, but he's nuts. He cooked Chinese when we got home from the fire on Monday night. Everyone was upset about Jerry, and I guess Trevor wanted to distract us with a fancy dish in his new wok. He burned the shit out of his hand. It'll take weeks to heal."

"I don't know him very well, but Trevor seems to run hot and cold when I talk to him."

"You got that right. He's one moody Scotsman." Ralph took a sip of beer. "But, he's one hell of a cook. You know what they say, with great talent comes some crazy. He's the Van Gogh of firehouse cooking."

Lexi couldn't help but smile. "Oh, is that what they say. We have one of those at the bakery. Our head baker can be volatile. He's a wonderful baker and decorates cakes beautifully. He is an artist. But when he goes off—"

"Stay out of his way," Ralph finished her sentence, put his beer down on the bar and ordered another.

Even though she hadn't been at the bar for long, Lexi wanted to go home.

"Listen, I'm going to take off." Lexi turned to leave when she spotted Detective Reiger at the other end of the bar. He motioned for her to join him. She pushed her way through the crowd until she was standing next to him. For the first time, she noticed there was only one other African American in the saloon, a fireman sitting with a small group at a table near the bar.

"Drinking on duty?" she said to Reiger. He gave her a wink.

"For your information, young lady, I'm off duty. I came as a professional courtesy."

The fireman sitting next to Reiger got up, and Lexi sat down. Reiger nodded to the African American fireman, who nodded back. It seemed to Lexi like a nice courtesy since there were so few African Americans she could remember on either the police force or at the fire department. There had been no Black firemen on Jerry's crew. It occurred to her for the first time that she didn't know what it was like to be the only white person in a room. She wondered if Beverly felt as self-conscious about being the one person of color working at the bakery as Lexi felt about being the only woman sitting in the Gold Spike at this moment.

It was noisy in the bar. Reiger leaned closer to Lexi and said, "That firefighter over there introduced himself to me at the church. Trevor Hayes. You told me that he came in the day of the fire. He asked me why you came to the memorial."

"That's funny. I was just talking to the guy who told me about the memorial, Ralph Murphy. He said it was Jerry's friends at the station who suggested that I come."

"Maybe Trevor wasn't one of Jerry's friends?" Reiger eyed Lexi closely. "Or, Ralph didn't mean it and was just being polite when he invited you?"

"Then I should have declined. Don't I have egg on my face." Lexi laughed, but it was a thin laugh and caught in her throat.

"What about your friend Victor? I thought you said Jerry and Victor weren't in contact, but he was at the service today."

"And I thought you said this investigation was just standard procedure," Lexi said, only partly teasing. She continued, "I told you I didn't *think* they were in contact. I still don't." It was easy to talk to Detective Reiger. *He must be good at getting people to open up to him.* "And why are you calling Victor my friend? He's my boss."

"Didn't you two go to the opera together?"

"Yes, but you knew the answer before you asked me." Lexi decided to stick with the truth, at least about that. "Why do you want to know? Are you investigating me?"

Detective Reiger frowned and shook his head. "I'm wrapping up loose ends."

"Okay. I went with Victor because I wanted to see an opera, and he had an extra ticket."

Reiger looked doubtful. Lexi continued. "Believe, me, it's not how I want to be remembered. I let him take me because it wasn't a date, and I wanted to see it."

"You don't remember the name of the opera, do you?" Reiger laughed.

"It's... you're right. I can't remember." Lexi laughed, too. "How could I forget? It was a big deal. Victor even bought me a program. I could tell you what it was about."

"Why would Victor take you to the opera? As you said, he's your boss. Seems tricky."

"Tell me about it. Victor isn't someone I want to get involved with. Trust me. For the record, Victor has a woman that he lives with, and he's dating one of my co-workers. After meeting his parents—"

"You met his parents?" Reiger shook his head.

"Yeah. It sounds, well, wrong. He really isn't interested in me, I promise. I think I've figured out what he was up to at least where I'm concerned. It has to do with his messed-up relationships with all the women in his life, including his mother."

Reiger looked amused. "Let me have it, Detective Fagan."

"Why are you so interested in what happened between me and Victor when I was dating Jerry?"

Reiger leaned on the bar and said, "Humor me."

"Ok. Here's my theory. Victor's parents want him to marry the girl he lives with, his girlfriend or fiancé, or whatever she is. I think her name is Jennifer. She's a big wig at a bank."

"If you're going to be a proper detective, you need to be specific. What position does she hold at what bank?"

Lexi thought for a second and was surprised that she had the answer. "She's a Vice President at Bank of the West."

Reiger said, "Better, but I still don't get why he's got you on the line as well."

He drained his beer and tried to get the bartender's attention. He asked Lexi if she wanted another drink. She shook her head. Another martini and she would be useless to herself and to the detective, but the buzz was helping her put Jerry at a fuzzy distance, at least for this moment. Reiger let his hand drop. The bartender was swamped with firemen calling for refills at the other end of the bar. It was noisy, and Lexi had to shout.

"He doesn't have me on the line! Asking me out had nothing to do with me, particularly. Victor wants to break up with his girlfriend—Jennifer—and openly date his lover from the bakery—"

"A Ms. . . .?" Reiger interrupted.

Lexi laughed at the detective using the term "Ms." He smiled that she had noticed.

"Beverly Roy, but he's in his parents' pockets and needs their approval. His parents are a powerful old-money family and they want him to marry Jennifer."

"Go on; you're still missing the point of the story," Reiger took out a fresh packet of cigarettes and banged it against his wrist. "The story is about you."

"Me?" Lexi laughed. "I'm not even part of the equation. The McCrackens wouldn't be happy to have their son date a girl who works at their bakery, especially one whose parents are from India. It wouldn't matter to them that she's studying pre-med and both her parents are doctors. Victor wanted me to meet his parents to get them used to the idea that he's breaking it off with Jennifer and bring poor Beverly out of the dating closet, so he used the opera and picking up the tickets at their house as a way to lay the foundation. Even the idea of an Indian girlfriend is too much for the McCrackens." Lexi pushed herself away from the bar. She felt loopy from the drink. Reiger nodded.

"I know!" she said loudly. "It's completely messed up."

"So, a red-headed Irish shop girl, as you say, is better than an Indian one? You have a vivid imagination, Ms. Fagan."

"You have parents? Didn't they have expectations of how your life would turn out?"

"Sure. My dad came from Mississippi to work in the shipyards during the war. He married a San Franciscan. They were trying to make ends meet most of my life, but they had plans for their son. I was to become a preacher." Lexi was surprised but pleased at his candor.

"Are they proud of you?"

"My dad died 10 years ago from asbestosis. It's a disease that hardens your lungs. A lot of pipefitters developed the disease from inhaling asbestos particles when they insulated the pipes. The insurance company blamed his smoking for his death, but it was asbestos from the pipes. That's what killed him."

"I'm sorry. Is that why you wanted to be a detective? To get at the truth and make people believe it?"

"That's quite a leap, young lady, but who knows? I never thought about it much. I do want to get to the bottom of things."

"What about your mother?"

"My mother's still alive. Lives in the Avenues. What about your folks?"

"They died in a plane crash when I was a baby." The noise of the bar filled the silence between them.

Talking about her dead parents was a conversation killer. Lexi said, "A preacher, huh?"

"Enough small talk. Let's get back to Victor," said Reiger, tapping his empty glass in one last attempt to get the bartender's attention.

"Well, my theory about Victor is the only explanation that makes sense."

"Who said things always have to make sense?"

Lexi laughed. "You have a point. But honestly, he is *not* interested in me. His mother tried to cover her surprise, but I could tell she and Victor's dad were shocked to meet me. I think Victor's easing his folks into accepting, one, that he's not marrying Jennifer and, two, that he's dating an Indian pre-med student. He's just using me as a stepping stone to Beverly."

"Your hypothesis is a stretch, and it doesn't explain why you dated two St. Andrew's boys in less than a matter of months."

Lexi was stunned. So, this really was about her. She felt dumb trying to explain Victor's behavior when Reiger was thinking the whole time about Lexi's dating history.

"Well, Henry says—"

"Henry, your PI friend from the bakery."

Lexi nodded. Her head bounced up and down, the alcohol loosening her up.

"Henry said that everyone in this city knows each other. If you were going to a Catholic school, you probably went to St. Andrew's. So why would that be unusual?"

"Slow down," Reiger leaned closer to Lexi. She looked into her empty glass pebbled with vodka drops and a lone olive.

She took the olive out of the glass and popped it in her mouth as she said, "What can I say, Catholic boys are my thing. I just hope Victor doesn't get killed after two dates with me." She meant it to be funny, but it fell flat. Maybe she did want another martini.

It had been smoky when she walked into the bar, but now it was hard to see across the room. Reiger took a deep drag off his cigarette and said, "Is there anything you're not telling me?"

"Oh, no." Lexi reached for Reiger's cigarettes. "May I?" He nodded, taking out his badge and flashing it to the bartender, who finally acknowledged him with a nod and headed their way. Handing the bartender his empty beer bottle, Reiger ordered a dirty martini.

"Make that two," Lexi said.

Detective Reiger had offered Lexi a ride home, but she wanted to sober up and decided to walk, forgetting that there was a borrowed VW parked on Lombard Street. The Gold Spike wasn't far from her apartment. Like most places in San Francisco, it was one giant hill away. By the time she got to the top of Union Street, she was out of breath and slightly less woozy.

When Lexi opened the mailbox outside the entrance to her apartment, there was a stack of bills, a letter from her grandmother and a postcard of a cable car overlooking her favorite view of Alcatraz Island. She had neglected to check her mail since the fire.

Lexi turned the postcard over, her heart pounding. On the back she read, "I'm crazy about you." She turned it back to the photo. She had pointed out that exact view of Alcatraz to Jerry as they drove away from her apartment the night of their first date. The world swam away as her tears flowed. She couldn't see a signature. There was nothing else on the card; only her address and the postmark from the day of the fire.

18

DECEMBER 28, 1983 – THE NOTE

It was cold in her apartment when Lexi's alarm blared at 5:00 a.m. She crawled out of bed, wrapping the blanket around her like she used to when she was a child. She wished that her grandmother were in the kitchen with the oven on, the door open to warm her, the blender pulverizing a breakfast of eggs, milk, sugar, and vanilla, her grandmother's version of eggnog. Lexi would pull on her school uniform in front of the oven and drink her breakfast before running to catch the bus to Holy Name Catholic School.

"Oh, that reminds me. I forgot my uniform," Lexi said to Saxman, who followed her into the bathroom, forgetting the bow she'd been batting around only moments before. "It must be in my purse."

She looked at her face in the mirror. The red indents on her cheeks from her pillowcase looked like scars from an old wound. She squinted at her reflection, her head pounding from a vicious hangover. She had taped the postcard from Jerry on the bathroom mirror and looked at it, picturing him the day they had met at the bakery. Instead of focusing on what might have been, she set her mind to trying to find out what had killed him and why. Knowing she had to move on from the fantasy of a future with him, she mentally moved Jerry to the part of her heart where her parents lived. She carefully removed the tape and the postcard from the mirror. Not sure what to do with it, she set it on the sink.

She pulled her messy hair into a ponytail, threw on jeans and a turtleneck, fed Saxman and grabbed her purse, digging deep to the bottom to find her dirty uniform. She felt the strings of the tie and yanked it out of the purse, shaking out the wrinkles. A balled-up piece of paper fell onto the floor and hit the ground, bouncing as it landed. Her attention drawn from her breakfast, Saxman pounced, batting the paper across the floor and under the dresser.

Lexi found the bow that had fascinated Sax until this new paper toy arrived and threw it in the opposite direction to distract her. She knelt down to find the crumpled paper among the dust balls.

Smoothing the note flat, Lexi read aloud: "STAY OUT OF THE FERGUSON CASE." The letters were taped to the page, each from a different source like a ransom note in a movie. Some of the letters were shiny, taken from magazine pages, and others were a dull matte cut from a newspaper. It had the opposite effect the author must have intended—instead of feeling scared, Lexi got mad.

"Happy almost New Years to me," She said to Saxman, who had finished torturing the bow and resumed eating.

She thought about calling Detective Reiger, but she wanted to hear what Victor had to say about Stuart first. If there was more to the Stuart case than what Victor had told her, maybe it had been he who slipped the note in her purse. Besides, she wasn't going to let him weasel out of telling her what happened, note or no note.

Leaving the note on the table, Lexi left early to retrieve the VW parked in North Beach and drive the car to work.

Once at McCracken's, the morning flew by. Lexi was wiping down tables when Paula came in.

"I didn't expect to see you today."

"I had to get out of that shop. It's boring around the holidays. Everyone's out of town visiting family, or if they're in town with family, they're all at Fishermen's Wharf eating sourdough bread bowls full of gloopy chowder, or on a freezing cold cable car. I'm not good when I'm bored."

"I feel sorry for the people with no place to go, the ones with no family or friends." Lexi poured Paula a cup of coffee when it dawned on her that Paula might be one of those people, though she didn't seem upset to be alone.

Paula took the cup and sat down. "Listen, Lex. I'm sorry about your friend. I know you really liked him."

"Thank you." Lexi touched Paula's shoulder. "That means a lot to me."

"I feel like a shit for teasing you." Paula patted Lexi's hand awkwardly. That was as touchy feely as Paula got. Paula picked up the newspaper and started reading.

For the rest of her shift, Lexi was a ball of nervous energy, dropping cookies and giving back the wrong change. She wanted answers from Victor and couldn't focus on work. Ben had already yelled at her for acting like what he called "a dingbat," but Lexi didn't care. He suddenly seemed to be the least of her concerns.

Timm had come and gone. Lexi was amazed that Stella and Henry were sitting at the same table. She was looking forward to telling Henry, Stella and Timm about the memorial and her conversation with Detective Reiger later that night; they'd made plans to meet at Sam Wo's for dinner so that Lexi could update them without being interrupted. It occurred to her that she'd been feeling lonely since moving to San Francisco, but there were people she liked right here. She had some time before meeting Henry, Stella and Timm for dinner and decided to walk to the church after work to talk to Father Doyle. If she could get more information about Stuart from Doyle, she would know if Victor had been lying when they talked.

Standing outside the church, Lexi stared above the door at the carvings of saints armed with swords. Twisted between them were leafy vines and grapes with what looked like a Celtic four-leaf clover in the center. It was an overcast day, but the clouds seemed to be lit from below, as if the city were shining a spotlight into the sky. She pulled the door open and stood in the entryway as it closed behind her. She was still until her eyes adjusted to the dim lights. Then Lexi walked through the entrance and into the nave past rows of wooden benches, toward the altar. The church was gloomy and smelled of stale incense. The ceiling stretched overhead; the stained glass dull and flat with no light to carry the color. The cold winter day felt even colder inside.

It was a few minutes after 3:00 p.m. Because it was just after Christmas, Lexi expected the church to be crowded, but there seemed to be no one inside but her. Approaching the altar, Lexi noticed someone kneeling in the first pew. It was a man, his head bowed in prayer. As she drew next to him, she noticed something familiar about his frame, the short military-style cut of his hair. He lifted his head, and Lexi found herself staring into the pockmarked face of McCracken's head baker.

"Ben?" she asked.

Ben's eyes focused on her. "Lexi?"

"What are you doing here?" They echoed each other. Smiling, Ben pushed himself off his knees and sat on the bench. He patted a place next to him. Lexi sat down.

"This is a surprise," he said. "I didn't know you were Catholic?"

"I'm not. I mean, I am, but I'm not practicing. I was raised—" She was babbling and cut herself off. It was shocking to see Ben outside of work, in a church and in such a good mood. He smashed the fisherman's cap he'd been kneading between his fists onto his head.

"What are you doing here?" he asked.

"What are *you* doing here?"

Ben laughed. His rough features softened into a broad smile. "I'll start."

His face sobered into the blank mask she was used to seeing at the bakery in between his angry flashes.

"I come here to pray. To ask for forgiveness. For the pain I caused in Nam. The pain I cause others, and for how I've treated myself." Ben was looking at the plain wooden cross of thick plants above the altar. He talked as if Lexi wasn't there, as if he were confessing. "I pray for my past, and I pray for my future."

As if waking, he shuddered and turned to look at Lexi. "And," he paused, "this was my high school."

"You went to St. Andrew's with Victor? And Jerry?" Lexi remembered the comment Father Doyle had made at the church. He had mixed up Ben and Victor. She hadn't even considered Father Doyle was talking about her Ben.

"I did."

"But, wait—" There were so many questions Lexi wanted to ask, she couldn't get them out fast enough. "Did you know Jerry?"

"It's a small school. We weren't buddies or anything. I didn't play football. Victor and I were closer." *Why didn't Victor tell me this?*

"But you knew Jerry?"

"Hey, I'm sorry about you and Jerry. Him being dead." Ben looked away, his eyes lingering on the statue of Saint Joseph in the corner. "You know what I mean."

Ben looked back, studying Lexi's face. She hugged her arms around her waist. "You're shivering."

Ben stood up and tugged at Lexi's sleeve like a little boy with his mother. "Let's take a walk. It's got to be warmer outside than in this frigid church."

They headed out a side door into a small garden. The afternoon sun made deep shadows below the bare tree branches. It was warmer outside, though not by much. Bright holly leaves with red berries made the most of the dull winter light. The sun felt good on Lexi's face.

As they walked around the enclosed space, Lexi asked, "Did you know Stuart too?"

Ben stopped walking, his face stern. Lexi stiffened, waiting for the volcano.

"I did." His steady eyes dared Lexi to ask another question.

"I, um, think I know what happened," said Lexi tentatively. Ben was still, unblinking.

"So do I," he said coldly.

Ben continued walking to a cement bench and sat down, motioning for Lexi to follow.

"I'm not talking to you about Stuart. And I don't know much about Jerry except that he and Victor were tight. I was a scholarship kid who ended up in Vietnam while the football players went to Stanford and some other schools back east. That's how it worked. Victor took over the bakery. I needed a job. End of story."

"Is there a connection between Stuart's death and Jerry's? Did you put a note in my purse or my pocket telling me to stay out of the Stuart case?" It was a shot in the dark, but Lexi was starting to suspect that the cases might be connected.

"Of course I didn't, but it's good advice." Ben's body went rigid. His back straightened, his eyes narrowed. "Lexi. I come here to pray. You interrupted me. There is no connection between Stuart's death and Jerry's. As far as I know, Jerry was a fireman who died in a fire." Ben looked away from Lexi but continued talking. "I know that you dated the guy for a second. Why are you digging into this? Are you trying to make trouble?"

"Trouble?" Lexi didn't care anymore if she sent him into an emotional eruption. "Of course not. I don't understand why you're so angry? Can't you just tell me—"

Ben interrupted her before she could finish her sentence. "We're done," he said, standing and walking away, leaving Lexi alone in the garden.

19

DECEMBER 28, 1983 – SAM WO'S

Lexi, Stella, Tiny Timm and Henry were seated at a round table in the warm dining room of Sam Wo's Chinese Restaurant. The smell of garlic and ginger, soy sauce, fried onion and bell peppers hung in the air. Ford Fong was nowhere to be seen. The restaurant had no holiday decorations. When she first walked into the dining room, Lexi had noticed a small dusty shrine above the door that she hadn't seen before. A young waitress in a high-collared silk shirt with knotted silk buttons brought tea, won ton soup and pot stickers they hadn't ordered. Tea was poured and dishes were rotating around the lazy Susan. All eyes were on Lexi.

"Remember I told you that Victor and Jerry went to St. Andrew's together," Lexi said. "Well, I went to the library and found out that there was a hazing incident at the school when they were there, and shortly after that the student involved with the hazing committed suicide." Lexi paused. Blank stares looked back at her. "The death was linked to the hazing and the parents of the kid who died, the Fergusons, were convinced he was murdered."

"Oh my God!" Timm stopped mid-bite lowering his chopsticks. Stella put down her tea.

"Go on," Henry said, extending his hand in Lexi's direction. They devoured their dinner while Lexi told them about the library, the memorial and her conversation with Detective Reiger at the Gold Spike. As she was telling them about the warning note, Stella interrupted. "That's it, Victor killed Jerry to cover up a murder at St. Andrew's when they were teenagers."

"Why would he wait so long?" asked Timm. "Why kill Jerry now?"

"Good point," said Henry. "Sometimes the obvious answer is just a distraction from the truth."

"How about this: Beverly killed Jerry to protect Victor," suggested Timm, helpfully encouraged by a nod from Henry.

"A pillow talk confession?" Stella's magnified eyes looked at them, her expression serious.

"So now every single person we know is a suspect?" Lexi laughed, and everyone laughed with her.

Henry said, "Kids die in hazing accidents. Have you considered that it could have been an accident, and Victor and his friends staged the suicide to stay out of trouble?"

"You'd never get the truth out of Victor." Stella was incredulous. "He's a smooth talker. He could talk Jesus off the cross. If you ask me, they're all covering up for each other."

"Let's not get ahead of ourselves," said Henry. "All we know is that the police and fire departments are looking into things. That's not unusual. And, as far as St. Andrew's is concerned, there would have been an investigation at the time of the hazing incident and that young man's death was ruled a suicide despite what his parents believed.

"What did Detective Reiger have to say about the hazing?" asked Timm.

"I didn't tell him," said Lexi sheepishly.

A collective "What?" rose from the open mouths at the table.

"I want to hear Victor's side of it first."

They let it drop. Henry fiddled with his cuffs. Stella sipped her tea and looked around the room. Timm picked up and then set down his chopsticks a few times.

The waitress came and spooned out more soup into their small bowls. Lexi's eyes were on Stella's spoon. It was a mystery how someone who supposedly smoked as much pot as she did was never hungry. Stella ignored the soup and reached for the teapot.

"I have an idea," said Henry. "I know the head coroner, Dr. Yu. He's an old buddy of mine from my P.I. days. He might have performed the autopsy on Jerry's body."

Lexi recognized the name from the article on Stuart's suicide. A chill came over her.

"Henry," Lexi said in a soft voice. "Dr. Yu was the coroner on the Stuart Ferguson case eleven years ago." She couldn't shake the feeling that, if it weren't a suicide, she might know the person responsible for Stuart's death.

"That's not surprising. He's been working for the county health department for 30 years. I think we should talk to Yu."

Lexi put down her pot sticker, resting the chopsticks on her plate. "How are we going to do that?"

"That's easy." Henry said casually, but Lexi could tell he was excited to be in the thick of things. "I'll ring him."

"Well, if you can get a meeting with Dr. Yu, let's do it." She hesitated. "But visiting a morgue—"

"Honey, you've got to toughen up." Stella gave Lexi a smack on the arm with her tiny fist.

Timm looked at Lexi with a sympathetic grimace. "It smarts when Stella hits, doesn't it. She's stronger than she looks."

Henry suggested they visit Dr. Yu on Friday the 30th after confirming with the doctor that he would be in.

"It's always dead around New Years at the morgue," said Timm.

"Har har," Stella said scornfully, but she was smiling.

"I'll pick you up at your apartment." Lexi squeezed Henry's arm. "That is if you give me your address. I have no idea where you live."

Outside the restaurant, they said their goodbyes. Henry hung back as Timm and Stella disappeared down the street toward the bus stop. At this time of night, the sidewalks were cleared of produce stands and wet from the shopkeepers having hosed away the day's grime. The low lights in the closed shops cast a yellow light over Chinese dolls and lucky cats, their paws still waving, their faces smiling eerily. Henry's bus pulled up. Lexi said goodbye as Henry got on.

She walked down Stockton to California to catch the cable car. It was chilly on the street, and she was cold even after she got inside the car. She watched the driver outside rock back and forth, pulling and pushing with large gloved hands the levers that gripped and released the cable underground. She waited until they were a block away from her stop before stepping outside onto the running board next to the driver. She hung unto the brass pole and stepped onto the street as the car slowed near Larkin Street. She was the only passenger. Waving to the operator, she stepped onto the street.

"Happy New Year!" the driver sang as he rang the bell and worked the cable to continue the ride.

When she put the key in the front door of her apartment, Lexi thought back to the thrill of the night Jerry had stood so close behind her on these steps. It seemed a distant memory now, but also one to have filled every moment of her life before now.

20

DECEMBER 29, 1983 – THE HIPPO

The next day at work, Lexi checked the clock every few minutes, waiting for Victor to show up. He finally came in at 11:00 a.m. She told Claudia she was going on a break. Claudia looked at the clock on the wall and gave Lexi a sour look because it wasn't her break time.

Victor was looking for something in a file drawer in the office. Lexi walked up and said, "Why didn't you tell me Ben went to school with you guys?"

Victor deflated in front of her. His body collapsed into the chair near the desk.

"Oh," he said, his face contorting into an ugly grimace as if he were in physical pain. "I didn't want to talk about Ben. Let's discuss whatever it is you want to discuss after work. Not here, Lexi."

"Victor, there is something going on around Jerry's death. The fire department wrapped up their investigation of the fire, but the police are still looking into Jerry's death. Please tell me what you know."

"Ben's life is private." He straightened his back.

Lexi knew she should wait until she and Victor were at the restaurant to talk as he had requested, but she couldn't help herself. She was so angry.

"There must be some reason you protect him? What is it?"

"What Ben tells you is his business, but I'm not going to talk to you about him. Drop it, Lexi."

"And what about Stuart Ferguson?"

"What about him?" Victor's eyes narrowed. "What does he have to do with anything?"

"You don't think Ben could have hurt Stuart?"

"No way. He was a different guy in high school. Nam messed him up. He was traumatized and started using drugs—"

Lexi opened her mouth, but before she got anything out, Victor said, "Listen to me. When Ben got his draft card, he went to Vietnam, but when Jerry and Ralph and I were drafted, our deferments lasted through grad school. Ben was the only one we were close to who was sent to Nam. Did we feel guilty? Hell, yes."

"So, that's why you let him terrorize everyone? You do know that he's using again." Victor shot Lexi a skeptical look. "I know everyone thinks I'm a country bumpkin, but I have seen him using cocaine, and so has Dean."

Victor sat back and said, "I've heard them call you 'Alaska.'" He reached his long arms above his head and put them behind his head. "But I wouldn't call you a country bumpkin."

"I guess I'll take that as a compliment, but don't try and make this about me, Victor. I grew up in a small town. High school fraternities, hazing and suicides, and learning my boyfriend has been killed in a suspicious fire—this is all new to me. Right now, I'm asking about Ben."

"I'm sorry, Lexi. I can't believe Ben's dirty. I've sent him to rehab a couple of times. But you have to believe that there's more to Ben than his drug habit. Please don't talk about Ben to anyone. He has nothing to do with Jerry or Stuart. Trust me. Just leave him alone. He needs this job."

Lexi wasn't ready to give up. "But Ben was part of your group in school? Right?"

Victor put down his hands, laced his fingers together and rested them on the desk. Looking down at his hands, Victor nodded slowly and whispered, "Yes."

After work, Lexi sat at her kitchen table, Saxman in her lap. She was meeting Victor at Hippo Burgers in less than an hour, where they'd continue their conversation. The restaurant was on Van Ness Boulevard close to her side of the hill, near the Broadway tunnel.

Lexi arrived early. A decorated tree with smiling hippopotamus ornaments took up most of the entrance. The hostess waved her in and motioned her to a booth in the back corner. Lexi slid into a booth and put up two fingers. The hostess handed her two menus and retreated to the entrance. Lexi glanced at the menu before looking around. Tinsel streamers hung on the walls and fluttered in the warm air that blew from the heating vents on the ceiling. It was warm, so Lexi took off her coat and set it on the seat next to her.

Victor walked in. He saw Lexi and headed to the back of the restaurant, his steps heavy. He squeezed into the booth across from her. The note warning Lexi to stay out of the Ferguson suicide case was in the pocket of her jeans. She was convinced that Victor was the one who had slipped it into her purse. If there had been any doubt he wanted her to stop asking questions about Stuart's death, it had been dispelled during their talk in the office.

Lexi said, "You look terrible." Victor's eyes were red, the circles underneath as dark as bruises. She hadn't noticed it earlier.

"I'm not sleeping. I haven't thought about Stuart in a long time." He shifted in his seat, making the leather squeak. "It's not easy for me to talk about."

"So I gather," Lexi continued. "Please make an exception. Tell me what happened."

After a sigh that was loud enough for a mother seated with her kids in another part of the restaurant to look their way, he said, "I was in a fraternity."

Lexi nodded. Victor had gone silent, staring at the Formica table. She prompted him, "In high school?"

"Yeah. St. Andrew's is an old school with a lot of history. I don't know about other schools, but at St. Andrew's we had fraternities. Let me back up. Jerry, Ralph and I were all on the football team."

"Why wasn't Ben on the team?" asked Lexi.

"I guess it seems odd because he's so big and tough now, but he was a skinny kid and got picked on. Not as badly as Stuart, but boys can be mean. All the guys in the fraternity were on the football team except Ben. Stuart wanted to be in the fraternity, and when we said it was just for football players, Stuart pointed to Ben. He begged us to join, but we didn't want him. We used football as an excuse."

"Why didn't you want him?" Lexi asked.

"We were stupid kids. He was a junior, and we were seniors, but, honestly, I don't even remember. I'm not proud of this, Lexi. Stuart was a smart kid, but he wouldn't let the fraternity thing go. That's when Jerry and I came up with a few challenges to discourage him. Stu was very devout, so we thought if we asked him to do anything sacrilegious, he'd tell us to forget it. But that's not what happened."

"You hazed him." Lexi said as the waitress came to take their order. They ordered quickly, burgers, fries and sodas. As soon as the waitress was out of earshot, Lexi said, "And?"

"His first test was to steal hosts from the tabernacle."

"What?" Lexi couldn't believe it. Having been raised a Catholic, she knew how serious and disrespectful it would be to steal consecrated hosts ready for communion.

"We couldn't believe it either, but Stu showed up with the lot of them. He had a whole stack in one of those red barrels that hold plastic monkeys. I remember it like it was yesterday. He said, 'The body of Christ' and handed us the barrel." Victor smiled and shook his head thinking of it.

Lexi looked into Victor's eyes. It was the first time he hadn't looked ill since he'd walked in.

"It seems obvious now that Stuart was going to meet any challenge we threw at him but, as I said, we were stupid jocks. Now we had to think of something that would scare him. I don't even remember whose idea it was. We set up a baptism. It was senior year. There was a special mass for the Feast of the Nativity at the beginning of every school year. See, Stuart was an altar boy, so we knew he'd be at the mass. There was a deep baptismal fountain in the church. We knew it would be filled with water because of this mass." Victor stopped talking and bowed his head.

"We dunked Stu's head in, and held it there." Victor was quiet for a long time before continuing. "We nearly drowned him."

Lexi couldn't hold her tongue. She blurted, "You almost killed him. Maybe you really did kill him and tried to cover it up by staging the hanging."

"You've got it all wrong," Victor sputtered, keeping his voice to a whisper. "Stu didn't die during the initiation. That kid was brave. He didn't cry out or tell on us. We were all impressed and unanimously accepted him into the club, so there was no way that was the reason he killed himself. He was a member. There must have been something else that was upsetting Stu."

Victor sat back and looked toward the door as if wanting to escape. "My biggest regret in life is that I wasn't Stu's friend long enough to figure out what was really troubling him."

He looked at Lexi, his face drained of color. "Lexi, Stuart committed suicide. His parents couldn't accept that so they kept after the school to investigate. They got the police involved. It just made things worse. They found out about the hazing and were convinced it had gone wrong, and that we were covering up an accidental death, or worse. It was terrible for everyone. In the end, I think they believed us. The autopsy showed that he hadn't drowned and that Stu had killed himself."

"Why should I believe you?" Lexi asked.

"You don't have to." Victor sagged in his seat. Tears formed in the corner of his eyes. "But it's the truth. Do you know why we won that stupid championship?"

Lexi shook her head.

"We did it for Stuart. We worked our asses off. Ralph got injured during the game, and Jerry had a concussion, but we played through. Nothing was going to stop us from winning."

Victor shook his head as if waking from a bad dream and said in a low voice, "His death ruined everything. We were all going to college together, but after Stu died we applied to different schools. That's why Jerry and I weren't friends anymore." Victor wiped his brow. "I haven't seen Ralph since graduation, until Jerry's memorial."

"I want to show you something." Lexi pulled the note from her pocket and flattened it on the table before handing it to Victor.

"What the—" Victor looked as baffled by the note as she had been.

"I found it in my purse."

"When?"

"It could have been put there any time on Tuesday, during work, before the service or even at the service." Lexi took a drink of water. "Who else would care about Stuart enough to threaten me?"

The waitress brought their food. Her cheerful bounce deflated when she saw the dour mood at the table. Lexi picked at her burger, and Victor took a few bites before pushing his plate away.

"It's been years since I've thought about Stuart. I can't imagine who would write this. Who else knows you're digging into this and asking around about Stuart?"

They sat silently, picking at their food.

Lexi hesitated. "Father Doyle?"

"Father Doyle!" Victor was sweating and yanked his sweater over his head. "Did you talk to him at the service?"

"Oh, no. I talked to him at St. Andrew's." Lexi expected Victor to pepper her with questions, but he smiled. "Father Doyle."

"I also ran into Ben at St. Andrew's."

Victor's smile disappeared. "We talked about Ben. You promised you'd leave him out of it."

"I didn't promise anything, and I wasn't looking for Ben when I went to the church. He just happened to be there when I was looking for Father Doyle."

"Well, Ben wouldn't threaten you."

"Really? That's not what I get from Ben."

Victor grabbed his coat and sweater and struggled out of the booth.

"Where are you going? Why are you protecting Ben? It makes me think he had something to do with Stuart's death."

Victor stopped, slumped back down in the seat and crumpled his coat and sweater in his lap. "It's not that. Ben really only hurts himself. We were the only ones who kept in touch after high school. He wrote to me during the war. But this is private business. Let it drop."

Victor stood again. "I have to get out of here." He took out his wallet and tossed twenty dollars onto the table before walking to the door. Lexi grabbed her coat and scrambled after him. She wasn't hungry anyway.

Outside on Van Ness, they said an awkward goodbye and walked in opposite directions. Once at home, Lexi thought about what Victor had said. The hazing at St. Andrew's could have led to Stuart's suicide, but not if Victor was telling the truth. Even after all these years, Stuart's parents were sure he had been killed. Who would kill him? Did the other boys cover up the hazing? And there was the note. Someone wanted her to stop digging. Why would someone threaten her if Stuart's death had been a suicide? She believed Victor, but what if she was wrong? Stella had repeatedly pointed out that he was a good liar, at least when it came to the women in his life, but Henry had also been right. People told lies all the time to get what they want; it didn't make them killers. Victor certainly used people. But that wasn't the same thing as covering up a murder.

The more she found out about Victor, the less she felt she knew. At the memorial, Lexi heard several of the firemen ask Victor how things were going with his girlfriend. She overheard him say that they were consulting with a priest. So, she's a nice Catholic girl, Lexi thought at the time. She had guessed as much. If they were engaged, it blew her whole theory that Beverly was his true love. Would he really break up with his fiancé for a fling? And what was the point of taking Lexi to the opera? Just to mess with his parents? It seemed pointless to guess.

There was so much more she needed to know about Jerry and Stuart, and Ben and Victor.

Lexi stood in the kitchen, waiting for the tea water to boil. The rabbit-ear television on the counter had snowy reception, but Lexi could see a ghostly image and hear reporter Carolyn Wilson on KRON news report on the fire.

> ...the firefighter killed was identified as seven-year veteran, Jerry Stevens. According to the Fire Chief, George O'Conner, Stevens's life might have been spared if the hotel would have had a sprinkler system.

There was no mention of the police or fire investigations.

21

DECEMBER 30, 1983 – THE MORGUE

Lexi had borrowed the VW from Victor to drive herself and Henry to the morgue at San Francisco General Hospital. She could hardly stand that she thought of the Orange VW now as Jennifer's. It was a rainy cold day, and Lexi hadn't wanted to wear Henry out taking buses, even though the last thing she wanted was to ask Victor for a favor. She intuitively felt that an unfamiliar environment would throw off Henry's confidence, which was based on his well-honed sense of where everything was. She suspected that even he didn't realize how bad his sight had become.

At 11:00 a.m., she picked Henry up outside his apartment on Leavenworth. They drove down Van Ness past City Hall and the Opera House before crossing Market Street. It was easy to avoid first gear—which didn't work in the old VW—while driving downhill. On the way, Henry explained that most post-mortems took place outside the city. His friend, the coroner, had told Henry that since this case was under investigation, Jerry's body would still be at General Hospital south of Market Street on Potrero Hill. Because General Hospital was a teaching hospital, it housed the University of San Francisco Department of Pathology and Laboratory Medicine.

When they arrived at the hospital, Lexi drove around the block several times before a parking spot opened up in front. She parked, and after she got out of the car she walked around to the passenger side and opened Henry's door. She gently took his elbow as they walked to the morgue. The sidewalk was slick, and she could feel Henry relax as she guided him inside. Once inside, the receptionist directed them to the basement. They took the elevator to the bottom floor. Paint was peeling from the walls, and there were pipes secured to the walls near the ceiling with rusty brackets.

Lexi said, "It has a 'behind the scenes' look to it. The place is falling apart. Like the guts of the building are exposed, right?"

Henry replied, "There's no love for the coroner, even though it's one of the most important positions I can think of."

They found Dr. Yu waiting in his office. The door was open.

"Henry!" Dr. Yu stood up, walked around his desk and gave Henry a squeeze. He looked close to Henry's age. His broad smile and warm eyes took some of the edge off Lexi's nervousness. She was terrified to see Jerry on a slab. Dr. Yu extended his hand to Lexi and introduced himself as Edward.

Lexi had hoped they would start in Dr. Yu's office, looking at the autopsy report, but instead Dr. Yu led them down a small corridor to a door that looked like a restaurant freezer. He was excited for Henry to see the body, and to bounce ideas off him. She could tell it was something they used to do and both looked forward to doing again today. As sick as it sounded—a man was dead after all—Lexi kind of understood their enthusiasm. It had been years since Henry had worked as a PI, and he was enjoying getting back into old habits.

Henry had explained that when there was a suspicious death, the first thing he would do when he was a PI was look at the body. That's how he and Dr. Yu had become friends in the freewheeling '60s and '70s when the rules were more of a concept than a practice. Lexi didn't have the heart to chicken out. She would try thinking of Jerry's body as an object and not as someone she had touched and who had touched her.

Dr. Yu pulled the handle of the heavy door, and the seal broke with a loud rushing sucking sound. They stepped inside, and the cold air hit Lexi like a hand to the face. There wasn't exactly a smell. She imagined the molecules moving slowly around and not generating enough heat to emit smells. There was something in the cold air, but she couldn't put her finger on what it was.

Dr. Yu walked to a wall of large drawers. The morgue looked to Lexi like the one on the television show *Quincy*. She winced when Dr. Yu pulled out the drawer. She closed her eyes for a split second.

"I'm ready for this," Lexi said mostly to herself. She could feel Henry lean forward. A white sheet covered a figure lying in front of them. *A sheet is okay*, Lexi thought. Dr. Yu pulled the sheet back, past Jerry's neck. Lexi gasped. Her heart felt as if it were breaking open as she looked at Jerry's waxy skin. His eyes seemed to be staring at the ceiling. Dr. Yu quickly closed the eyes, apologizing.

"Dreadfully sorry. It's a habit to keep them open," he said.

A huge gash ran horizontally across Jerry's chest. In the middle of his chest was another cut, which disappeared beneath the sheet. Huge stitches resembling those on Frankenstein's monster closed the wound. Jerry's face was badly burned on the right side, but the left side and part of his neck were not. *This is what a dead person looks like,* Lexi thought, trying to breathe. She started to sweat and was sure that she would throw up; bile bubbled in her throat.

"You see here where the skin is purple," Dr. Yu pointed to the neck. Lexi felt as if she was looking down at Jerry's body from high above the others. She was aware of having an out-of-body experience, as if she were floating near the ceiling. There was a mark that looked like a purple fingerprint on the left side of Jerry's neck. Where had she seen a mark like that before?

"You can see the pressure on the neck here," Dr. Yu traced Jerry's throat with the point of his pinky finger as if talking to an anatomy class. "Collapsed the bones, blood vessels and trachea. This was a violent blow."

Henry asked, "Caused by a pipe falling on him during the fire?"

"Not necessarily, it could have been a beam. Something very heavy."

Dr. Yu pulled the sheet over Jerry's head and pushed the tray back into the wall of cabinets. The sound of the suction from the freezer vacuum resealing unnerved Lexi more than she thought possible after seeing her lover's dead body.

As they walked back to Dr. Yu's office, Lexi asked the doctor, "Can you tell us anything about the 1972 St. Andrew's church suicide of Stuart Ferguson?"

"Ah," said Dr. Yu. "Henry mentioned that case when he called. Stuart Ferguson. I remember it was a very sad case. Suicide. In my experience, when someone hangs himself someplace other than the home, it's a message."

"But what was the message? One of Stuart's classmates said that after the hazing, which was supposed to be the reason for his suicide, the fraternity had accepted Stuart into the group. So that couldn't have been why he killed himself."

"I have a feeling it was more of a message to the church than to those football players," Dr. Yu said, shaking his head.

"What do you mean?" Lexi asked.

"There have been rumors about St. Andrew's for years, but that's not my area. Priests. You know. But I'm only concerned with what I can learn after a person becomes a body." He nudged Henry as they walked. "Present company excluded." He and Henry chuckled.

Once in Dr. Yu's office, he motioned to the files on his cluttered desk.

"If anyone were to accidentally find my files from the Stevens autopsy when I was out of the office—" His sentence trailed away as he left the room, leaving the door ajar. Lexi looked at Henry. He sat down at Dr. Yu's desk and opened a folder marked "Jerry Stevens."

"What does it say?"

Henry took black-rimmed glasses with thick lenses from his inside pocket.

"I didn't know you wore glasses?"

He looked guilty and said, "They don't help much, but it's so dark in here I need the magnification."

Despite the glasses, he held the file close to his eyes and read for some time in silence.

"There was no smoke in Jerry's lungs." He kept reading to himself. The ticking of a large institutional-looking clock on the wall was the only sound in the room.

"That's not all. The cause of death is listed as strangulation. That would make Jerry's death a murder."

"But it was a pipe or beam that hit him and knocked him unconscious. It was the smoke," Lexi said in a hollow voice. "I thought it was only murder if someone set the hotel on fire. Could he have survived the blow?"

"Not according to this."

Lexi looked at Henry. "I don't understand."

"I'll explain later." Henry stood up. "Let's skedaddle before we get my friend Dr. Yu into trouble."

22

DECEMBER 31, 1983 – NEW YEAR'S EVE

Lexi knew there was something wrong when she put the key in the lock to open the bakery door. The outdoor floodlights were casting an eerie glow onto the sidewalk. The key was hard to turn, and she could see that the lock was mangled, but she managed to force it open. She thought maybe an early New Year's party had gotten out of hand and revelers had tried to break. San Franciscans loved a party. Maybe they couldn't wait one more day. There's no telling what people will do when they're drunk and hungry.

Lexi saw the light from the warehouse shining through the window of the swinging door. She relaxed a little knowing that she had company. Ben and Dean would be frying donuts and taking sheets of pastries out of the ovens. Once inside, she left the front door closed but didn't bother trying to lock it. She didn't want to risk not being able to open it again if the lock got stuck.

Lexi checked the register. The cash drawer was open and empty as usual. Once in the back, Lexi turned off the switch to the floodlights. Dean was banging a basket of donuts onto wax paper on the table before sprinkling them with sugar. Ben was concentrating on a cake and didn't look up. There was a small parking lot in the alley, with a separate entrance for the employees who drove, so the bakers might not have seen that the front door had been tampered with.

"I don't know what you're babbling about, Dean, but I'm busy," Ben snapped. At least things were normal here. Dean looked up from dusting the donuts and gave Lexi a wink. It was 6:45 a.m. The bakery would be open soon. The widows would arrive at least ten minutes before regular opening hours, but they wouldn't think of trying the door before 7.

Trays of pastries and warm donuts were stacked on racks ready to be put in the cases out front, but first Lexi wanted to check the office to see if anyone had made it into the bakery or just damaged the lock trying.

The desk was as messy as ever.

Since, as usual, the whole office was covered in a fine dusting of flour, Lexi looked for clean spots. The numbers on the adding machine were dust free. A roll of tape spilled out of the back like a swirl of icing that disappeared out of sight. If anything had been touched by a thief, there would be a nice set of prints visible through the dust. She knew she should call Victor or tell Ben, but she didn't want to bring Ben into it until she knew if anything was actually wrong. She unlocked the safe and counted the money. Nothing was missing, and the door didn't look tampered with.

Who would try and break in? An addict? Other than the guy throwing a muffin in her face, Lexi thought that they weren't known for action. On the other hand, nothing was taken, and that was more like a heroin addict's behavior. She imagined that if an addict had managed to break in, he or she would have probably nodded off in Victor's chair.

"Lexi!" Ben roared. "You better get those donuts squared away."

Lexi jumped and looked at the clock on the wall of the office. The glass was cloudy, and she couldn't make out the time. She looked at her watch. It was five to seven. She needed to get the cases full and the coffee brewing in five minutes. She left the office and watched Ben and Dean for a moment. Ben's body language was normal. He was usually on edge, but nothing signaled that he was about to blow. Their relationship had been tense before she ran across Ben at the church; now there was a new level of hostility she felt from him.

Dean was making room on the table for more trays coming out of the oven. He gave Lexi a smile. With his finger on the side of his nose, he breathed deeply while nodding. Ben was high. Lexi shrugged. She couldn't worry about that now. She was thinking about calling the police to check things out, but decided it should be Victor's call, if she could reach him. It was his bakery. She walked back into the office, cleared away order books and old message pads until she found his number in the same spot as on the day of the fire. With a sense of déjà vu, she dialed the number. Only this time, Victor picked up on the first ring.

"Victor, it's Lexi. Someone tried to break into the bakery."

"Holy hell," Victor said. "Was anything taken?"

"It doesn't look like it. The cash drawer was in the safe, but the front door lock is damaged. I had a hard time getting it open."

"I'll be right in. If Claudia comes in before I get there, head to Paula's to get a new lock."

Lexi hung up, took the first rack of baked goods to the front and started filling the counters as fast as she could. She finished putting the sheet pans of raised donuts, bear claws and fruit Danishes away, then rolled the empty rack to the back. Before taking the second rack out, Lexi motioned for Dean to follow her. Once out of earshot of Ben, Lexi asked Dean if he had noticed anything strange when he came to work.

Dean was quiet for a moment. "I could see the lights on in the front when I drove past. I've never seen them on before. I just thought the closer left them on last night by mistake."

"Nothing else?"

"No." Dean turned to go but stopped. "You know," his voice dropped to a whisper, "Ben wasn't in when I got here. He came in at 4:30 a.m. And, he's high as a kite today." Dean paused. "Please don't tell him I told you."

Lexi rushed to put the rest of the donuts out. The smell of fried dough, sugar and chocolate made her hungry. She stuffed a chocolate-cake donut in her mouth.

It was after seven. The pound cakes could wait, and she could check the dates on the cakes later. She saw the widows standing outside but pretended not to see them when she put the coffee pots on the burners near the front door. At 7:15, Lexi made a big show of opening the doors, even though they were already unlocked. She'd have to live with the widows clucking over the delay unless Howard came in to distract and frighten them.

It was a busy morning. Lexi didn't have time to think about the break-in or anything else. The widows had their plain-cake donuts with coffee and free refills; there were German tourists eating cream puffs and a few people her age that looked like college kids on a winter break, with dirty backpacks and hiking boots. The only people missing from their usual places were the heroin addicts from the methadone clinic. She guessed the clinic was closed.

At 9:10, Victor arrived. Lexi was cleaning a table and said over her shoulder, "This is your idea of coming right in? Hey, I need to talk to you when Claudia gets here." He nodded his head before disappearing into the back. Twenty minutes later, when Claudia arrived, the place had cleared out. The widows returned to their Tenderloin apartments on Polk Street above small corner markets and video stores with special rooms for gentlemen viewers in the back. The tourists had finished their breakfasts and Lexi watched them pile onto cable cars headed to Powell Street and the turnaround at Market.

"This used to be a nice neighborhood but now, only hoodlums." Claudia was staring out of the front window. "I'm going to ask the union man to transfer me to downtown."

Lexi shook her head and, before walking into the warehouse, said, "I don't think it was the crime of the century." Victor was in the office. She asked him if he had called the police. She didn't tell him that Ben had been late or snorting coke. After his reaction at dinner at The Hippo, she knew there was no point. Victor never listened to anything negative about Ben. *Better not stir up a hornet's nest,* she thought. Things had been pretty quiet in the back, and she didn't want that to change.

"Nothing seems to be missing. I think some kids must have tried to break in as a prank. A real burglar wouldn't have given up. Besides, who would rob the bakery so close to New Year's Eve? There are cops all over the place this week."

"It's your call." Lexi said, leaving the office and walking to the front.

Tiny Timm was struggling to get in the front door.

Lexi rushed to the door and said, "Let me get that." Timm looked relieved.

"Your usual coming right up," Lexi said in a sing-song voice, following Timm into the bakery. "As soon as I put the fresh ones out for you."

He sat down and turned to Lexi, who was now behind the counter pulling out a tray of hamentashen and tea cookies.

"Lexi, my dear. Come viz me to the Kasbah!"

Even though Timm said it nearly every time he saw her, it still made her laugh.

"After you have your cookie, the Kasbah," Lexi said, picking out a large Russian tea cookie and pouring his coffee before joining him. She sat down, moving his crutches to the other side of his seat.

"What happened to the door?"

"Oh, you noticed. Somebody tried to break in here last night, or they did break in, but we don't think they made it into the bakery."

"This neighborhood is getting dangerous." Timm took a bite of his cookie. "You never know who's going to get robbed or killed."

Lexi looked across the street at the burned-out hotel. Timm noticed and said, "I'm sorry, Lexi. I can really put my foot in it sometimes. Speaking of Jerry," he looked up at Lexi sheepishly. "What happened at the coroner's office?"

Lexi had been so distracted she had almost forgotten about Dr. Yu and the morgue.

"Timm, it was horrible. It was so awful to see Jerry lying on that table." Lexi's eyes were moist, and she stopped talking until she could calm herself, blinking back the tears.

"Take your time, my dear," Timm said tenderly.

She took a deep breath before continuing. "Henry and I saw bruises on his neck. Then Dr. Yu let us look at the autopsy report. Jerry had been strangled. None of it makes sense. Trevor told me he'd been burned badly, and, as awful as this sounds, his burns didn't look that bad. Not that I expected—"

Timm watched Lexi intently and put his hand on her arm to slow her down.

Taking a deep breath, Lexi went on. "Jerry didn't have smoke in his lungs." The clarity of the statement, of saying it out loud, was overwhelming to her. They looked at each other for a long time before Timm said in a whisper, "Then he didn't die in the fire?"

"No. That's what Dr. Yu thinks. Maybe Jerry was murdered someplace else and then his body was moved to the hotel?"

"Then why did the fire marshal close the investigation?"

Before she could answer, Victor pushed through the swinging door. "Lexi, can you get the new lock from Paula? But I want it to fit the old keys, so bring your key."

Lexi agreed, said goodbye to Timm and told Claudia she would be back soon.

Outside on the street, Lexi turned right and walked up the hill toward Post Street. The key store was several long blocks away, and she was out of breath by the time she reached the store.

"Hi, Paula," Lexi said as she walked in. Paula was matching a key to a blank from the wall behind the counter. The most common keys were hanging closest to Paula's height. The more unusual sizes gathered dust at the top. She stepped on a small box to reach a blank near the top of the pegboard. Lexi saw a fresh bruise around Paula's wrists as she took the key off its peg.

"Give me a sec," said Paula as she moved to the key machine. She unscrewed the block and put the blank into the holder below the metal guide. Lexi knew it was an unusual key because of where Paula had taken it off the board.

Without looking up, Paula tightened both screws on the blocks, then moved the arm holding the guide and blade over the original key. The room filled with the sound of grinding as the blade sawed through the metal sending tiny metal shards onto a pile below. Next Paula ran the arm up and down the keys several times to make sure each groove of the new key was identical to the master.

When she finished, Paula pulled the arm back, unscrewed the cut key and ran it under a swirling metal brush, sweeping away the metal shavings. Paula's left index finger was gnarly from rubbing against the brush. Lexi imagined Paula must have made hundreds of keys, each time wearing more of her flesh away.

"Almost done." Paula sandwiched the keys together and eyeballed them to check that they were identical. Lexi watched as Paula put the keys in a tiny envelope and wrote "Hearn" on the side. She opened a drawer stuffed with envelopes and filed it under "H."

Finally looking up, she asked, "What can I do ya for? I have a pile of trophy plaques to tackle, but I have time for you."

"We need a new lock for the bakery door. The front door. Someone tried to break in."

"First the fire, you lose a friend and now a break in," Paula shook her head in disbelief. "What happened?"

"They damaged the lock, but I don't think they got inside. Nothing was taken that I could tell. Victor doesn't think so either, but it would be hard to tell in that office. It's such a mess." Lexi realized that Paula's store was, in many ways, as cluttered and unkempt as the office at the bakery.

"The safe wasn't touched," Lexi said, trying to change the topic. "We need a lock to fit this key." She handed Paula her key.

"Why doesn't Victor just put in a new lock with new keys?"

"I have no idea, but if I were to guess, this key also fits the lock on the back door, and Victor doesn't want to change two locks. It's silly, but he's the boss."

"It was probably a heroin addict trying to get sugar," Paula said with a laugh as she took the key.

"I thought of that," Lexi agreed. "The fact that whoever tried to break in gave up so easily confirms it."

Lexi thanked Paula and asked if she could come back and get the lock before the end of her shift.

Paula looked skeptical. "This will take some time. I'll need to rekey an existing lock. It's really a pain. Try me in a couple of days."

"I'll tell Victor." Lexi waved goodbye and walked to the door. "It was a struggle to get the door open this morning, but I think we can wrestle with the lock until the new one's ready. I'll call if Victor doesn't want to wait."

Paula said, "Maybe he'll go for a new lock after all. I could give you one right now." She waved over her shoulder before turning back to her work. "Sure, leave me to engraving kiddie bowling trophies."

Lexi laughed. She put a quarter on the counter. "I'm taking an *Examiner*."

Things were slow when she got back to the bakery. She told Victor that the lock wouldn't be ready for at least a couple of days. While Lexi had been at Paula's, Victor had messed with the lock and decided that they could manage. It locked after a bit of back and forth with the key. Lexi asked Claudia if she could take her break early and sat down to read the paper. She flipped through the front section and stopped when she saw an article on the fire.

> The Fire Department's investigation of the Cathedral Hill Hotel fire that killed firefighter Jerry Stevens and two guests staying at the hotel—at the corner of Van Ness and Geary Boulevard—has been closed. The report issued by the Fire Marshal's Office found no signs of arson. When the hotel formerly known as the Jack Tar was built in 1960, sprinklers were not required. The fire code was changed in 1975, but this regulation applied only to new construction. As a result of the December 19th fire, Mayor Feinstein and Fire Chief O'Conner are calling for a law requiring sprinklers and smoke alarms to be installed in public areas as well as guest rooms in all hotels.

Lexi wanted to go home. She poured a cup of coffee and walked into the office.

"Your drawer is always wrong," Victor said without looking up from the adding machine. He was more amused than annoyed.

"Victor, doesn't it bother you that someone might have killed Jerry?"

"What are you talking about?" Victor looked up.

"A detective from the police department told me that Jerry's death was suspicious," Lexi lied. She didn't want to tell him she'd seen the autopsy report.

"I don't think so." Victor was irritated. "My buddies at the fire department say it was an accident and the case is closed. It wasn't arson. Jerry died fighting the fire. There's nothing suspicious about it."

"Just like there was nothing suspicious about Stuart Ferguson's death."

Victor looked hurt. Lexi regretted saying it. "I'm sorry," she said. "That wasn't fair." She fidgeted with her watch. "How well do you know the guys Jerry worked with?"

"After we graduated, I wanted nothing to do with any of them. Stuart's death changed everything for me. Jerry and I lost touch. Ralph drifted away. I wanted to be a fireman, but you've met my parents. And there was no way I was going to Nam. I went to college and my folks set me up at the bakery. I went along with the program and never looked back."

Lexi started to leave the office, but stopped when Victor stood up. There was enough covering up going on. She said, "I saw Ben snorting coke."

She expected Victor to be shocked, but his expression was blank.

"I give Ben a lot of rope. He wasn't as lucky as me. He's never been the same since Nam. That doesn't mean I'm not disappointed, though." Victor's eyes moved from the flour-coated window to Lexi's face. "I think you need to let this go, Lexi." His eyes narrowed. "Did you sleep with Jerry?"

"What?" Lexi was flustered. "That's none of your business."

"I'm trying to figure out why you can't accept that Jerry's death was an accident, and that Stuart died a lifetime ago. You're merging two things in your mind that don't have anything to do with each other, and now you're trying to drag Ben into it."

"That's why you let Ben act like a nut? Because you feel guilty about how his life turned out?

"A little more compassion wouldn't hurt, Lexi." Victor slumped onto the edge of the desk, his weight crushing the papers beneath him. "You're young. You don't know much about life."

"Maybe not, but I'm getting a crash course."

"In compassion or life?" Victor folded his arms.

"Both," Lexi said and left the office, walking back into the bakery. She straightened a row of cookies and watched the clock, but all she could think was that Victor had made everything her business.

When Beverly's shift started, Lexi could tell that she was in a bad mood and guessed that she had had a fight with Victor. Once the afternoon crowd thinned out, Lexi asked her what was wrong.

Beverly frowned and said, "It's nothing. How are you doing after the memorial?"

"I'm okay. There's a lot we need to catch up on, but not here. Thanks for asking. Now your turn. What's the matter?"

"Oh, alright. It's your date with Victor."

This was not going to be good. She hadn't told Beverly about the opera.

"It wasn't a date. You must know that. I'd never been to the opera and have always wanted to see one."

"You never told me that you liked the opera. The word opera never left your mouth. You just made that up!"

"It never came up." Lexi sounded lame even to herself. She continued even if it was digging a bigger hole. "Victor told me that you hate the opera. You know I don't give a hoot about Victor. It was Mozart. I know I should have asked you first. I'm sorry. Victor doesn't care about me. Did he tell you we went together?" Lexi felt awful.

"He didn't. He hid it like a coward. More lies. More deception." Beverly shifted the pastries on the Danish tray by filling in the empty spaces near the counter window.

"If he didn't tell you, how did you find out?" Lexi busied herself checking under the cakes for expiration dates. She was relieved when Henry walked in, but instead of coming to the counter he stopped when he heard Beverly interrogating Lexi and helped himself to coffee. He took the paper from the garbage can and sat down to read.

Beverly continued, "I looked in his jacket pocket and found the tickets. I confronted him because, of course, I thought he had taken her, but he was almost proud when he said he'd taken you."

"Oh, no. This is all mixed up. There's nothing going on between us. I promise you." Lexi put her hand on Beverly's arm. "Listen, have you ever met Victor's parents?"

"No. How could I?" Beverly shrugged off Lexi's hand. "They don't know about me."

"Exactly." Lexi felt she had to have reached the bottom of the hole she was digging. "I met them." Beverly's large brown eyes got bigger.

"Victor made a point of taking me to his parents' house to pick up the tickets. It wasn't until I talked to Detective Reiger that I put everything together."

"You're talking to a detective about dating Victor?"

"No," Lexi said. "I was talking to him about the fire. It had nothing to do with you and Victor, really. Let me start over. Victor keeps his girlfriend around to make his parents happy. In their eyes, she's more of an acceptable partner than you are. You must know that. You work at their bakery. She's a blonde, blue-eyed vice president of a bank."

Beverly looked down. Her expression changed.

"But, I come from a good family. My parents are doctors. My family are Brahman. I'm in pre-med. We only left India because of the opportunities for me here."

"I know. But the only culture the McCrackens want is at the opera."

Lexi knew what she was telling Beverly was upsetting, but there was no going back now. Time to crawl out of the hole.

"I thought he loved me," Beverly said softly as tears welled in her eyes.

"I think he does love you. He never made a move on me, honest. Victor was proving something to his parents. I'm sure he was trying to let them know that things aren't working out with his girlfriend. I was the Irish version of you."

Beverly looked skeptical.

"We work at the bakery. The bakery they own. That's not okay with the McCrackens. I know for sure that his grandparents were dirt poor when they came to this country. Your parents had more to lose coming here than they did. But Victor's parents have forgotten where they come from. They are snobs, and so is Victor. Hell, you're a catch compared with me. I'm not even in school."

Beverly couldn't help a tiny smile.

Lexi continued, "It's as simple as that. Victor took me to the opera because he wanted his parents to meet me. He was giving them the message that he's stepping out on what's her name." Lexi stopped short. "Jennifer. Let's call her by her name. We should give her a little more respect. It's not her fault Victor is a wimp."

Beverly shrugged and said bitterly, "I thought her name would be Fiona or Leprechaun, something super Irish."

This time they both managed to laugh.

"Listen, Victor has to accomplish two things. First, he needs to get his parents to accept their precious son dating someone that isn't a professional, at least not yet. Then he just needs to get them over the second hurdle—not having an Irish daughter-in-law."

Beverly wiped her face and gave Lexi's hand a squeeze. Lexi looked at her smooth skin, straight nose and large dark eyes. Even smeared mascara couldn't diminish her beauty. She didn't tell Beverly that Victor was talking about finding a priest at Jerry's memorial and that the leprechaun and Victor might be engaged.

"I know it's the '80s, but people are still clannish. Look at Claudia. She came to America from Russia, but she lives in the Avenues surrounded by Russians and sends her kids to Russian schools. She wants her daughter to marry a nice Russian boy."

"A White Russian boy," Beverly pointed out.

"Of course. Look, Victor might not be giving his folks credit. They'll love you once they get to know you. He's afraid of them, you know. My advice, worth zilch, is that you force Victor's hand. Make him choose you. You make it too easy for him to see you and Jennifer. If you walk away, at least you'll know how much he does or doesn't love you if he'll fight for you."

"The funny thing is," said Beverly sheepishly, "that I've never introduced him to my family. He's way too Irish for them." She shrugged.

Lexi walked to the coffee table and grabbed some napkins, handing them to Beverly. She wiped the mascara from her face.

"You have to start somewhere, so why not start with your family?"

Before Lexi dropped the subject of Victor, she wanted to make one more point.

"And don't ever take that VW again. That piece of junk is a hazard. Use his car. Let him drive that orange death trap. You take the Mercedes."

Beverly gave Lexi a hug. "Thank you. I feel better. And, I'm sorry about Jerry. Look at me. I'm a wreck and you're stoic and brave."

"You don't see me at night in my little apartment huddled in a ball hugging Saxman."

Though it was New Year's Eve, Lexi was grateful to have no plans. She put on her pajamas and watched on her snowy television as the ball dropped in Time Square 9:00 p.m. East Coast Time. Saxman was purring in her lap. She imagined Victor and Beverly happily married with kids running around, and then felt a stab of guilt for thinking that Jerry was the kind of guy who would have stood her up.

23

JANUARY 1, 1984 – STELLA BROOKS

It was the first day of 1984 and Lexi was meeting Henry and Timm at Stella's apartment on Geary Street in the heart of the Tenderloin District, the area between Van Ness, Market and Geary streets. There were blocks of neglected pre-war apartment buildings, residence hotels, porn shops and liquor stores. A heavy concentration of homeless people, drug addicts, prostitutes, hippies and runaways made their home at the Civic Center in the elbow of the Tenderloin triangle near City Hall.

Lexi hadn't seen where any of her bakery friends lived except for the lobby of Timm's building. She was curious about Stella's life outside of the bakery. At eleven in the morning she, Henry and Timm met Stella in the lobby of her building. The Art Deco interior was still beautiful but shabby. It had good bones, as Henry put it. The marble flooring in the foyer was cracked and covered with grime, but Stella pointed out that it had been imported from Italy in the 1920s. A heavy gilded mirror hung above a narrow table with stacks of flyers and unclaimed mail in neat piles.

They crowded into the elevator. Henry closed the cage door, and Stella moved the metal handle all the way to the right. "Number 10," she said in a faint voice. The elevator shuddered and slowly ascended to the top floor. When it stopped, Henry slid open the rickety door and they entered a dark hallway with faded red carpet. Stella led them to number 52, took a key from her jeans pocket and let them into a narrow entryway.

A framed poster from the 1950s of Stella performing at the Purple Onion on Columbus Street hung in the hall. In the living room were two club chairs and a love seat. They sat down. Stella went into the kitchen and put the kettle on for tea. Lexi looked around the room.

Memorabilia from her singing days at the Hungry I in North Beach hung on the walls. Old black and white photos of Stella with jazz musicians, programs from Greenwich Village jazz clubs, knick-knacks and mementos covered every surface. In the photos, Stella had the same short bangs and straight bob, only today her hair had silver steaks breaking through the black. Next to the radiator was an old microphone stand with a large round mesh screen attached to the front.

Lexi could see into the kitchen and noticed that Stella, not surprisingly, wasn't a cook. The countertops were overflowing with stacks of papers, framed photos, a bowl of faded matchbooks and song sheets stacked where there would have been appliances. There were no family photos that Lexi could make out.

Stella had told Lexi that by the time prohibition gasped its last breath, she had moved from Greenwich Village to San Francisco and was singing in speakeasies and nightclubs. She sang whenever a club owner would let her. Sometimes a trio accompanied her, but mostly it was Stella and a bass player crammed in a corner, opening for acts like Lenny Bruce.

Stella came into the room with a tray of teacups, each with a dry tea bag inside because the kettle hadn't boiled yet. Lexi watched Henry as he looked around the room, eyes landing on various items. Lexi wondered how much he could make out in the dimly lit room. He stood and walked to a framed piece of yellowed parchment. He put on his glasses to take a closer look.

"I wrote that song," Stella said proudly.

"I thought it was a poem." Henry read the title, "Little Piece of Leather."

"It is a poem," she said, looking at Lexi, "It's a love poem to the Blues."

"I've never heard you sing," Lexi said. "Can you play us something?"

Stella nodded, picked up a Folkways record from a nearby shelf and said, "This one is called 'As Long as I Live.'" She gently took the record out of the sleeve and put it on the stereo console behind Timm.

"This is an old Arlen and Koehler tune from the '30s," said Stella.

They listened until the song's refrain. Henry said, "It's beautiful, Stella. It takes me back." He paused to listen before asking, "Do you mind if we talk while it plays?"

Stella smiled her ascent.

Timm piped up. "First. Let's toast the new year!" They raised their empty teacups.

"To a good year."

"Hear, hear! To 1984!"

Once they had settled down, Henry started the conversation. "Maybe Jerry's killer set the fire to cover the murder?"

"But we know it wasn't arson according to the fire marshal's report," Lexi answered.

"The whole fire investigation seemed so rushed," said Henry.

"Maybe that's the answer," said Lexi. "It's not about the fire."

The group set down their cups and looked at Lexi.

"I keep thinking about a scene in *Cosi fan Tutte*." She hesitated unsure of how her theory would sound when she said it out loud.

"What do you mean?" Stella asked.

"It's a long story, but when I was at the opera—"

Timm said, "Ooh, the opera. Aren't we fancy."

Henry gave Timm a look and said, "Go on, Lexi."

"Well, there's a scene where the fiancés of two sisters are dressed in disguises to try and fool the sisters into thinking they are different people. They wave at the sisters, but the sisters don't recognize them."

She was met with blank stares.

"What if the person that waved at me from the hotel wasn't Jerry? What if it was someone trying to make me think it was him?"

"It would have to be a fireman. Who else would have access to a suit?"

Henry said, "That seems farfetched. Let's take it at face value. It was just a fireman waving at the bakery to thank you for the donuts."

"It's possible," said Lexi. "I just have a funny feeling about it. Maybe it was someone pretending to be Jerry to throw off the timeline of when he was killed."

"Are we looking in the wrong place?" asked Timm. "We shouldn't forget how crazy Ben is. He might be in love with Lexi and jealous—"

"Now, that is nuts," Lexi said. "Mr. Squared Away practically hates me. I don't think he loves anyone or anything. Except maybe drugs." Lexi paused. "I've seen him snorting coke at work."

"Honey, that's not news," said Stella.

Henry, Timm and Lexi looked at Stella and said, "What?"

"I know his dealer. But drug use doesn't make you a killer. I'd have murdered any number of people by now if that were the case."

They laughed before Henry got them back on track. "Let's get back to who could have killed Jerry."

"Well," Timm said. "It was pretty chaotic with the evacuation and firemen and paramedics everywhere. Jerry could have been killed by anyone."

"But what's the motive?" asked Henry.

The kettle whistled. Stella got up and went into the kitchen. She came out and poured hot water into their cups. Timm struggled with the cup and saucer in his small hands.

No one had an answer, so Henry continued, "What about Victor? You said he knew Stuart and Jerry."

Lexi explained that she had confronted Victor about Stuart's hazing. Victor told her that Stuart had been accepted into the fraternity but, though he could tell there was something going on with Stuart, Victor had never asked what had been bothering him, and then it was too late.

Lexi dipped the tea bag in her cup. "Victor is full of regrets."

"Yeah," said Timm. "Why would the kid kill himself if he got into a fraternity he wanted to get into?"

Henry, who had been looking out the window, roused himself and said, "We're kind of where we started."

They sat quietly as the song played on the record player.

What if I can't live to love you as long as I want to?
Baby, I'm gonna love you as long as I live.

The record ended. Stella took off the crocheted vest she had on over her turtleneck. She picked up a half-smoked joint from an ashtray and lit it with a small lighter. After taking a long puff, she handed it to Timm. He took a hit and gave Henry a dubious look. Henry shook his head, as did Lexi.

Stella got up and motioned for Lexi to follow her down a narrow hall lined with pictures into a tiny bedroom. Stella picked up a small oval box and handed it to Lexi, who turned it over in her hands. It was two abalone shells fastened with a gold clasp. Lexi started to lift the hinge, but Stella stopped her.

"This is for you, dear. Open it later," Stella whispered in a stuttered voice. "I want to give something to you for all the donuts and coffee."

Lexi protested, but Stella insisted, pressing the box into Lexi's hand. She said in a soft whisper, "When I was young, I wanted to tear through life. And I did. I grabbed it with both hands and planted a big smacker of a kiss on it, and you should do the same."

Lexi put the shell box in her bag, and they joined the others in the living room as Henry was saying, "Anyone is capable of killing under the right circumstance."

"But especially under the wrong circumstance," Stella interjected in her shaky falsetto.

24

JANUARY 1, 1984 – RALPH MURPHY

Once she was at home, Lexi sat at her kitchen table and turned the shell box over in her hands. The latch was easy to open, and she found a joint inside the smooth sides of the shells. *That is so Stella,* she mused. She put the joint back in the shell and closed the latch.

Lexi was exhausted from trying to solve the mystery of Jerry's death. Even though he was dead, he was the most vivid person in her life right now. It seemed impossible to imagine moving on. In an uncomfortable way, the situation reminded her of her childhood, when her world revolved around her dead parents. Back then total strangers would walk up to her and tell her stories about them. Lexi was sure they had meant to comfort her, but it was uncomfortable to hear things about her parents;

mostly because she didn't know them, but, because it was such a small town, it seemed like everyone else did. And now Jerry was showing up in her days and also in her nights; in her dreams.

Lexi jumped when the phone rang. She picked up the receiver. "Hello?"

"Lexi, it's Ralph. From the fire station."

"Oh," said Lexi. "Yeah. Hi Ralph."

"I have something I need to talk to you about."

"Really, what?"

"I can't talk about it over the phone. Can we meet for a drink?"

"I guess so. When?"

"Tonight." When Lexi didn't respond, Ralph said, "It's important."

"Okay." Lexi felt a tug in her stomach. Ralph was the one person Lexi tried not to think was involved. She had liked him the first time they had met at the firehouse. "How about Royal Oaks on Polk?" Whatever it was Ralph wanted to discuss, Lexi hoped she could find something out about Jerry and Victor.

They agreed to meet at seven. Lexi left early for the bar, but when she arrived, Ralph was already there. He motioned for her to take a stool next to him at the bar. He was dressed in jeans, a turtleneck and a puffy ski jacket. She'd never seen him out of uniform.

"Lexi, you look lovely."

"Thanks, I guess." Lexi sat down. "Can you tell me what this is about?"

“I want to apologize that I didn’t spend more time with you at the memorial or at the Gold Spike after.”

“That’s why you wanted to meet me? To apologize?”

“Well, I need to apologize for something else.” Ralph motioned for the bartender. “What are you drinking?”

“Whatever you’re having.” Lexi was impatient to know what was going on. Ralph ordered two B52 shots with beer backs. He looked at Lexi, his brows furrowed, his eyes squinting with worry.

“Can you please tell me what this is about, Ralph? You’re scaring me.”

“I put the note in your pocket.”

“What?!” A couple seated next to them looked. She lowered her voice, “Why? When?”

“At the memorial when I hugged you outside the church.”

The bartender set two shot glasses on napkins in front of them along with two bottles of Anchor Steam beer. Ralph drank his shot and chugged the beer.

“But why would you do that? That was a terrible note, Ralph.”

“I know. It was stupid. Father Doyle told me you were talking about Stuart, and I didn’t know how to tell you to stop digging into it without you figuring out that I knew Stuart, and that I was in the fraternity with Victor and Jerry.” Ralph was speaking fast.

Lexi said, “And Ben.” Ralph nodded.

"Why are you all so afraid to talk about Stuart if you did nothing to cause his suicide?" Lexi took a sip of the shot, the alcohol burning her throat. "You know, the more you try and cover it up or send threats warning people to stay away, the more it looks like you had something to do with Stuart's death." Lexi gingerly drank the last of the shot and looked at Ralph. He picked up a cocktail napkin and wiped his eyes.

"Everyone has secrets, Lexi." Ralph finished his beer. "Things they don't even want to admit to themselves."

Lexi put her hand on Ralph's arm. "What happened to Stuart?" She wasn't sure why, but she didn't feel afraid of him.

Ralph gulped hard, looked at Lexi and said, "Stuart was gay."

Lexi knew there was more to it. She waited what felt like several minutes for Ralph to continue.

"We were lovers." Ralph dissolved in tears. "Nobody knew about us. They still don't know. They didn't know I was gay, but Stuart—"

Lexi asked, "That's why he was bullied so badly?"

Ralph pointed to Lexi's beer. She nodded for him to drink it. He drank deeply, set down the bottle and called to the bartender, "Another round here!"

He lowered his voice. "That's why Stu killed himself."

Lexi didn't know what to say. The bartender put their shots on the bar, and Ralph downed his in a flash.

"I've never talked about this with anyone, but I hoped and prayed that if I told you the truth, you'll drop it. If the guys at the station found out—I can't lose my job, Lexi. I love my job."

25

JANUARY 2, 1984 – LOCKS AND KEYS

McCracken's Bakery was open every day of the year. It was a place many in the neighborhood considered a home away from home. Lexi had hoped the New Year would bring a fresh start, but nothing felt new today.

Victor called her into the office.

"Paula called. The new lock is ready. Can you pick it up for me?"

Lexi agreed.

"I have a locksmith coming tomorrow to install it. Things will finally start getting back to normal around here."

Lexi felt far from normal but nodded.

"Who's covering the counter?"

"I will until Beverly starts her shift in a few minutes, then I'll go to Paula's."

Happy to be outside in the fresh air, Lexi left the bakery, forgetting to take off her uniform. She crossed the street and stopped to look at the burned-out hotel. She had never been nearer to it than where she was standing now. On an impulse, she decided to go inside. Since the Van Ness side had been where the fire started, the only usable entrance was on the Franklin side. She wasn't sure if she could get inside, but she wanted to try.

When she'd reached the front of the building, Lexi thought it looked normal, almost as if there hadn't been a fire. She walked through the large courtyard between the towers that ran the length of the blocks on the Geary and Post Street sides. Benches and plants surrounded a fountain in the middle. To her surprise, the glass doors opened silently as she approached the entrance. She stepped over the police caution tape into the building. The stale smell of old dust and window cleaner hit her before the lingering scent of burned plastic and charred wood.

The reception desk was deserted, and the lights were off. The deep shadows and dead air made Lexi uneasy. She walked to a large table in the foyer with a bouquet of drooping flowers; the murky water smelled of decay.

Lexi headed toward where the fire had started. Thick particles floated in the air around her as she walked down the hall, in and out of a sunbeam. The soot got thicker on the walls as she continued toward the rooms closest to the Van Ness side. There was only a shell of a first floor. There were charred beams where walls should have been. The exposed metal beams were what kept the structure standing. Lexi took the stairs to the second floor. She could feel goose bumps on her arms. Yellow police tape stretched across the hall. Lifting the tape, Lexi ducked under. She could see only a few feet ahead. She walked gingerly to where the floor ended at a black hole and peered over the edge, down to the first floor.

Light filtered through the dust. She could make out pieces of upholstery that clung to what had once been the arm of a chair and what might have been a couch among the blackened rubble. She felt dizzy and backed away from the edge. She looked up. The ceiling had been streaked with smoke stains but was mostly intact. *This was where he died,* she thought. The light shifted and an exit sign with the "t" melted away came into view at the end of the corridor. The idea that Jerry had died right here took her breath away.

She remembered Jerry's body at the morgue and tried to bring back the detached feeling she'd had while looking at it, not Jerry, but a body; like something that wasn't real. Then she remembered Jerry's open eyes, and she started to shake. As a child, she had never imagined her parents' actual death, but seeing Jerry's dead body and the devastation that came with the fire, her mind brought up disturbing thoughts of her parent's bodies after the plane crash. *Had their remains been found? Were they even recognizable?* She didn't know.

Lexi turned away from the melted carpet and black walls. What had she wanted to accomplish? Was it morbid curiosity? Did she think she'd suddenly remember something about that morning? She was about to leave when something caught her eye. Just under one of the crumpled beams she saw a flash. She bent down and fished out a small lump of blackened metal from under a wooden beam. It fit in the palm of her hand. Lexi felt the weight of the condensed metal. With her finger, she rubbed the remaining black soot from its surface, uncovering more of the silver underneath. What had it been? A doorknob? A hinge? She put it in her pocket and absentmindedly rubbed the ash caked to her fingers onto her apron. Then she suddenly had to get out. She felt as if her life depended on it.

Lexi sprinted down the stairs through the empty lobby and into the courtyard where she sat on the bench, taking deep gulping breaths. Her limbs were heavy, and she stared at the fountain. Her face was wet with tears. She didn't know when she had started crying. She felt as if she couldn't hold onto anything. Trying to compose herself, Lexi wiped her face on her sleeve and looked at her watch. She'd been gone for twenty-five minutes already, and Victor would be wondering what was taking her so long.

She got up slowly and walked to the street, turned onto Franklin, looped back to Van Ness and continued to Paula's store. The late winter sun was sinking fast. Despite the walk, the January chill had settled in her bones.

Still shaken from the images at the hotel, Lexi opened the door to the key store. Paula sat straddling the engraving machine. She looked up and lifted the arm that held the small pen-shaped device used to trace the letters that were being engraved by a corresponding pen. A diamond head cut the letters onto a small silver object.

It occurred to Lexi that there were a lot of devices that required restraint in Paula's business and personal life, with vices for holding keys and the engraving machine. Lexi tried not to judge her friend after their trip to the S&M club. As far as she was concerned, Paula wasn't hurting anyone but herself.

"Hi!" Paula waved. She seemed skittish and stood up quickly as Lexi walked over to the machine. Glancing at what Paula was engraving, she saw that the vice held a lighter.

"Another boyfriend?" Lexi laughed, but Paula quickly stood in front of the engraving machine to block Lexi's view. It was too late. Lexi saw the word "Trevor" engraved at the top of the lighter. A shiver ran through her. She remembered Paula telling her she liked a man in uniform. But that man?

Lexi looked at Paula and was about to ask if this was the Trevor she knew but stopped when she saw Paula's eyes. She already knew that it was. Another thought flashed through her mind; she remembered where she'd seen a thumb print like the one on Jerry's neck. She'd seen variations of that thumb print on Paula's neck and wrists off and on over the time they'd been friends.

Paula moved to the front door and locked it as Lexi looked around the room for another exit. In a flash, Paula turned the "Open" sign to "Closed" and pulled down the shade. Lexi thought about Henry telling her that anyone was capable of killing.

A siren in the distance focused Lexi's attention. A dog howled nearby.

"Happy damn New Year!" Paula's voice was loud, verging on hysteria. She noticed Lexi looking toward the door. "No one's coming, Alexandra," said Paula coldly. No one had called her Alexandra since she was a little girl. Lexi stammered, "How the hell do you know—"

Paula cut her off. "I see you're surprised I know your real name. Remember when I made you a key to your apartment? Well, I made myself an extra. Don't look so shocked. I've been through your entire apartment. I looked at your papers, hung out with that cat with the weird name. I made myself at home." A malevolent smile passed over Paula's lips.

Lexi saw a door behind the counter and thought about how to reach it. She remembered the lump of metal in her pocket. She pulled it out.

"This was Trevor's lighter?" Lexi said, the thought and the words forming at the same time. Lexi threw the dense metal at Paula's head. Bull's-eye. Paula screamed. Her hand shot up to her forehead.

"Sit down." Paula's voice was stern. She pointed to a straight-backed chair near the counter. Lexi ran for the front door, but Paula stopped her with a blow to the stomach. Lexi doubled over in pain and thought she would pass out when Paula pushed her into the chair. Lexi tried to raise her head above her knees, but a wave of nausea kept her head down.

Paula grabbed a rope from the back of the counter, took Lexi's wrists from where she held them across her stomach and forced them behind the back of the chair. The strain was so great and the pain so severe that Lexi thought her arms would break. She forgot about the pain in her stomach. Her arms pressed sharply into the chair, and she winced as the rope dug into her wrists. She pulled hard against the rope to try and create a space as Paula made another loop around her arms. She couldn't resist the pressure, so she balled her hands into tight fists.

"What happened to Jerry?" Lexi pleaded. "What did you and Trevor do?"

The strain on Lexi's arm muscles was becoming too great. Paula yanked the rope one last time and stood in front of her. Lexi released her grip and felt a slight give in the rope between her hands.

Paula paced the room and started talking.

"Trev and I couldn't resist the idea of getting it on at the fire house. We thought everyone was gone on some training exercise. We were turned on by the idea of getting caught while I was tied up, but we didn't know anyone was there. It was just part of our game. And then Jerry walked in when we were going at it in the kitchen. I was tied up. Jerry thought Trev was hurting me. I was screaming and carrying on." Paula sounded almost wistful, her voice dreamy.

"What a fucking mess," she said, losing her train of thought. She lifted the blinds on the front door to look outside and turned around to Lexi.

"Well, he was hurting me, but I think you've guessed that I like that. Jerry came at him, and I don't know what happened. Trev just went nuts. He was always pretty rough with me. More than I'm used to or usually allow. But I've never seen anyone with that kind of rage. He had his hands around Jerry's throat and wouldn't stop."

Lexi could see that Paula was enjoying telling the story. The thought crept into Lexi's mind that she wasn't getting out alive.

Paula kept talking. She shifted in her chair and jabbed the diamond-tipped pen into the slot.

"I tried to stop him, but by the time I got out of the ropes, Jerry was limp. He was fucking dead." Paula's face was ashen. Lexi thought that Paula's eyes shined with tears but realized that they were glassy from some kind of mania. It was as if someone else was talking through her.

"We had to do something. We were going to set Jerry up in the bathroom, tie him up, and the police would think that he strangled himself while masturbating."

The image made Lexi feel sick, but she tried to focus on how to keep Paula talking. She twisted her arms to loosen the ropes binding her, trying to move as little as possible.

"Did you set the fire at the hotel?" Lexi asked in a quiet voice.

"No, we didn't set the fire. The fire alarm went off when we were cleaning up the kitchen. We knew the place would be crawling with firemen in no time."

"How did Trevor know that it was the Cathedral Hill Hotel?"

Paula whirled around.

"He didn't know, you dumb shit. That was luck. We heard about the fire over dispatch. What a lovely way to cover our tracks. Besides, most of the firemen were already out. There was only one truck's worth of guys at the station. And poor Jerry, of course. Nobody saw us put Jerry's body in the trunk of my car. I drove to the hotel while Trev went back into the firehouse, put on Jerry's facemask and fire gear and jumped on the back of the fire truck as it was leaving. Trev and Jerry are about the same size, so everyone thought it was him. It was Trev's morning off, so no one was expecting to see him until dinner. People see what they expect to see."

Paula gave Lexi a cold look and said, "The reality of getting caught turned out to be very different than the fantasy. But I did like the idea of you working a stone's throw from Jerry's body burning." Lexi held her breath. She didn't want Paula's rage to turn into any more violence. "I could have had him, you know! I chose Trevor. Jerry was a loser. A spineless, gutless loser!"

It made Lexi sick to think that Jerry died trying to save someone who didn't want or need to be saved. What a pointless way to die. She needed Paula to stay focused on the fire, to keep talking.

"So, Jerry couldn't have waved to me." Lexi felt nauseous and light-headed. "It was Trevor."

All she could think of was to keep Paula talking, and maybe someone at the bakery would realize she'd been gone for a long time and come to investigate.

As if reading Lexi's mind, Paula blurted, "And you little judgy bitch! That club. What was it called at the time, Whipped Cream? Cool Whipped? You looked at me and saw a monster, a pervert. I was a friend, and you turned on me."

Paula didn't seem to hear Lexi whimper, because she kept talking.

"It was a good plan, and we were lucky. The fire was already out of control when Trevor's company got there. Everyone knows their job. It's automatic. They don't take roll call. They saw who they thought was Jerry on the back of the truck. The power of suggestion is strong. You fell for it." Paula gave Lexi a swift kick to the shin. Lexi screamed. Paula grabbed Lexi by the hair and yanked her head back.

"You scream again, and I'll knock you unconscious."

Lexi closed her mouth and tried to nod. Paula let go of her hair. Lexi gasped for breath. Paula continued talking as if she hadn't just yanked Lexi's hair at the roots. "By the time the fire chief checked in with the crew, everyone thought Jerry was in the hotel." She looked at Lexi menacingly. "And he was."

Paula was getting excited as she told the story. *Good,* thought Lexi. *Keep talking.* With the tiny bit of slack in the rope, Lexi wriggled her hands, but she couldn't risk drawing more attention to herself. She still couldn't get a finger outside the small loop in the rope that she had created with her fist.

"I drove to the front of the hotel. People were coming out onto the sidewalk in their pajamas. I think they were headed to the church across the street. There were cops and fireman everywhere. I had to be careful that one of my cop friends didn't see me. Trev came out of the hotel and motioned for me to drive into the service entrance. He grabbed a laundry cart and dumped Jerry's body inside. It was so chaotic, nobody even noticed. I stayed ducked down in the car while Trev took Jerry inside. He dressed him in fire gear and left him in one of the rooms he was sure would be burned up. Trev got out just before the room went up in flames but not before burning his hand pretty badly."

"That's why he made Chinese food the night of the fire," Lexi said. "He intentionally burned his hand to cover the burn from the fire."

"Now you're catching on." Paula leaned over her and laughed, her face inches from Lexi's. Lexi kept her eyes trained on Paula's. She started sputtering and her eyes bulged. Lexi's head ached and her shin was throbbing. She thought she might pass out, but knew she needed to stay awake. Lexi thought if she kept Paula talking, she'd have a better chance of surviving. If she were passed out, there would be no telling what Paula would do to her.

"But you didn't kill Jerry." Lexi said. "You couldn't kill anyone. Why tie me up?"

"Shut up!" Paula screamed as she walked to the phone on the counter next to a bowl of Bic lighters.

Paula dialed the phone.

"May I speak with Trevor, please?" Her voice was even and friendly. After a short pause, Paula spoke into the receiver, "We have a problem. Get over here right now. Lexi knows everything."

Paula put down the phone and sat on the stool in front of the engraving machine. Lexi heard the metal arm run back and forth in the grooves as the diamond head pressed into the metal of the Zippo lighter.

"I'll tell you what it says," Paula voice was getting shrill.

"TREVOR,

IT HURTS SO GOOD.

PAULA"

"Other people know what happened," Lexi tried to keep her voice from shaking. "You can't do this."

"Bullshit. You didn't even know what happened." Paula sounded confident but said, "Who knows something?"

If Paula thought that Lexi was the only person that knew the truth, she would certainly kill her. Paula would know from Trevor that the fire department had finished their report and concluded that it wasn't arson, and that Jerry's death was an accident. Paula also knew a lot of cops. They would probably have told her if there had been a break in the case. Lexi chose the one person she thought could figure it out, "Henry."

"That old geezer from the bakery? His mind is going. He still thinks it's 1950."

"He was a detective, and I know he was getting close to putting everything together." Lexi was getting desperate, and her arms were growing numb from the strain. She suddenly thought of Susan Hayward and said, "I want to live."

Paula made a hollow sound, her mouth stretched into a smile. "Nice one. No matter now. You are on death row. Trevor's on his way." She continued to trace the letters that Lexi knew were already permanently etched onto the lighter.

There was a loud knock at the door. Lexi's heart pounded. She was sure she would die of a heart attack before they had a chance to kill her. Paula went to the door and peered around the shade to confirm it was Trevor. She unlocked the door and let him in.

They didn't speak but eyed each other with cold calculation. Trevor disappeared through a small door at the back of the shop. Lexi's eyes didn't leave the door until Trevor came out a minute later. He was carrying something in his hand that Lexi couldn't see.

"Brilliant," Paula whispered into Trevor's ear as they moved closer to Lexi. There was a flash in front of Lexi's face, and she felt something being forced into her mouth. It was a hard rubber ball. Trevor snapped the straps behind her head, ripping Lexi's hair out. She winced but forced herself not to cry. Her mind raced. They liked to see pain. *How am I going to get out of this alive?*

Paula kissed Trevor.

"Oh, that's the ball I had in my mouth when you killed Jerry."

Lexi's blood ran cold. The idea of killing her was turning them on.

"We can always have another fire." Trevor gave Paula a passionate kiss. Lexi thought they were going to have sex in front of her. She closed her eyes. She needed to concentrate. Her head throbbed. She could barely breathe through her nose and couldn't stop obsessing over the idea that she was suffocating. Panicked, she tried to calm herself down before she hyperventilated and passed out. She needed to stay awake and alert, it was the only way she could hope to figure out a way out of this situation.

26

JANUARY 2, 1984 – BEN

Timm used to have his particular seat by the window; Stella read the paper by the door, and Henry sat as far away from the widows as possible at a table near the front counter but today they sat together talking quietly. They looked up as Howard's wheelchair approached the front door. Lexi hadn't returned from the key store, so Beverly walked to the front and, remembering how Lexi would handle this situation, asked if Howard would like her to open the door.

He looked fierce but nodded. He maneuvered to the counter and said, "Aut my mow-nee."

Beverly was getting Howard his coffee but didn't realize he was talking to her.

"Henry," Stella asked. "Where's Lexi?"

"She's been gone for a really long time," Henry said with a worried tone. "I didn't realize it until Howard came in."

Stella got up and approached Howard.

"I need to ask Beverly a question. Is that alright?"

Howard's agitation was growing. He rocked back and forth until his wheelchair looked like it would tip over.

Stella didn't give up. "Howard. I need to ask Beverly about Lexi."

At the mention of Lexi's name, Howard started to calm down.

"Le-I" he said. "Wa Le ey?"

"We need to find her, Howard. I need to talk to Beverly."

"What's wrong?" Beverly asked, setting down Howard's coffee on the counter in front of him. She had forgotten his straw, but Howard wanted to know about Lexi so he stayed quiet.

"We don't know where she is," Henry said, approaching the group. "I'm getting worried."

Beverly said, "She went to pick up the new lock from Paula's." She looked at her watch. "She left just after I got in and that was over an hour ago. Victor stepped out. Let me get Ben."

Beverly disappeared into the back. She told Ben that Lexi left to pick up the new lock but had been gone for more than an hour. She didn't think it was anything to worry about, but some of Lexi's customers were upset that she had been gone for so long.

"They do depend on her. Howard was asking for something, but I didn't know what he was saying."

"He probably wanted you to get his money so he could pay."

"How do you know that?"

Ben said, "I keep my eyes and ears open. Howard's needs are simple: open the door, bring him milky coffee with a straw and a messy donut, and occasionally count his money." Ben was annoyed that Beverly hadn't figured that out after all this time. He walked to the front, approached Henry sitting with Stella and Timm and asked brusquely, "What's up with Lexi?"

"I'm really worried," Henry answered softly. "She's been gone for over an hour."

"I'll go check it out." With that, Ben left the bakery and walked up Van Ness toward Paula's Keys.

Lexi tasted blood. Her nose was bleeding, and it was becoming nearly impossible to breathe.

Paula and Trevor were huddled together talking about the lighter Paula had just given him. Since they were distracted, Lexi worked on the knot that tied her wrists. If she didn't get her hands free soon, she would choke on the blood and draw their attention. She couldn't lean forward to stop the bleeding the way Jerry had taught her, so blood was running down her throat into her stomach. The thought of throwing up with a rubber ball in her mouth entered her mind.

Ben saw the blinds drawn and the "Closed" sign on the door of Paula's shop. He looked around the street, his eyes scanning the area, his muscles tense. He walked to the side of the store on Austin Street, which was more like a small alley than a street. A motorcycle was parked behind a garbage can. He walked up to the bike and put his hand on the engine. It was warm.

Ben walked back to the front of the key store when he heard a loud thud coming from inside. He froze and listened. A faint moan and another thud came from inside.

Quickly, Ben moved to the back of the building and checked the back door. It was locked. It was a key store, so it might be more secure than it looked. He opened his wallet and took out a credit card. If he couldn't jimmy the lock, he'd just break down the door. If Lexi was in trouble, there had been plenty of time for the worst to have already happened. The building was old, and he could see between the door and the frame that the deadbolt wasn't engaged.

He eased the credit card above the lock and moved it down to the latch. It clicked open. He pushed the door open slowly. It squeaked so much, he decided to just get it open quickly. He was calm. His mind was sharp, and once the door was open enough for him to slip inside, he waited for a beat, looking for motion that would indicate he had tipped someone off. There was no movement, so he slipped inside, leaving the door open. He might need to make a quick get-away, and he didn't want to make more noise than he already had.

Ben was inside a small storage room. He let his eyes adjust before taking in his surroundings. There was a bare bulb with a chain. Shelves along three of the walls were stuffed with open boxes of key blanks, broken equipment and merchandise. The door to the bathroom was open. Ben spotted a gym bag with leather straps and a spike collar inside. What the hell? He could hear voices from the front of the store. He couldn't tell what they were saying, but could make out a man and a woman. The voices grew louder. Ben looked for a place to hide and slipped behind the bathroom door, his senses on full alert.

"Did you hear that?" Trevor pulled away from Paula's embrace.

"Baby, you are paranoid."

Lexi hadn't heard anything. She looked toward the back door.

"Snap out of it," Paula said and slapped Trevor across the face playfully. Trevor returned the slap twice as hard.

"I know I heard something." Trevor's voice was harsh. Lexi watched him move to the door behind the counter and thought, *It's now or never.* She had managed to free one of her hands. She screamed into the ball in her mouth to draw Paula to her. Blood spattered where her mouth met rubber. Paula looked up. Blood ran from Lexi's nose and down her face.

"Why are you bleeding?" She approached Lexi with a raised fist. "I'm the one who was hit."

Before Paula could land a punch, a crash from the back room distracted her. She turned as Lexi raised her free hand and punched Paula in the chest as hard as she could. Paula lost her footing and fell to the floor. Lexi stood up and untangled herself from the ropes. Her legs were shaky as she took a step toward the front door. In a flash, Paula tackled her to the ground. They landed on the ground with full force. Pain shot through Lexi's left side. Her head hit the floor.

Ben didn't wait for the man who came into the storage room to find him. He jumped him from behind the bathroom door and pummeled him in the face. The guy was caught off guard, but he started counter-punching almost immediately. Each punch to Ben's body was a solid hit. Shit! I'm out of shape. Trying to catch his breath, Ben grabbed the guy and hugged him close, like a prizefighter playing for time. How am I gonna take this monster? The time-out renewed the guy's strength, and he broke the embrace and slammed a fist into Ben's face, breaking his nose. Remembering the gym bag, Ben twisted his body to fall closer to the wall. He grabbed one of the leather straps, threw it over the guy's head and turned around, pulling hard at the ends. The strap landed around the man's chin, and Ben eased up just enough to get it around the guy's neck as the guy squirmed under him. He screamed and pulled at the strap, but Ben had a tight grip on the straps. He easily moved out of the way of back kicks coming at him. Ben had promised himself that he would never kill again if he got out of Vietnam, but he recognized that might not be an option today. He knew this guy would kill him without giving it a second thought.

Ben heard a thud coming from the store and figured that it was Lexi and that she was in trouble. He decided to break the guy's leg in order to spare his life. Ben waited for the guy's left leg to come back toward him before stomping on it as hard as he could. An ear-splitting shriek cut through the air. The bloodied man fell forward, and Ben let go of the leather strap.

He didn't wait to see if the guy was all right. He wouldn't be going anywhere with what Ben knew was a compound fracture, so Ben left him writhing on the ground and ran into the store.

Hearing Trevor's blood-curdling scream, Paula let go of Lexi, stood up and ran to the back door. Lexi scrambled to her feet and ran after Paula. As soon as Lexi reached her, Paula turned and shoved Lexi to the ground, jumping on top of her like an animal. Her fist was raised when Ben ran out of the back room.

"Hey, Paula!" Ben screamed and knocked her off of Lexi. "Call 911!" he yelled to Lexi.

27

JANUARY 2, 1984 – CITIZEN'S ARREST

"Another ambulance is on the way," the police officer announced as he cuffed Paula and led her outside to the squad car. Ben had told the officers that he had subdued the guy in the back and that he was in pretty bad shape.

"Oh, and Lexi and I need a ride to the hospital."

Even though the rubber ball was gone, Lexi found it hard to open her mouth.

"What took you so long?" she asked Ben in a weak voice when her mouth started working again.

"It was muffin time at the bakery," said Ben with a grin. "Those prune muffins are in high demand."

After the hospital checked for broken bones and pronounced her beaten but whole, Lexi talked to the police. It took several hours to tell them the whole story.

At 11:00 p.m., a squad car dropped her off at her apartment and waited until she turned a light on inside before driving away.

Lexi peeled off her bloody uniform, T-shirt and jeans and dropped them in the garbage can; she never wanted to see them again. She stepped into the tub and turned on the shower. Her nose was clotted. Blood ran down the drain. The steaming water ran over her body until the tension finally left her body.

As she stepped out of the shower, she winced with pain and slowly dried herself off. Saxman was crying loudly outside the bathroom door. Lexi opened the door and picked up her cat, stroking her fur and nuzzling her until her nose hurt.

She crawled into bed, wrapped the blankets tightly around her sore body, snuggled Saxman and fell into a fitful asleep.

28

JANUARY 3, 1984 – AND SO IT GOES

Lexi sat next to Henry. Across the table, Timm and Stella watched in rapt silence as Lexi told them what had happened.

"So, it wasn't arson at all, just a coincidence," said Lexi. Henry nodded and put away his notebook.

"And Trevor had planted the idea with Lexi that Jerry was fighting the fire by waving to her from the hotel—"

Timm interrupted Henry's story. "To cement the idea."

Lexi said, "That's right. I thought of the wave as an illusion after seeing the opera where two men fooled their fiancés by disguising themselves, but never suspected Trevor might be pretending to be Jerry."

Stella croaked, "What a ridiculous opera!" Everyone laughed but no one harder than Lexi.

Henry smiled weakly and said, "If we had listened better, we might have been able to figure it out before you were nearly killed."

Lexi shrugged. "There's no way we could have known about Paula and Trevor. Besides, there was a lot going on. The hotel wasn't obligated to have sprinklers. They'd been grandfathered in. Once arson had been ruled out, the fire marshals wrapped up their investigation before the coroner filed his report. It might have ended there except that I told Trevor the police were investigating, so he came up with a plan to implicate me."

"That seems like a dumb plan. Why finger you?" asked Stella, edging closer to the table and nearly knocking over her coffee. "Was that the break-in?"

"It wasn't a great plan. I don't think Trevor or Paula were thinking clearly. It was like they were living in a fantasy. They had hatched a plan for Paula to break into the bakery to plant evidence against me. But when Dean showed up for work, she had to leave. Paula's Plan B was to plant the evidence in my apartment. Paula had a key to my place from when I had it copied shortly after I stared at the bakery. She just never got a chance to make Plan B happen. She did tell me that she had used the key to enter my apartment and hang out when I was at work."

"That sends shivers up my spine," said Timm. Everyone nodded in agreement.

"Why didn't she just plant the evidence in your apartment to begin with?" asked Henry. "It would have been easier to use the key to your place than to break into the bakery."

"The only thing I can guess is that Paula likes danger," said Lexi. "She and Trevor were addicted to it. Using the key to my place was too easy. If Ben hadn't come to the key store to look for me, I'm sure that I'd be dead."

"Then we did help save your life," said Timm proudly. "We raised the red flag because you were gone for so long."

Lexi didn't understand.

"Howard came in." Henry continued, "He was lost without you, and that's when everyone realized that you had been gone for over an hour."

Stella interrupted, "Yeah, yeah, we're heroes. Finish telling us what happened, Lexi."

Lexi tried to remember where she had left off.

"After Trevor came to the key store, everything moved so fast. Ben must have come through the storeroom, because we heard a noise in the back. That's when Trevor went back to check on the noise, and then we heard fighting. I finally got the rope off my arms, but couldn't get away because Paula jumped me. Ben appeared out of nowhere and dragged Paula off me. I called the police. I had the phone in one hand, and I was fumbling with the strap on the contraption around my head."

"It's like something out of a movie," Timm said breathlessly.

She told them how she couldn't wrestle the gag off because the straps were too slippery with her blood for her to get a firm grip.

"The woman on the phone at police dispatch kept asking what the emergency was, and if anyone was on the line. Maybe she thought it was a hoax.

"And you couldn't talk!" Timm had stood up and was pacing with nervous energy, his crutches moving fast between tables.

"The operator told me to stay on the line so they could trace the call. I guess they could hear the fight between Ben and Paula. I was still holding the phone when the police broke down the front door."

"Guns blazing!" Timm said.

"Actually, no, but their guns were drawn. I think I dropped the phone and passed out when Ben cut the strap off my head with his knife."

"Honey, that's what I call action," said Stella.

"I hope I never see action like that again."

As she talked, Lexi realized that she had moved from Alaska to San Francisco to try and meet people her own age and had ended up with friends her grandparents' age. Stella and Henry were at least as old as her grandparents, but they were able to hear a story about danger and not freak out. If these were her people, then she was glad. Paula was closer to her age, and look how that friendship turned out.

The door opened and a cold wind made Lexi shiver. She looked up as Detective Reiger walked to their table.

"Hi, Detective," Lexi stood and extended her hand. "These are my friends. The ones I was telling you about."

Everyone was introduced before Lexi excused herself to talk to Reiger.

"Tea, Detective?" Reiger nodded, and Lexi poured hot water into a cup, dipping a teabag into the water. She went to join him at what was becoming their regular table away from the other customers.

Reiger filled her in on the blanks in the case. He confirmed that the fire marshals that had come into the bakery had seen Trevor walking into the hotel.

"That's why they ran out before asking any questions. Trevor was trying to find evidence of something he could say had landed on Jerry's neck."

"Planting evidence is more like it," Lexi said. "It wasn't much of an investigation."

"It's true," Reiger agreed. "They believed him, but why wouldn't they. I see people turn on each other a lot in my line of work, so nothing surprises me, but it would be hard for any firefighter to understand what Trevor did. Any organization, especially when you're on the front lines, can be as myopic and self-protective as the police sometimes. Internal investigations can be less than perfect. It's often difficult to suspect the worst of a brother-in-arms. Trevor managed to slip out of the hotel before they arrived. When they questioned him later, he made up an excuse about looking for a piece of equipment the guys had told him was missing."

Lexi said, "That's right, he wasn't supposed to be working that day. It was quite a risk for him to come into the bakery. What if another firefighter had come in at the same time?"

"Those two were addicted to risk. They were a dangerous Bonnie-and-Clyde combination. But you did notice, and mentioning it put Trevor in the middle of the investigation. It's the reason Trevor and Paula were looking to implicate you. As long as the fire and Jerry's death were accidental, they would have left you out of it. You were their back-up plan." Reiger looked at Lexi, shook his head and said, "After Paula was arrested, she was ranting about how you took her man. As if Jerry was her boyfriend, and you stole him away."

"She said something like 'I could have had him' when she was screaming at me. It was all in her head. I don't think Jerry even knew who she was."

Lexi told Reiger that, for a time, she had suspected their head baker, Ben.

"But when I finally asked him why he had been late the morning of the fire, he told me that he was late more often than that. Dean only noticed it because something unusual had happened, the fire. It was pure coincidence. He's ex-military and so rigid that I just assumed he was on time and always 'squared away,' as he puts it."

"So why *was* he late?" asked Reiger.

"He's dating a woman who works a nine-to-five job, and he overslept. It never occurred to me that Ben would have a girlfriend."

"So, you see how important it is not to get stuck on one theory. It's dangerous for a detective. You have to keep asking questions to either confirm your suspicions or prove them to be wrong. Once you start looking for patterns, you see them everywhere and sometimes they're just coincidence." Reiger didn't just look like a professor, now he sounded like one.

"I'm not a detective, Detective." Lexi protested.

"You never know where life might take you. I have guys on my team that aren't as sharp as you, Lexi."

Lexi looked at Reiger's thoughtful face. His eyes were soft, and his mouth was open slightly as if he wanted to say something else.

29

JANUARY 16, 1984 – FAMOUS IN SMALL CIRCLES

Two weeks had passed since Paula and Trevor's arrest. It was mid-January and just starting to feel like a new year to Lexi. Trevor's leg was badly broken, but it would heal. Ben was proud of the fracture. Lexi had overheard him tell Victor, "That broken leg saved that bastard's life. I would have killed him if he'd have kept coming at me." Paula's injuries were minor. Getting beat up was nothing new to her.

Detective Reiger came into the bakery one last time to see how Lexi was feeling.

"Bear claw and tea, right?" Lexi asked with a smile.

"That's the ticket. I love marzipan. You have a good memory. You should try out for the police force. We could use good people like you."

"I was practically a detective the last time I saw you. Now I'm a cop."

Reiger smiled.

"Doesn't it get you down?" Lexi asked. "Murder."

"I suppose it's more of a disappointment. Believe it or don't. I like to see the best in people, but we haven't yet evolved out of being deadly predators." Reiger paused. "At least some of us."

"And that makes the rest of us prey." Lexi put the pastry on wax paper and placed it onto a plate.

"Ah, but you won't make a mistake of becoming prey again now, will you? Trust your gut. And, that's to go." Detective Reiger pointed to the Danish. "While I'm at it, give me a Danish ring. The marzipan one."

"For the guys at the station?" Lexi asked.

Reiger smiled and leaned across the counter conspiratorially. "It's for the Monday prayer group at my church."

Lexi rang up five-fifty. Reiger put six dollars on the counter and said, "Keep the change."

Reiger juggled his cup of tea, the bag with the bear claw and the pink box with the Danish ring, and left.

An hour later, Dean came in. He was dressed in a suit and tie, his hair freshly cut and his mustache trimmed.

Lexi said, "Well, Dean, look at you."

"I'm getting married today."

"Married? I didn't know you were engaged." She came from behind the counter and gave Dean a hug.

"This is my man." Dean beamed at the tall handsome man who had walked in with him. He put his arms around Dean and smiled at Lexi.

The widows watched and clucked with disapproval.

"We came in to get a groom-and-groom for the top of our wedding cake."

"Oh, no. You're too late. I sold them all!"

"It's your fault," Dean's boyfriend said crossly. "You told all our friends McCracken's had them, and now there aren't any left for us."

Lexi told them to hang on a minute and went in the back to the office. She pulled two bride-and-groom boxes from the top of a filing cabinet. She opened the boxes, took the plastic tops out and set them on the desk. Grabbing the bride, she snapped it off at the base and did the same for the groom of the second top.

She searched the desk drawers for glue, feeling a bottle of something deep in the center drawer among the pens, scraps of paper, and a letter opener. She pulled the bottle out and to her great relief it was Elmer's Glue. There were receipts and bits of adding machine tape stuck to the open spout. She picked up the scissors and cut the spout below the tip. She glued the groom where the bride had been, moved a plastic flower at the base to cover the mismatched feet and put it back in the box. It looked perfect.

Dean and his boyfriend were standing at the counter, looking perplexed. Lexi handed them the box.

"It's on the house."

Victor walked in through the front door and, seeing Dean with the box in hand, smiled and said, "I hope she gave that to you free of charge." He looked at Dean and said, "It's her specialty." Victor winked at Lexi and walked into the back.

Lexi turned scarlet and said to Dean, "Thank you for making me the number one seller of groom cake toppers in San Francisco."

"Try the top seller in the world, honey." Dean kissed Lexi on the cheek, and he and his fiancé disappeared out the door.

"Not bad for a 'country bumpkin,'" Lexi said with pride.

30

LIFE AFTER LIFE

When she thought of Jerry now, Lexi's heart ached. She missed loving him, but she also felt lucky to have known him for even a short time. It reminded her of a song by Rupert Holmes, "The People That You Never Get to Love."

Lexi knew that love was not just about loss. Love was also something that could expand your world. When she had moved to San Francisco, she worried about leaving the physical beauty of Alaska. It had been the one thing she could always depend on. It fed her life when she was a child. She loved how her hometown stretched like a ribbon along the bottom of Deer Mountain. She knew that she would always miss the view of the waterfall out of the kitchen window, the patter of rain as she walked through the forest and the boats rocking in the harbor.

But to her delight, even though she had grown up in a dramatic and beautiful place, loving one place didn't stop her from falling even harder for another. San Francisco was a city with its own breathtaking landscape. The rolling hills and valleys made its own urban mountain ranges: Twin Peaks, Cole Valley, Pacific Heights, Hayes Valley, Potrero Hill, Noe Valley and Cathedral Hill where the fire had taken place, and even her own neighborhood of Russian Hill.

As different as her hometown and the city seemed, San Francisco was also a fishing town. Boats bobbed along the wharf; the smell of the ocean filled the air. The people weren't that different either. Lexi often thought Ketchikan was like something a writer might have imagined; a town filled with eccentrics living among dreamy landscapes, more a figment of the imagination than a real place. There were plenty of eccentrics at McCracken's Bakery too, and most of them were her friends.

Gold rushes had defined both of her beloved homes and had attracted adventurers and hucksters alike. People came to the edge of the Pacific Ocean to rewrite their stories, and Lexi was no different. In her small town, everyone thought they knew everything about her. To them, her story was already written, the past, present and future.

Lexi had called her grandmother to catch up before heading out for her morning coffee and a cigarette she'd bummed off the kitchen staff.

"How have you been, Alexandra?"

"Fine, Grandma. How are you and Grandpa?"

"We're doing ok; nothing to report. I'd put Grandpa on, but he's asleep in his chair. Did you find a boyfriend down there in San Francisco yet? I hear it's full of gays, so you picked a town worse than Ketchikan to try and find a man. At least we have a bunch of roughnecks to choose from."

"No, Grandma." Lexi looked out from the bay window onto Larkin Street. "I don't have a boyfriend." The street was wet and deserted. It was just-before-dawn dark, and an hour earlier in Ketchikan. She knew her grandmother, who barely slept four hours a night, would already be on her second cup of coffee.

"And I am home."

After getting an update on the doings in Ketchikan, Lexi said goodbye and hung up. She sat still, watching the morning light slowly bully away the fog. Saxman circled her legs, her golden eyes bright in the emerging light. Lexi rose and, throwing on her warmest sweater and a worn pair of jeans, left the house and walked to the cement steps at the end of Fisherman's Wharf. She smoked the Players cigarette and drank the coffee she'd picked up at the Buena Vista. The fog had burned off, and the light around Alcatraz brightened and darkened as clouds passed overhead, their trails whispered away like shadows. She felt that her days at McCracken's were ending. She had moved to San Francisco to lose herself, to stop being the orphan whose parents had died. But she also didn't want to be the tragic girl whose boyfriend had been murdered, a newspaper story like Stuart Ferguson. She took Jerry's postcard from her pocket. It was spotted with water-marks from hanging on the bathroom mirror.

She said goodbye and threw it into the Bay.

The two places she loved most were different in one important way. Unlike Ketchikan, San Francisco hadn't written Lexi's story yet. Maybe it was big enough to erase her past, to allow her to start over; Lexi would move on to a new job and a new adventure. If not, there was always the Kasbah.

THE END

ACKNOWLEDGEMENTS

My most heartfelt thanks go to my readers, who allow me to live and flourish in my imagination.

I also owe a great deal to Pamela Hearn, my first reader. Her encouragement and love for me (thus, her love for anything I'm working on), gave me the courage to continue writing. I owe her everything.

Next, with whole-hearted gratitude, I want to thank the following people for their support, feedback, editing, suggestions and much-needed pep talks while I worked on the Lexi Fagan Murder Mystery series: E. Lynn Malchow, Theresa Dailey, Robin Hall, Janis Petrin, James Goldin, Pamela and Craig Hearn, Suzanne Doerr, Anthony Geraci, Barbara Lebow, Jan Weinberg, Heige Kim, Susan Fogel, Michael Barish, Liz Malchow

Price, Alicia Ulrich, Stephanie Bowen, Elizabeth Meeker, Valerie Tesauro, Desmond Mascarenhas, Bee Ottinger, Lisa Memije Jennings, Charla Thompson, Kelly Ireland and Natalie Chovancek Ebnet. Their fresh eyes and constant encouragement—along with a friendly "How is the book coming?"—were just what I needed.

Special gratitude is owed to my dear sister, Heather Doerr-Ruiz, who came through for me at a low point when the book's timeline was in tatters. She put her superwoman cape on and helped me put it back together. As L. Frank Baum put it in *The Patchwork Girl of Oz*: "A little misery, at times, makes one appreciate happiness more." Thank you, Heather, for getting me through the misery and back to the happiness.

Finally, I thank my editors: Tatjana Greiner, Nicole Gurley, Sandy Weinberg Kristen Weber. It does take a village.

COMING SOON

In book II of the Lexi Fagan Murder Mystery Series, *Free For All*, office intrigue turns deadly as we find Lexi working as a receptionist at a San Francisco think tank. Also reappearing from book I is Detective Robert Reiger, who leads the investigation; he uses Lexi as his eyes and ears inside her office where suspects seem to multiply by the day.

In *Sins of the Mother*, the third book in the series, Lexi returns to her hometown of Ketchikan, Alaska, for her grandfather's funeral. While there, she's forced to face the truth about her own parents' untimely death 20 years earlier. As she digs for clues, Lexi starts questioning everything she thought she knew about herself and her family.

Made in the USA
San Bernardino, CA
10 August 2017